One Day

By the Same Author

Beach Boy

One Day

ARDASHIR VAKIL

HAMISH HAMILTON
an imprint of
PENGUIN BOOKS

HAMISH HAMILTON

Published by the Penguin Group
Penguin Books Ltd, 80 Strand, London WC2R ORL, England
Penguin Putnam Inc., 375 Hudson Street, New York, New York 10014, USA
Penguin Books Australia Ltd, 250 Camberwell Road, Camberwell, Victoria 3124, Australia
Penguin Books Canada Ltd, 10 Alcorn Avenue, Toronto, Ontario, Canada M4V 3B2
Penguin Books India (P) Ltd, 11 Community Centre, Panchsheel Park, New Delhi – 110 017, India
Penguin Books (NZ) Ltd, Cnr Rosedale and Airborne Roads, Albany, Auckland, New Zealand
Penguin Books (South Africa) (Pty) Ltd, 24 Sturdee Avenue, Rosebank 2196, South Africa

Penguin Books Ltd, Registered Offices: 80 Strand, London WC2R ORL, England

www.penguin.com

First published 2003
1

Copyright © Ardashir Vakil, 2003

Grateful acknowledgement is made for permission to reproduce extracts from the following:
   The Inner Game of Tennis by W. Timothy Gallwey, published by Jonathan Cape. Reprinted by
permission of the Random House Group Ltd.
   'Night Nurse': words and music by Gregory Isaacs and Sylvester Weise; © 1982, Splashdown
Music Inc/Tammi Music Ltd, USA. Reproduced by permission of EMI Copyright Holdings Ltd/
Charisma Music Publishing Ltd, London WC2H OQY.
   'Home Again': words and music by Carole King: © 1970, Screen Gems-EMI Music Inc., USA.
Reproduced by permission of Screen Gems-EMI Music Ltd, London WC2H OQY.

The moral right of the author has been asserted

Set in 12/14.75 pt Monotype Dante
Typeset by Rowland Phototypesetting Ltd, Bury St Edmunds, Suffolk
Printed in Great Britain by Clays Ltd, St Ives plc

A CIP catalogue record for this book is available from the British Library

ISBN 0-241-14132-X

To Georgia

One

Start high above this city. Descend in a slow circle. Through a window in the grey clouds what do you see? Neat straight lines of houses. A snaking ribbon of silver river, steeples, a long flat roof, the famous clock, squares, crescents, playing fields, stadiums, thin lines of dinky cars. A great expanse of red brick, patches of green, banks of grey. Rows and rows of identical houses, some joined together like Siamese twins; others packed tomes on a shelf leaning against each other. In one of these – a turn-of-the-century house in the north of this city – side by side, in their basement bedroom, lie husband and wife, Ben Tennyson and Priya Patnaik. Whacka, their little boy, sleeps in the room next door.

Quarter past midnight, 15 March 1999. They had just returned from a dinner party. A party, thought Ben, where once again so much time, too much time, had been spent talking about the problems of getting one's child into the right primary school. The Millennium Dome. Plans for New Year celebrations. Talk like that was for the middle-aged middle classes. So what did that make him, this thirty-one-year-old school-teacher? It made him feel small, vengeful, angry.

Spreadeagled on the left side of their queen-sized bed, Priya was rubbing her vulva, tweaking and pulling at the engorged lips. Ben wasn't up to joining her. He fished out his book – *The Inner Game of Tennis* – from the debris of knickers, tapes, lost socks, 'shag-rags' and 600,000 dust mites under the bed.

He shoved his orthopaedic pillow under his aching neck, and studied the introduction.

As Priya manipulated, knees bent, thighs fanned out, soles of her feet meeting like an Indian dancer's, a diamond shape in the bedclothes between her naked legs, Ben read:

Each game is composed of two parts, an outer game and an inner game. The outer game is played against an external opponent to overcome external obstacles, and to reach an external goal. Mastering this game is the subject of many books offering instructions on how to swing a racket, club or bat, and how to position arms, legs or torso to achieve the best results. But for some reason most of us find these instructions easier to remember than to execute.

A year ago, in the time of innocence, the time before the tearing apart had started in their family, Ben remembered, he had picked up some special advice from this book about hitting a forehand. His flat stroke had turned into a topspin. For a few games he had hit rasping winners every other shot. He had trounced Mauro, his long-time friend and opponent, three times in a row. No inhibitions. And Welsh, his fellow teacher, had hardly won a game. That kind of form had never returned. What was he looking for now? Advice on the mental side of the game? A way out of this losing streak, a couple of wins over Mauro, revenge for the humiliating defeat he had suffered last week at the hands of Welsh? He had meant to return to the book to relearn the lesson; instead the book had ended up as a window jamb in the room where he worked, to be made soggy by the rain. Was it the sodden state of the pages or his dodgy forehand that had prompted him to bring it down to the bedroom? He hated himself for these pointless reflections.

Priya had laughed at him when she saw the yellow book in

his hands. 'You're not reading that again!' Ben was convinced there was some nugget of advice that he could recover and reabsorb, something that might change his life, not just his tennis. He saw himself as a small man spading earth into a hole. Effort, commitment and discipline were necessary for this vital task. The crevasse of self-doubt must be filled with hard work. It was the last thing his dad would say when he dropped him off at Haylesbury, his boarding school – 'Get some good work done.' In his daydreams, he saw himself having finished the job, smoothing over the cracks, patting the mud, proud of his immense dedication and sacrifice, administering the last cursory dabs and prods. After that, he could see himself walking away from his great work, as if he were watching the movie of his life, walking away towards satisfaction for the rest of his days. Ben was in search of a solution. Somewhere, there was someone or something, a machine, a book, a person, that would provide the missing piece, stop the constant sense of souring inside him, stop the ever-increasing urge to lash out, that crucial bit of advice – *always lean forward when you hit those ground strokes* – that would staunch his hidden suppuration, even for a little while.

He skipped to the first chapter, 'Reflections on the Mental Side of Tennis'. He could hear Priya's fingers furling and unfurling her flaps, making a mixture of rough papery and unctuous liquid sounds. Just briefly, he asked himself what she might be fantasizing about – his blood raged at the thought. He should have left immediately. He shouldn't have waited. Was it too late now? Too much reflection. He should have taken Whacka and driven to his parents' house in Amersham. Perhaps he should have left the first time, years ago, before Whacka was born, when the Marcus thing happened. 'Don't go there,' Ben said to himself. 'Stick with the book.'

Beside him, the focus of Priya's activity had narrowed. Ben was familiar with the pattern. Since the beginning of their long relationship, almost nine years ago, they had masturbated freely in each other's company. Sometimes they would do it side by side, enjoying their own private fantasies, sometimes she encouraged him to tell her his. That had been before the rupture. At times like this, when one or the other wasn't in the mood, more often him than her, they masturbated in the first person singular. No big deal. In fact, Priya masturbating was Ben's favourite aide-mémoire when he went solo.

His glance caught the pads of her forefinger and thumb, pressed together as if holding a guitar plectrum, thrumming the delicate walls of her moist vagina. She was gathering her resources, like a weightlifter summoning his strength for an almighty heave – knees pushed out, stomach distended, left hand pressed against her navel, next to the black mole that sat like a graphite jewel on her sun-starved cinnamon skin, breasts erumpent (where Ben liked to put his hands), face contorted. An other-worldly expression. This face belonged to him alone. How florid it looked. (Once, in mid-flight, she'd opened her eyes, seen him looking at her and spluttered with laughter.) Here was a look of childlike absorption. It reminded Ben of a black and white photo of Priya, as a toddler, grimacing at the camera, in the Delhi glare. The image sent a ray of old love through him as he lay watching. Pursed lips, straining neck, cheeks tremoring like jelly, stretched, in an effort to contain her great inhalation. Such concentration he envied. The longer it continued the more her face tended frighteningly towards explosion. Like an overripe fig.

It's not that I don't know what to do, it's that I don't do what I know! This, Ben's book said, was the common complaint of sportsmen down the years. He did not agree. He had read the instruction manuals, but when things heated up in his tennis games, especially over the last year, he wasn't sure which bit of advice to follow. There were too many instructions in his head. Too many options. If you were at set point, or even, as happened last week against Mauro, if you had two set points in hand, leading 5–4, how should you play the next point? Should you just block the ball back and play safe? Should you try to blast the opponent with a winner? Or should you hedge your bets and try a bit of both?

Priya let out a strangled grunt from the pit of her stomach. It reminded Ben of the noise women tennis players made when hitting their big shots. He laid his manual to one side and focused on his wife. Her free hand slid down from her stomach and held on to the soft inside of her thigh. The face twisted another gothic notch. Anticipating her exhalations, Ben pulled his trapped balls from between his legs. At last, Priya's brown throat opened, her agonized growls torched the polluted air of their bunker bedroom. Broad flaming brands of sound. With each cry of pleasure and liberation her lower half shuddered and rocked as her hands whirled in a paroxysm of twisting delight. Until, finally, with a prolonged sigh she opened her eyes and her body slumped; release had soused the sheet between her resting thighs. People in the street must hear these euphoric roars. Nights were punctured by shouting humans and booming stereos flashing past. Sometimes he could hear a distressed woman's ululation from the flats behind their walled garden. Lines from the text he was teaching came to him:

The time has been my senses would have cooled
To hear a night-shriek.

From the upstairs flat – even through the intervening ground floor – you could sometimes hear a mixture of sobbing and unintelligible accusations hurled by Carol at her man. A piteous wailing at the far reaches of her voice box. Some mornings, Ben bumped into her in the communal entrance hall – eyes darted away from his gaze, a defensive, unfriendly reply followed his greeting. The Scotsman Mick's voice was never to be heard. Only the sound of T. Rex or Guns N'Roses turned up loud after Carol had finished her screaming. Mick was charming, with a slurring drunken Caledonian charm. Ben imagined him in a Tintin comic, pissed, tottering down a backstreet in some harbour town to be slammed on the head with a truncheon.

Through the wall beyond Priya he could hear their Polish neighbour, Rosa, still practising her accordion. She started at seven in the evening, pumping and squeezing on into the early hours, night after night, folk songs full of mourning for the lost Eden of Poland. She described other European cities as 'sonshiiiine, boootifoool bildings, boootifoool kaantreee', while this city, London, was 'derrtty, feelthy peepplle, robbberrs, creemeenaals, derrty feelthy houses, horrriible wehzerr'. She rarely left the confines of her one-bed, net-curtained, spic-and-span housing-benefit flat, but on occasion Ben and Whacka would be accosted by this squat, bow-legged, fur-encased caricature hobbling down the road towards them. She would bend down to Whacka, bringing her gnarled, fag-breathing face close to his. 'Boootifoool baaabby, boootifoool hair, so daaark, so handsooome, like hiiis maaather, eh?' Whacka looked at her in a daze, at her bulging eyes, at her goblin expressions, transfixed by the marble-sized wart sitting on her bottom lip.

Sometimes, in the middle of the night, Ben would start up in their queen-sized bed, and wake the light-sleeping Priya. 'What's wrong?' she'd ask.

'I don't know. It's nothing. Sleep.' He would fall back on their mattress and listen for the distant humming. No television sounds, no cars passing, no next-door voices, no Alsatians barking, no sirens, no airplane drones. No accordion from next door. In this ancient city of partial darkness, a stillness had snatched him from his slumber.

Priya pulled the quilt over her naked front. The days when he wanted sex every night were gone. Now he was more than happy – a perverse satisfaction perhaps – to let Priya please herself.

'Sorry,' she smiled. 'Was that really selfish of me?' Slipping an arm round his waist, she lay her head in the cup of his shoulder. 'Come on, we've got a big day ahead. Let's get some sleep.'

'Can I read a bit?'

'If you have to. Ten minutes.'

Eight years of marriage and still he had his reading in bed rationed. It was like lights out at boarding school. Sometimes he longed for his childhood bedroom in Amersham. But his parents had sold that house now.

'I need you to be on the ball tomorrow,' said Priya. 'We've invited a lot of people for Whacka's birthday. You need to do your schoolteacher bit with the games.'

'What games?'

'Pass-the-parcel.'

'Are you sure they're old enough for games?'

'Of course. Whacka's all excited about pass-the-parcel and

musical chairs. We've got to make sure that every child gets a present from the parcel. I'll never forget the face of that little girl at Jessie's party.'

'The one who was missed out?'

'And nobody seemed to have noticed. She looked sadder and sadder as the game went on. Other children kept unwrapping the parcel and getting a present but the music refused to stop for her.'

Ben said, 'It slightly ruins the point of a game to think that every child has to get a prize.'

'Games are not meant to be cruel.'

'Somebody has to lose. It can't be avoided.'

'Then you end up depressed for days like you do when you lose at tennis.'

'Remember in India,' Ben said, 'when your mother made them rerun the egg-and-spoon race at that school fête because she insisted that Whack hadn't had the rules properly explained to him?'

'No, it was because the other children hadn't followed the rules. She wanted a rerun for everyone. She hates the thought of injustice.'

'Like it was some kind of life-and-death matter,' said Ben.

'She'd say, "I don't care who wins or loses. The game has to be played in the correct spirit."'

'Believe that, and you'll believe anything.'

A silence. Ben tried to return to his book, worrying about how many of his ten minutes he had already wasted. He read a few more lines.

I was beginning to learn what all good pros and students of tennis must learn: that images are better than words, showing better than telling, too much instruction worse than none, and that conscious trying often produces negative results. One question perplexed me: What's wrong with trying? What does it mean to try too hard?

'Who's going to help me with the games?' asked Ben. 'You'll be in the kitchen setting up the kids' tea.'

'Anya's au pair is coming to help. Oh God! I haven't phoned that Nazir, about the samosas and kebabs.'

'How are we going to afford all this? Surely my biryani will be enough?'

'We have to feed the adults properly, Ben. Have you made sure you've got enough beers?'

Ben didn't answer. Another birthday, another party, not just for kids, but adults as well. More money spent from their mushrooming overdraft. Before they had started their joint account, he'd rarely ever spent more than he had in the bank. He'd made do with his teacher's salary, and the occasional present from his parents. It was a simple case of stop spending when you run out of money. Live within your means. That's how he had been brought up. He had kept one current account, which usually had money left in it at the end of the month. Priya had had two or three current and savings accounts, and while she was hugely overdrawn in one she saved money in another. When they started living together, the arguments about money got worse. They started a ledger, on his suggestion, in which they were meant to write what each of them had spent in the month. Priya called it the 'divorce book', because they always argued about the sums. She accused him of being petty, he accused her of being wasteful. Then one day Priya's cousin suggested that they start a joint account for all the household expenses and keep separate deposit accounts for personal funds. Ben was sure he would lose control of the finances.

For a time, it relieved the tension between them, until, according to him, Priya's excessive spending meant that their joint account was always in the red. More brawling ensued, arguments that led to tears, to screaming condemnations. Couples talk about other couples. They'd compare themselves to Jane and Crispin, or Leo and Jan, or Jehan and Rebecca. They fought as if it were not the case that every couple in the world, rich or poor, had disagreements about money. Priya had some ridiculous notion that her parents, however fractious they might have been otherwise, had never quarrelled about money. In her family, she said, they'd believed there were more important things to discuss.

So Ben changed his strategy. He secreted money in his deposit account like some Barings slyboots. Then when their joint account was hugely overdrawn he would transfer to it reparatory sums. Now, they both had to pour their savings back into the current account. In a circuitous way, they had ended up doing the same thing – only their attitudes to each other remained different. He believed that she was overspending, while she thought she was making savings and resented his accusations. Ben tried his best to stop worrying about it and respond to Priya's view that there was nothing worse than seeing oneself behave like a miser. Fretting about who was going to buy the next round in the pub. Like his father, counting the pennies and putting them in neat piles to buy the papers on Sunday.

Still, he couldn't help feeling, especially at times like these, that she was spendthrift. Earlier in the evening he had found it hard to keep quiet about it, about all the things that Priya had found it necessary to spend money on: absurd amounts of food, lavish party bags, clothes ordered from catalogues, far too many presents for Whacka, new plants. His objections had only sent her into a tirade. 'I've been sweating my guts out for this party. I did all the invitations. Do you have any idea how long that took, the shopping, the presents, the decorations for the flat, the cake, the jellies? And all you can do is complain and criticize.'

Ben had wanted to say, 'If it caused you so much exhaustion, why did you do it? I didn't ask you to, no one asked you to.' Instead he heard himself say, 'Let's not go over the jellies again.'

That Sunday afternoon there had been yelps of anguish from the kitchen. 'Ben! Ben! I can't believe this! After all my efforts, this fucking jelly is stuck to the mould. I asked your mother a hundred times.' Priya, like the rasp of braking tyres. Everything with her was a hundred times, or a thousand times. 'I asked her a thousand times, "What do you do when the jelly has set in the mould?" "Oh," she said, "just turn it over", and now look what's happened. It looks like a cat has clawed into the face of the fucking fish! Don't just stand there!' Ben had stared ruminatively at the scaleless and mangled scarlet blob. 'Do something, damn it! You're meant to be the cordon bleu chef.'

'Priya, I can't think straight with you shouting.' Ben was inwardly smirking. He had warned her not to overstretch herself. 'Switch the kettle on. Let's try and dunk the tins in hot water. That should loosen the bits of jelly.'

'The bits!' screamed Priya. 'Half the frigging fish is stuck to the mould!'

'That other one is all right.'

'I'm never doing this again. I don't care what you say, it's all your bloody fault. I don't have time to sit here making jellies. Life's too short. It ruined my morning and look at the result.'

Ben carefully overturned the fish-shaped moulds into warm basins of water.

Priya sat down at the kitchen table and wept. 'It's because you keep hassling me to save money. That chocolate cake is rock hard, inedible. I can't serve them that. I'm going to have to do the whole thing again. These jellies look like dog food.'

Serves you right, Ben thought. Saving money – you wouldn't know how to save money if there was a world war on. He tried to find a surface on which to stand the bowls of hot water. But all the kitchen surfaces were cluttered with dirty pots and other paraphernalia. 'Why do you always leave behind such a mess?' he mumbled.

'What was that?' Priya retorted. 'What did you say?'

'Nothing, just talking to myself.'

'You better be.'

Priya wasn't cut out to be a cook. After she had finished assembling a dish there were always stacks of soiled pots and pans littering the kitchen as in some student squat. For her, making porridge required six packets of oats, three pans, four pints of milk and six ladles. It was almost as if she despised the kitchen and its utilities, and they bore her a reciprocal grudge. Like a sensitive horse tiring of an inadequate rider, the kitchen lurched and frothed and fumed at her as she flailed hopelessly at its unyielding rump. If Ben dared enter this war zone to give a little advice or help, Priya would erupt. A dish was being massacred, but he was meant to turn away and ignore the scene. Equally, he would get it in the neck if she asked for assistance and he didn't immediately find a solution for some curdled undertaking.

Once she had decided to make a daal, from a recipe given to her by her mother. In her normal style, Priya had invited five or six people to join them for dinner. At the end of two hours of tense chopping and stirring, during which Ben had cooked the other parts of a delectable Indian meal, washing up his and her mess as he went, Priya had finished cooking her daal and was out of the kitchen. Ben sneaked a spoon into her slop and couldn't help being surprised at how subtle the flavours were. But she had forgotten to add salt. Impulsively, he chucked in a spoonful and ruined the daal. He was desperately stirring the mixture just as she reentered the room. Ben complimented her. Priya smiled triumphantly. 'It needed salt, so I put some in.' The fleeting moment of goodwill vanished, sucked out by Priya's industrial fury. Thank God it was close friends who were coming to dinner. Ben's oily red butter chicken was flung on the floor, some of it splattered the wall; he had to wrestle the salt-tainted lentils from Priya's grip as she was trying to slosh the yellow liquid down the sink. A warrior-like anger scarred her face. That's where Whacka's behaviour came from, thought Ben. Priya stomped off to the bedroom, leaving Ben to stare at the carnage.

A scene impossible to forget. He had been horrified at what he had let loose in her. Ben was anguished and confused by the hurt his small error had caused Priya. She had seen it as an attack on her attempt to produce something acceptable in the kitchen. Perhaps she was right, Ben thought. (It struck him that carelessness often hides cruelty.) This was a long time ago, but he remembered that the evening had been painful and stilted; even with the help of their friends and a couple of joints Ben couldn't rid himself of the feeling that he had sullied something more than a tasty daal. It was to be one of their first and last joint enterprises in the kitchen. Now it was he by far who did most of the cooking.

★

The jellies, Ben felt as he lay in bed, fitted into the story of how their marriage had developed since those early days. By dipping the moulds in bowls of hot water for a few seconds, he had salvaged some of the scales and the mouth and eye of the fish: these bits he had delicately sutured on to the wounded carp. The result was more than a little smudged, but the whole jelly could now conceivably be taken for a flounder. He grinned to himself at the thought of quizzing Whack as to the identity of this animal. He remembered Whacka sitting on the floor one Saturday morning, holding up a toy tiger, and demanding, 'Is this a sheep or a tiger, Daddy?'

'It's a tiger, like you.'

'Look, Daddy,' Whack sniggered, 'the tiger's got a string tied to its bum!'

Priya had watched Ben the surgeon, while wiping her cheeks of tears and melting jelly. She looked up at him, looked at the fish and started laughing and mock-sobbing at the same time.

'It'll be fine. The kids want jelly, they won't care what it looks like,' he lied, putting his arm round her slender shoulders.

'Whacka wouldn't notice if it was a perfectly moulded peacock,' she said squeezing up to him.

'He would if it was a sword.'

Priya had grand ideals, grand ambitions, grand plans for her life. Desires and dreams beyond her means. On her mother's side, she came from a well-established Hindu family who had been leading figures in the struggle for Indian independence. Politics and law and writing were in their blood. Her grandfather had been gaoled during the freedom struggle, his brother had been finance minister in the first Indian government, other relatives had continued serving the Congress Party until recently. Her mother was one of the pre-eminent writers of post-independence India. Her brother, an affluent solicitor in Bombay, travelled the world and aspired to the titled panache of his forefathers.

After coming to England at seventeen – since her grandfather's time most of her relatives had gained a degree from a university abroad – Priya had returned to live in India for two short periods only. She found her family history cumbersome. The widespread net of influences and assumptions that came from her mother's background in India seemed to find her out wherever she went. In England she felt she had made her own life. The fierce independence of mind and the self-reliance she had inherited from her mother had helped her in her adopted home. In Priya there beat the heart of a dissenting radical. She saw herself as a person who could never be forced to sit back if something unjust were going on in her presence. But much as Priya liked to think of herself as a doer, a joiner of unions and cooperatives, a walker on marches against racism and pit closures, she was, like her family, most at home in the world of ideas. She had an irrepressible natural intelligence. If a discussion started in the room she would enter the argument at the right moment and sear her way to the nub. This Ben loved to watch. The way she could seem lazy, even shabby, distracted, while her brain leapt into action with the clarity of a first-rate barrister. She wasn't one of those who looked to put others down with a caustic remark or show off the knowledge she had of Gramsci, Marx, Freud or Fanon. Hers was a questioning kind of intelligence.

But there was a dark side to her character. She was subject to violent mood swings. Her father had turned to alcohol, destroying his marriage, and after an idyllic first five years of childhood Priya had seen him only occasionally. Her mother eventually achieved a separation from a by then deranged husband – in the final months, he had become incensed whenever he came upon his wife writing anything. As a result, guarding her privacy became the foremost concern in Mohini Patnaik's life. Priya always felt, as did her brother, that for her mother reading and writing books came before any other kind of human activity. She wanted never to have to live under that kind of subjugation herself. She saw writing as a means to an end and was sceptical of the creative imagination.

Priya, who was always fighting off the influence of her mother's family, was nevertheless steeped in their world view. They saw themselves as philosophers and thinkers. Money should not be talked about. It was vulgar. And yet no expense should be spared to procure what the heart desired. Financial troubles could always be sorted out at a later date by someone else. If you were having a birthday party, there *must* be champagne and beer and several sorts of fruit juice. If the weather was good, there *must* be or we *must* have a barbecue, and the meat *must* be marinated in three different ways, breasts in lemon and garlic for the children, hot sauce for those who like it hot, and not so hot for the rest. Then, should we have a biryani as well? Yes, why not? Ben, I loved the biryani you cooked last time – please could you do it again? Ben, with his cooking expertise, a sucker for flattery, caught in a weak moment, obliging Ben, how could he resist? Then there must be all sorts of snacks, peanuts and *chewda*, samosas and kebabs, watermelon and fruit salad. This was all very well in the motherland, where there were cooks and servants who could prepare all day, lay the tables, serve the snacks and wash up afterwards. But if Ben dared mention the word 'servants' to Priya another flurry of 'you don't understand anything about my culture' would come flying in his face.

No, no, no, it was nothing to do with servants, it was to do with Indian hospitality. People in India (Which people, he silently asked himself, beggars on the street?) entertained properly. You didn't ask guests to your house and then act stingy. There were no half measures for Priya. 'What do you want me to produce,' she would ask, 'curried eggs, pork pies, crusty sandwiches, Kia-Ora?' Cold British food was like the dirty baths, the net curtains, the grey winters, the empty milk bottles outside the door. Over my dead body. What about living beyond your means? Oh no, all their friends thought their parties so special that they came to them from right across London. There was boundless praise for Priya's resourcefulness: mother, host, broadcaster, political activist, party organizer.

How strange, thought Ben, no movement in the bed, no complaint about the light. Could Priya have fallen asleep? He returned to his book.

The player of the inner game comes to value the art of relaxed concentration above all other skills; he discovers a true basis for self-confidence, and he learns the secret to winning any game lies in not trying too hard . . .

The author repeating himself. Where's that advice on the forehand he was looking for? 'Relaxed concentration' – easier said than done. Nothing would make Ben happier than to stop having to make an effort. End the struggle. Allow himself to be permanently lazy, draped on the sofa like an Afghan hound, staring for all time at the box. Late as it was, and stupid as these thoughts were, he couldn't find sleep. The more he tried the more it moved away.

The peculiar thing about Priya, he thought, was that

although she was extravagant she wasn't interested in maintaining standards or proving herself to the Joneses: she despised the Joneses. Friends like Jehan and Rebecca who had to have five holidays a year, an *Elle Decoration* house and Nicole Farhi clothes, were disapproved of. Priya was more slob than snob. They had lived in this flat for four and a half years now and the level of untidiness and mess had reached epic proportions. Ben would never live like this if he had the choice.

Some years ago he had given up trying to do anything about it. Look round this room, he told himself, clothes slung on chairs, on the floor, on an old towel rack, hanging from open cupboard doors, on the edge of their bed. Dirty cups, books and newspapers, crayons, broken toys, magazines, tapes and catalogues strewn about. A desk and a mantelpiece piled with hillocks of junk, boxes lurking in the corners. Over four years in this flat and there were still half-emptied cartons left from the move. Letters, bills, more books, slippers and shoes. The chest of drawers that never closed because there were too many socks and T-shirts stuffed into it, as in the cupboard with the doors hopelessly open. There was dust on the windowpanes, dust on the boxes, on top of the cupboard. And there were Whacka's toys to trip and break your leg over. He closed his eyes. O for his mother's neat piles of washing, socks sorted and trussed, handkerchiefs and towels colour-coded. Why had he started thinking about all this now?

Just after the Christmas of 1994, over a year before Whacka was born, Ben had kicked Priya out and she had slunk off to Camberwell, to the flat of that unmentionable man from her work. The giant. Ben had cleared the flat of all the mess, chucked things out, hoovered the carpets, washed the kitchen down – he'd even sponged the walls and mopped the dust off the skirting boards – put all the books back on to the shelves, sorted the tapes and CDs into their boxes, thrown away a lot of pointless papers, magazines, catalogues and mildewing food. It had taken him a whole Sunday. He'd finished at 10 p.m. There he was, standing in the middle of the spotless kitchen admiring his handiwork. Free at last from the Patnaik oppression. A song from an old tape he had uncovered came streaming through the disinfected air. 'Niiiiight nuuuurse . . . only you alone can quench this here thirst.' (Priya had taken him to the Brixton Academy to see Gregory Isaacs, three months after they had started going out.) He had sat down at the kitchen table with his mug of tea, looked round the room in its neatness, with its smell of bleach, its gleaming floorboards, looking for flaws, looking for something that still needed to be done, and then the corny words 'only you alone can quench this here thirst' brought on tears he couldn't stop. He sobbed like a toddler then – like Whacka, when he laid face down on the floorboards, weeping inconsolably for his departing mother. He wanted all that tidiness to be flushed down the drain, wanted Priya and all her mess back, and somebody to cook for and complain at. He had thought then she had really gone for ever. If only four years ago he had been sensible enough not to let her come back. No Whacka then, and he owned most of the flat, so there wouldn't have been much sorting out to do . . . A warning voice in his head again. Don't go there. Just don't go there. Stick with the book.

Four years ago he had made Priya leave. He had refused to answer her phonecalls. He had forced himself not to meet her. Within days she had left Marcus, the Camberwell giant. She wanted to come back. He was unable to sleep. When this condition continued for several nights running he decided to visit his doctor. The GP, a gallant fellow, with framed pictures of his daughters – ponytails, private schools – said it was as if he'd been bereaved and that he wasn't accepting this. Ben had to agree. 'I'll prescribe you these sleeping pills,' said the GP. 'They should help. And perhaps you should stop cleaning the flat.'

It reminded him of Sarah, his older sister who had 'gone for good' when he was eleven. Slipped in the bath, they said, hit her head, they said. Three months later he was sent to Haylesbury. Daddy was determined to go ahead with the plans he had for his son. Ben respected his father's stoicism. This reminded him of when he had first came across the word in school. Mr Oak, his classics master, explained that Brutus was an adherent of the philosophy of the Stoics. When, on the eve of the battle of Philippi, Brutus loses his temper with his ally Cassius over some petty instructions, he omits to mention the tragic missive he has just received. After the friends have embraced in reconciliation, Brutus orders a bowl of wine. Only then he confesses, 'O Cassius, I am sick of many griefs.' Cassius replies blithely:

> Of your philosophy you make no use,
> If you give way to accidental evils.

To which Brutus says:

> No man bears sorrow better. Portia is dead . . .
> . . . her attendants absent, she swallowed fire.

The first part of that, it seemed to Ben, could refer to his own father, the second to his sister Sarah. *Her attendants absent, she swallowed fire.*

★

'Time's up,' grumbled Priya. 'You've had much more than ten minutes. I want the light off *now*.'

He laid his book to rest in the darkness. No point in arguing. He thought she had fallen asleep. He should have known better. The servitude of marriage, the life-sucking subservience of it. Some nights he went up to the kitchen to read in order to avoid this curtailment, but tonight he was too distracted to read. He wanted to be near Priya and the dark was good for that. She was lying on her side facing away from him. He shovelled his specs and wristwatch under some crusty knickers on the floor and pulled up alongside. This was their favourite position. Like two foetuses fitted together, the smaller inside the larger. He wrapped his right arm round her shoulder and cradled her breast in the snug of his palm whilst finding the soles of her feet with his insteps. She replied by pushing her bum up against his lap till she found the right pressure. He nuzzled the back of her neck, displacing strands of her hair by breathing out through his nose. Priya let out a hum of tired satisfaction.

From somewhere above them, as if he were a bird on a branch, Ben observed this comfortable wedlock embrace: white brother, brown sister, like a swivel of layered chocolate, dark and white. He hated white chocolate, so he imagined a pudding, one layer meringue, or even nougat, the other chocolate, not slices, not a gateau, but in the shape of a voluptuous swirl, a multiracial lolly, with some sort of roasted nuts. Hazelnuts, perhaps. That should be his next recipe, number 32. He tried to find some way of making sure he remembered it before he fell asleep. Once, at a school lecture, he had heard the famous ornithologist-painter Rushman Lasdie say that he never went to sleep without a notebook on his bedside table. The middle of the night, according to him, was when one had great thoughts and great dreams. Lasdie regaled them with the story of Muriel Spark, who had woken up one morning to find that she had dreamed the entire plot of her next novel, from beginning to end, all in one night. Nothing left to do but reach for her sharpened pencils.

Ben had started writing the recipes for his East/West cookbook two years ago. It had seemed an original idea at the time; the editor of his first book was keen, said his agent. The opening chapter traced the history of cardamom and pepper – did people know, for instance, that in the sixteenth century Britain consumed more spices than India? The book would be a blend of recipes, history, sociology and anecdote. Like early blooms three lyrical chapters had written themselves, but then the plant had become stifled and withered to a dry stalk. As time hastened on, he saw more and more fusion cooking appearing in restaurants, and the more he read about it and the more he tasted it the more depressed he became about his own enthusiasm for the subject. This kind of cooking was everywhere, but only in a few places did it amount to very much more than the addition of spices to western sauces, with little understanding of their essential qualities. His book was subtle: he wanted to write about food in a way that harked back to the great French gourmands of the nineteenth century, such as Brillat-Savarin. Ben wanted to emulate the verve and the eclecticism of M. F. K. Fisher. Years ago, he had had his first pizza from a wood-fire oven in Umbria. On coming home he had been sure that if one could start a restaurant in London with a wood fire, people would be thronging at the doors. His friends had said it wouldn't be allowed because of the smoke laws. Five years later the first restaurant with a wood fire opened in Farringdon. It became a huge success.

Two

Lying in bed, with the memory of Priya accusing him of doing nothing for Whack's birthday, he couldn't help thinking, I bought some presents. I went to the bookshop, specially.

It was *The Fight* that had taken him to the bookshop. He'd come across an extract from Mailer's book in an anthology in the school library and liked the writing so much he had decided to go out and buy it. The title had made him think of Whacka. Whacka wasn't his real name. It had come of Arjun Tennyson's desire to be sung to at bedtime. 'Sing "Whacka", Daddy. I wan "Whacka"!' he pleaded, night after night. 'Whacka' was his way of saying 'Frère Jacques'. But it fitted in with everything he was. The hands and legs thudding inside her that Priya had complained of all through the middle of her pregnancy. Before he was born she'd imagined him as a fighter, and Ben, who'd been keen to stop this male-warrior phallic stuff, couldn't help but agree that it must be something in Whacka's genes.

Whacka was a kicker, a screamer, a street-fighter, a spear-carrier, a banshee all rolled into one. He came tumbling out of the womb and in his black eyes, as Priya said to her friends, into which she was the first to look, there was a green smouldering. Whoever you were, you couldn't help but marvel at the pugnacious energy that radiated from the toddler. Ben was no sportsman, his games of tennis apart. Priya had an intellectual's interest in sporting behaviour – for the actual games she showed no concern, unless India were playing in the cricket World Cup. But Whacka was already sport-obsessed. For hours at weekends he studied all sport on television, and nothing made him happier than kicking or hitting a ball round the garden or the park. His parents watched with growing fascination the foreign proclivities of their descendant.

In Books etc. on Victoria Street, at the end of a day's teaching, Ben found Mailer's book. He went on to the children's section after that, and there encountered the vivid Californian colours of the Maisy stories. He bought the most elaborate one, imagining what pleasure it would have given him as a child to have owned it. By the till he saw *Jimmy's Snowy Book*, on its cover a baby-blue background with balls of white flaking down, Jimmy in a multicoloured scarf and red cap, a bird and a yellow puppy. Ben remembered a book about snow that he had adored as a toddler: 'This is snow. Snow is very cold.' About a boy building a snowman with a carrot for a nose. He wanted to go back there, be there outside their porch on a bitter January morning, smacking the nougat-like snow-pack with his blue plastic spade. Stick a pipe in his mouth. A scarf round his neck. The carrot, the specs, the whole cliché. The silliest basic book you could find, but it had captivated him. To this day, when snow fell Ben stared out of the window like a rapt child, enchanted by the transformation of the air, 'gazing on the new soft-fallen mask'.

The snow book was expensive, and Whacka would yank all the tabs from their pull-out sockets, but in a self-indulgent mood Ben gave into his childhood fantasy. From somewhere came another fantasy: a whiteness in his underpants, a gluey residue in the seat of his crotch. Fucking Helen on the desk in her head of year's office.

*

Helen Finnegan had come to Tachbrook a year and a half ago to take up the post of head of year 11. She had become Ben's friend. She was a woman with a zest for life, two children (a boy and a girl), and a husband, Steven, a grey academic who had devoted his life to setting up a pressure group campaigning on behalf of injured industrial workers. He was writing his second book on the subject. It had taken him ten years so far. Helen told Ben laughingly that once, when she had complained too much about Steven's writing obsession, he had locked himself in the bathroom with his laptop and threatened to throw it out of the window.

Ben remembered sitting in the pub with Helen after a parents' evening a few months ago when she was confiding in him about her lack of sexual adventure because of her early marriage and parenthood. Like inviting butterflies, her eyebrows fluttered as she spoke. Ben tried to keep his gaze off her breasts as she flicked back the blonde-streaked hair that had fallen in her face. He had every right to take this chance, he wouldn't have to feel any guilt. Why hold back? Vengeance is mine, he thought. How could Priya object after all she'd put him through?

After the pub, on the way to the tube station, they twice stopped on a side street. It was dark. Their conversation came to a halt. Both times it seemed as if they would kiss, Ben thought he should take her in his arms, press her against these ornate London railings. She was waiting, but each time something held him back. He remembered her sigh; 'Oh Ben,' she said, then slipped her arm through his and walked him down the ramp of Pimlico station.

Some weeks after that evening, when Ben was at a crowded table of inebriated teachers in the George and Dragon, Helen's lips, all juiced with lipstick and red wine, came through the pub haze and landed like plush cushions on his mouth. There they waited while his tongue lay slack. A rotting smell, strong as garbage and old wine, made him want to retch. He opened his mouth and let her loll her tongue round. She straddled his knee with her leg. He knew that colleagues were watching. He had never been one for the standard drunken-teacher behaviour. He'd been faithful to Priya for eight years and now this. Is this what it felt like? He disentangled himself and went to the bar and bought some more drinks, Guinness to wash out the taste of her.

John Welsh, his opponent at tennis, slunk up to him with an empty pint glass. 'I wouldn't bother, she's not worth it. I don't know,' he said, shaking his head. 'How does a married man like you allow her to kiss you like that?' Using the soft of his thumb he twirled his gold wedding band ostentatiously. Ben ignored him. 'Mine's a pint of dry cider,' John said.

Ben paid for the drinks and went back to Helen without uttering a word to Welsh.

He liked Helen. He could always rely on her friendship. If it were not for her he might be forced to spend all his time talking to the likes of Welsh about football scores, and which of their colleagues had drunk thirteen pints last night. Helen and he talked about books and food and relationships and school kids and their own. She was smart, committed, hardworking. She had told him about her two lists. The first one was a list of the things she could do something about and the second was a list of things she could do nothing about.

Another night in the George, while they were talking, Ben was thinking he might tell her about how his life had been torn in two. He thought he might approach the subject obliquely: 'How would you feel if what you had always believed to be the truth was suddenly, dramatically, gouged out?' She would be the first person to hear his story. She was sufficiently distant from his world of friends and family. He felt the need to tell someone, other than Anouchka, Priya's and his therapist. Helen had stopped him with a drunken kiss. She dwelt on him with her steel-blue eyes. Something seized Ben's limbs, crept into his pants and sent his blood into a surging spin. He wanted her. He knew exactly how. He wanted her to lie face down on her desk, on her head-of-year desk, strewn with registers and letters, black skirt flung over the small of her back, bare breasts too full for his hands. She urging him to go in harder. He was a cliché from the end-of-term Christmas party. Helen was worth more than this.

The afternoon he had gone into the bookshop to buy his son a present he'd imagined an encrustation of sperm on his penis, Helen going home with no knickers, their joint juices dribbling down the insides of her legs. She had knelt down, taken his penis to her cheek, made him hard, working devotedly she had swallowed his turmoil. He was behaving like an animal – he could not explain it except as revenge. Where did these images come from? The public school in which they had wanked themselves sore on *Forums* and *Penthouses*?

On the way home, he had felt proud of his purchases: the situation was under control, he had bought two presents for Whacka's birthday and he had slipped in a treat for himself. Then he remembered that he should have warned Priya – she would have got Whacka a whole busload of gifts. If it had been up to him, these two books and perhaps a toy would have been enough. He remembered treasuring the few presents he had been given at Christmas and on his birthday. A sword, a shield, a skateboard, a scooter, a Scalextric set. But nowadays, birthdays were an obscenity, a week-long celebration, a confusing plethora of objects. He noticed the fleeting interest children showed in their presents. He remembered the pleasure of receiving a present lasting for days. Now it was just the frenetic desire to tear open the next gaily decorated wrapper and peer at the bits and pieces inside. One after another, until the inevitable built-in disappointment of the last one. End of the line. The tangerine in the toe of the stocking.

Priya showered Whacka with presents as if that disappointment could be forestalled, that sadness swamped by a further excess of rocking horses, play-kitchens and teddy bears. Battery-operated cars, flashing telephones, tricycles, garish doctor's kits. Chests full of toys and gadgets surrounded them. Even the so-called useful ones irritated him. The pram with its rain hood, the bouncy chair, the paddling pool, the swing, the car-seat, two pushchairs, the high chair, the travel cot, nappy bags, bottles, stair gates, safety catches for all the kitchen cupboards, socket and corner guards. All for one brattish badly behaved three-year-old.

Still awake. Still thinking. Still looking for a satisfactory exit. Tomorrow morning Ben had to wake up at six thirty. He had promised to stop on the way to work at an Oxfam outlet in Upper Street, to pick up an ancient rocking horse that Priya had reserved three weeks ago. Another present. 'A beautiful old-fashioned red horse,' she had said. Priya, in her Indian way, had done a deal with the man, or at least she thought she had. For thirty pounds, knocked down from thirty-five, he would even open the shop early so Ben could pick up the rocking horse on his way to school.

★

as if one day equals a lifetime. As if everything important that's ever happened to you finds its way into some recess of the brain where it reverberates for the rest of your days. The mind never forgets. If your sister committed suicide, or your father died when you were seven, or you were raped, or even the good things that have happened, like passing an important exam, your first sexual experience, these things, it's accepted, stay with you all your life, they are never going to go away. But what about the small things? The smell and touch of things?' Priya remembered the musky fragrance of the sheets in her childhood bedroom in Delhi, the warmth and weight of her mother's hand on her chest as she lingered and sometimes fell asleep beside her in the afternoon heat. Some days they were there, but only in the very far reaches of conscious thought, or in your dreams, but most days these memories gained a new encrustation, a new layer of misery or understanding. People talked about things getting better with time. They got better, maybe, but they also got worse. Because each accruing day the humiliations and pains and joys gained a further lamina of significance; another angle, a loss, a discovery, a struggle to recall. The June morning in Oxford, almost nine years ago when Priya heard she had got a distinction in her MPhil. She always remembered that day, the hot weather, the pride on her mother's face, the sun burning through the window of her room in St Catherine's. She would revisit that moment often and each time some transfiguration occurred. A little bit of that summer's day would peep out at her, like a ray of inviolate light, against which nothing could measure up. Or the afternoon she made her first broadcast from the World Service to the subcontinent. One of those London days when the air looks as thick as the dark water in a pond. She walked all the way home from Bush House even though she could have afforded a taxi, daydreaming of being the most famous broad-caster in the country, seeing herself appear on TV, in news-paper interviews and profiles, her memoirs lining the shelf.

The last time she saw her father at the sanatorium in his dirty kurta pyjamas: this *was* her father, and yet she felt in-different, neither sorry nor sad. The day Ben found Leo's letter, how careless were the moments before she breezed in through the door and saw him sitting there, an ashtray choked with butts by his side. And later when she noticed the colour of his blood on their granite table. She had become obsessive about the shade of red, like a dark cherry she had once seen immersed in liqueur. She remembered a phrase from Leo's letter: 'I want things to remain the same.' How reassuring that line had seemed to her at first. Now she saw it for what it was. A hollow wish. Nothing would ever be the same again.

So she lay there, her thoughts like those of a fox who finds herself penned in by baying hounds. Shutting her eyes, she pushed away the images that had harried her every hour since that holiday in Wales, and the ecstatic moonlit night in the open field with the sheep bleating. Could she go back and change what had happened? Would she, could she, react differently if the same situation arose once more? When she had tried to allude to this in therapy, Ben had kicked the table and walked out of their session. Taut-muscled grimace on his exiting face. Tonight she must box up these thoughts. She yearned for sleep to seal the lid.

Too many nights had been spent going over the whys and wherefores and the where-to-go-from-heres. Tomorrow, no, not tomorrow, this day, the day that had just begun, was her son's birthday, and she was going to try hard to get some sleep so she could be awake to enjoy it.

A few months ago she couldn't have borne lying here in bed with her eyes closed. Those nights when she had followed Ben from room to room in their flat, he trying to slam the door on her, holding his fingers in his ears and humming as she shouted herself hoarse, as if to be heard was all that mattered. To speak your mind, she had learnt from an early age, was one of the fundamental rights of every human being: with every drop of her freedom-fighter heritage she would strive to uphold this. She remembered the night when the neighbours had rung the doorbell; the same night Whacka had woken from his bed and they had fought over who would comfort him. Ben rushed out into the cold street, with Whacka in his arms, threatening to call a cab and run away unless she left him alone. Today, 15 March, the Ides of March, it must be past two, her son's birthday already, if only she could purge the thoughts from her head. Would she and Ben survive the day without an eruption? She was determined that it should be so. What were birthdays for, anyway? Fake celebrations? Reminders of the chance in a million that had brought us here. That's not the way Ben saw the date of Whacka's birth.

Fellow, come from the throng; look upon Caesar.

What say'st thou to me now? Speak once again.

Beware the Ides of March.

Priya could feel the roilings in Ben's head. She knew he was still awake. The heat of those revolvings in the bed, but he wouldn't let them out. He was so knotted up, his wiry muscles strictly plaited, the way her ayah used to yank her hair into

Priya remembered thinking, If only I didn't have to look any more. If only the producer could edit me out of this scene, like a piece of errant tape on a radio report. When Whacka was a baby and they used to go to the café at the bottom of Parliament Hill, she would see this woman, swaying backwards and forwards in her plastic orange seat. The woman would intone the same line over and over, 'No you're not, Mummy. No you're not, Mummy. No you're not, Mummy.' At first Priya was sure the woman was saying, 'Know you not, Mummy?' Back and forth, in a beige mac, like a pendulum, speaking in time with her movement, she would go on, 'Mummy phones me, she says, "How are you, my love, my darling, my sweetheart? How are you keeping, my darling, my sweetheart?"' Back and forth, back and forth, as Priya used to rock on the squeaky-springy sofa-swing at her uncle's house in Poona. Hours at a time, as a child, she would push with her little toes, up and away. Into the trees and out, into the trees and out. 'Mummy says, "I won't be able to phone you any more, my love, my sweetheart, my darling heart."' Priya remembered it all. '"Write to me," she said, "my sweetheart, I have to save money, so I can't phone you, my sweetheart, my darling, but you must go on writing to me, my love, my sweetheart, my darling, whatever you do, don't stop writing, my sweet love, my honey pet, my darling." "Yes, Mummy," I said, "Of course I will, I will write to you, I promise, Mummy, I will write to you of course I will."' And then back again to her pacifying refrain: 'No you're not, Mummy. No you're not, Mummy. No you're not, Mummy.'

What was it about the deranged woman that had touched Priya so? Was it her bravery? The way she came to the park each day, demanded her cups of tea with four sugars? The way she continued to want to live? Or was it the more obvious stuff about missing her own mother? Can any of us ever get enough of our mothers? Once, when Priya was three, her mother had gone away for four months, having been invited to be a visiting writer at Cambridge. Priya, her father and her brother, the three of them at home together. So she was told, but she couldn't remember any of it. Nor could she remember when her mother came off the airplane and Priya was standing at the bottom of the stairs on the tarmac, allowed there by special permission, waiting with her dad and grandfather to welcome her. Priya had shrunk from her mother's arms and called her 'Aunty', as if she were a stranger. That became a family joke. It was only now when she thought of the impossibility of leaving Whacka for more than ten hours at a stretch that the hurt of her mother's absence had begun to strike.

Once again her mind dragged her back to Leo's tears falling on the table. She hated him for crying like that. What right had he to cry? Pale-skinned, dark-haired oafish man's tears, dropping on their absurdly expensive granite table. Priya could swear that even with her head bowed, she had heard the patter of droplets. 'It's all over, it's all over,' he kept repeating, 'too late for this. I didn't want this.' Priya remembered feeling that clichéd numbness that takes over in the presence of uncontainable emotion. She couldn't feel anything just when she needed desperately to utter some words of comfort, or even of rebuke. Say something, make some gesture, either of denial, or love, or hate, she remembered urging herself. But it wasn't there and she didn't know how to fake it.

'Fuck you, Leo! You should have known better, you should have *fucking* known better, than to behave like such an ignorant twit.' Surely 'ignorant' wasn't the right word. Ben had spoken to Leo as if they were still the closest of friends, as if he still loved him. 'Stop crying. It's me who should be crying, it's my blood, my life, my baby.' Then Ben spoke to himself, as if Leo and Priya weren't in the room, as if they were doomed to be bystanders for ever, their fate to listen to and to suffer the course of events they had instigated. 'How could you have let her stay on her own? I loved her. I loved them both. I love my baby, my baby, my baby, my baby!' Ben's broken-backed cries. Priya stepped forward, glad to feel something. 'But, Ben, he's still your baby, he'll always be your baby, don't you understand?' He looked at her then with a primal hatred.

It was her, it was her he despised, not Leo. It was her he most wanted out of sight. It was that kind of woman-hating, she thought, that made men rape. From her bed, she saw Ben coming forward again, she watched him as he came, laid his hands, his monkey paws that had loved her so well, flat on the stone table, looked with gleaming eyes at the wall, and seemed as if he were going to butt Leo, who didn't flinch until Ben's head came tumbling like a cataract. The crown hurtling down on to the black stone, once, twice, three times – the fall of the torso as with a marionette folding at the waist – before they were able to dive in and pull him off. 'I trusted you! I trusted you!' he cried. Blood flying, animal howls. 'Get your hands off me! Stop crying! Stop that crying! You Judas! You pathetic . . . My heart hurts, it hurts . . . Do something. Tell me, what should I do? I'll take any kind of medicine. I'll die.' For a minute there were only two sane people in the room, she and Leo. Evil sanity. It filled her with self-disgust. Thinking about it now, almost a year after the incident, it struck her that it was probably what Ben had intended.

As if a plug had been pushed back into place, the flood had

stopped. Priya wished Ben had gone on till he was spent. 'Give me a cloth,' he said. And then, with icy politeness, mopping his bloody forehead, 'You'd better call me an ambulance.' As she went to the phone, Priya said, *sotto voce*, 'You're an ambulance.'

Ben drifted towards sleep. Uncoiling from his cramped position, he stretched out his thin legs. The accounting of his life was almost over. School tomorrow, nothing to worry about there. Possibility of tennis next Sunday. A recipe entered the recesses of his mind. Tumescence of something saporific. Number 33: Rice with Cinnamon and Cloves. Yes, that's what he was getting: the distinctive nutty whiff of steaming basmati. Serve it with Puy lentils and butterflied leg of lamb that's been marinated in yogurt, garlic, cumin and the sweet chilli powder that comes from Kashmir. Rice must be perfectly cooked. Each grain fluffy, standing on its own, but never al dente like we British cook it.

Two years of writing and still he was torturing himself with the unfinished book. Neither the publisher nor the agent called any more. No more free lunches. Remember when the TV company had courted him? How he'd stuttered in front of the camera. His face looked so angry in the screen test. How did Leo manage to play tennis and football and still work on his frames? He had admired Leo. The dedication, the craftsmanship, the hours, even at weekends, that he spent in his workshop. And sometimes, for months, there had been no orders, no pictures to frame, no tables to make, and still he had worked without complaint in his strip-lit, bare-boarded room.

They used to meet for walks when Whacka was a baby. They talked about friendship, while tramping round for hours on Hampstead Heath. Once Leo had said, 'When you're young, you think friends are dispensable, old ones go, new ones come, you think there'll always be more. But, recently, I've begun to realize how important to me my friends are.' Ben had no man he could talk to now. He missed Leo. There was no point in denying it. He should confide in someone. But he couldn't think who. 'I know it's selfish, but I don't want kids,' Leo had always said. Without kids, you could do anything. Run away. See the world. And yet, most people did nothing. Slumped in front of the telly after school or work watching *Countdown* and *Neighbours*.

Ben had slipped so far down the slope of sleep that only something grating could halt his progress. A whirring noise, like the heavy blades of a ceiling fan. Cricket. The 'pick, pack, pock, puck' remembered by Joyce in *Portrait*. Ben loved the game. He had only learnt to play it properly at Mayo College, the boarding school in India where he had been invited to teach in his year off from Oxford. He remembered the boys laughing at his attempts to bowl. At Mayo he was taught how to drive the ball with a straight bat by Nayyar, the beautiful south Indian chemistry teacher. Nine months in barren Rajasthan, which ended in the summer of 1989. He was happy there. Nayyar and he staying up late into the night smoking the local grass from a pipe. The boys used to tease Nayyar mercilessly. So lugubrious, so lyrical, such dark liquid limbs, his silken movements like thick sweet cups of Indian tea. He remembered the crispness with which Nayyar hit a square cut. Brilliantly caught in the gully by a tubby fielder. Ben's vision of himself at the crease used to send him to sleep on baking nights in Ajmer. Ben smiled as he saw it coming to him again.

★

He is standing at the crease, a cricket bat gripped in his hands, waiting to receive a bouncer. A giant bowler is pounding down a tunnel towards him. The man is lanky, like Kapil Dev or Curtly Ambrose. His arms and legs, as they get closer, scythe through the air like the blades of a windmill caught in a gust.

Ben can see the red ball cupped right up against the ear, the bowler's eyes pinned wide, like a racehorse in the home straight. He can see the high kick of the white-flannelled knees, the hard toes of the spiked cricket boots, the elastic limbs coiling up for the rocket release, a polished cannonball ready to be fired into the hot breeze. The silent stitches of the seam peek out at Ben from between the V-shape of the bowler's digits. The ball is hurled like a spear. It stings the dirt halfway up the wicket, ricocheting as it ascends towards Ben's brain. His bat swings upwards, backwards, sidewards. His eyes are trained on that shining missile. He spies the glint of gold, the lettering of the maker, '5 1/2oz, Made in Pakistan'. The bat comes back round his shoulders – the face open, the orange grooves carved for balance, the Gray-Nicolls signature, the oiled and pressed willow – and pulls at the ball. Ben strikes it at its apex, swinging long and hard and loose, correcting the flow of energy, not hitting against it. 'Thwack!' The maroon orb wallops the air, setting off on its loop round the world and into the stands, into the hordes, into their gaping maws. From his bed Ben sees the bowler, standing with his hands on his hips, looking out to the square-leg boundary, where a forlorn fielder gazes at the arcing ball, soaring like a comet, a rainbow, a half-moon smile for the nature of moving things.

Pillowed in a north London gloom, sliding down the glassy slope – the middle journey of his life – Ben tried in the far reaches of his falling to open his eyes but he was helplessly, hopelessly, tumbling into the wet, sweet, plunge pool of slumber. In the city darkness, not a real darkness – 'a brightness shining in darkness which darkness could not comprehend' – Priya turned, munched on her suspirating lip and soothed an itch on the left cheek of her burnished buttocks.

happily ensconced in the buttery folds of goose down, perhaps it was the heavy lunch, followed by the exertion of walking up Primrose Hill, and the satisfaction of sex before sleep.

The day before Whacka's birth they had been invited to lunch by Leo's mother, Jocelyn Batstone. Priya's mother, Mohini Patnaik, who had arrived from India ten days before, was staying with Jocelyn and her husband, Martin, until her daughter's baby was born. Mrs Patnaik intended, once Priya gave birth, to spend the days with Priya and Ben, helping them look after the baby. In 1987 and 1988, while she was an undergraduate at the School of Oriental and African Studies, Priya had spent nine months living in a top-floor room of the Batstones' house in Camden Town. She thought of them as her family away from home. Leo, who was learning his trade as a frame-maker, lived in the room next to hers. He and Priya spent many an evening in the pub with his friends. They talked late into the night and he played her his collection of singles and rolled large conical spliffs. She teased him about being dumped by his upper-class girlfriends. They watched Mike Leigh's *Nuts in May*, sick with laughter at the tuneless gathering of campers. Priya entered a London world that felt different, more real than the university hall of residence she had lived in and the students' bar she had frequented in her first two years of college. She loved Jocelyn's style of housekeeping, her disregard for order and tidiness, a long way from the elegance and simplicity of her mother's small house in Poona. When going to bed, Jocelyn, at fifty-seven, still stepped out of her clothes like a teenager, leaving them in a ruffled pile on the floor. She was a loud talker, eccentric, opinionated, but also full of curiosity. She represented that group of people who thought that no problem was insurmountable if only one applied a little common sense, although her version of common sense was often interpreted as provocative and perverse by its recipients. Priya loved her unfettered pronouncements, her lack of conventional understanding as to the right moment to stop. The world needed characters who were not afraid to blunder, who dared to test their emotions, who were not afraid to risk. Of Leo's sister Alice, Jocelyn confessed to Priya that she found her boring. 'She sleeps too much and she's not interested in anyone except her husband and her daughter.' Priya liked Alice, and would defend her, but she had to admit there was a smug languor evident in Alice's yawn-accompanied pronouncements. Of Leo, on whom Priya knew that Jocelyn doted, she said he was a waster, weak and easily influenced. 'Why should anyone choose to make picture frames for a living? I can see that one might be interested in carpentry as a hobby. But to spend seventeen days working on a chair! I ask you. It's all the fault of that school I sent him to. The only teacher who ever inspired him was the craft and design man. Oh, what was his name, Jim something . . . Jim Kelly. When I went to the parents' evenings, Mr Burleigh, the head of English, would say, "Oh Mrs Batstone, Leo's got such an original eye," and I would say, "But he can't spell." "Yes," said the silly man, "nor can I, and I'm the head of English at this school."'

'And then what did you say?' Priya would ask.

'I said, "Will he pass any exams?" They just weren't interested. Middle-class boy, he'll muddle along, was what they thought. And, of course, he failed most of his exams. He tried to cheat in the French exam and we were very nearly hauled into court.'

'But it all turned out okay for Leo. He's doing what he wants to do.'

'That's as maybe. I don't know if he really wants to be sitting in a loft on his own all day. There isn't a call for his kind of craftsmanship these days. He's a gregarious chap. He likes to chat, he likes to gossip, to be in the thick of things.' There was a grain of truth, hidden under a mattress of exaggeration, in everything Jocelyn said.

Priya loved Jocelyn because Jocelyn loved her people, Indians and Pakistanis, or perhaps it was that Jocelyn loved and hated in such strong measure. She hated her own sister, but she loved Priya's mother. She thought sex was overrated, but she loved food. She didn't ever drink but she smoked ceaselessly. Within seconds she might create animosity or, for that matter, delight in the heart of a new acquaintance. She was always spoiling for a good argument, but she would just as easily accept criticism. She had her loyal followers from round the world, who visited her annually.

The minute Priya dropped down into the armchair by the gas fire in Jocelyn's kitchen she felt like a teenage daughter coming home from college. Jocelyn had no airs, no manners, no ceremony. For Priya, honesty was more important than manners. At Jocelyn's you didn't need to ask, you could make yourself a cup of tea or hunt in the kitchen for the whisky bottle. Her open house was always well stocked with food and drink, and friends dropped in and stayed for hours.

And she loved Priya's mother. Ever since Priya had lodged in her house, Jocelyn had insisted that 'Lady Patnaik' – as she liked to call Priya's mother – must stay a few days with her when she visited her daughter. It was a strange, perhaps unlikely relationship. Priya was never sure what her mother thought of Jocelyn: people often misunderstood her loudness, mistaking it for boorishness, and Jocelyn made no attempt to correct them. Priya's mother, Mohini Patnaik, had poise, but she was shy. She spoke carefully and quietly, she smiled gracefully, she seldom laughed. Jocelyn guffawed and shouted and stuck her hand down her shirt, and even sometimes down her trousers to tackle an itch on her belly or to stroke the side of her thigh.

Martin Batstone, Jocelyn's husband, a sociophobe who hid away in his bedroom or ran round the corner, book in hand, to the pub whenever there was company, was also fond of Mohini, and spent some time alone with her, at breakfast normally, while Jocelyn was still bleary-eyed in her lavish bathroom, spluttering and spitting into the ornate basin. Martin served Mohini breakfast, and asked her in his tentative whisper about her writing. He had chosen the right person to talk to. Mohini wouldn't try, she had too much tact, to pry into Martin Batstone's mysterious layabout life. It was said that he was working on a business deal to import cheap globes and flip-flops from a manufacturer in Malaysia, but whenever he was asked about it he would shrink from the suggestion. 'Nothing more than negotiations, too early to talk about.' Mohini had used the lineaments of Martin's personality for a character she was writing about in her current novel. At breakfast it was Martin, in his hesitating voice, who asked the questions. She answered them and found herself saying something new about her writing. His were the usual questions, 'Are you very disciplined?', 'Where do your ideas come from?' When journalists and readers ask these questions, they want a neatly wrapped answer. Your life, in no more than fifty words. Martin was a sensitive, patient listener. He offered Mohini coffee, which she politely declined. She liked Darjeeling tea, black with a slice of lemon, and had an aversion to mugs, especially if they were chipped, as they often were at the Batstones'. Mohini would ask for a poached egg and Martin served her this like an intelligent and careful butler she remembered from a hill-station hotel in Musoorie.

On that afternoon, three years ago, the day before Whacka squeezed his fighting forehead into the thick heat of delivery room 2 at the Whittington Hospital, they were all sitting in Jocelyn's basement kitchen waiting for lunch. Leo was talking to Ben about the torso of a new TV cook. Martin was serving the drinks while being instructed in other menial tasks by Jocelyn, hunching round the kitchen in his cardigan, head tilted downwards in case somebody should attempt to speak to him. Jocelyn stood at the head of the table, introducing Mohini to an Indian writer whom she had also invited to lunch. He was a well-known member of the new breed, kept getting shortlisted for prizes, and Mohini, one of the old school, who still lived in the time before large advances and book tours, felt little interest in meeting him. It was a bumblingly well-intentioned move on Jocelyn's part. Mohini did not particularly like meeting other writers; she had told Jocelyn this, more than once, in her discreet way. But there were some things you had to shout, perhaps even strangle Jocelyn with, before she took any notice. 'Of course one Indian writer would love to meet another, it makes sense, the poor fellow is missing his Calcutta home.'

Arun Sengupta, gaunt, bespectacled, neatly bearded, sat very still in his chair, apparently suffering from some sort of depression or airplane-shock. He was finding it difficult to utter a word, and his intense eyes seemed fixed on the forsythia bushes in the garden. You didn't want to appear depressed or ill in Jocelyn's presence: she would hack into your shadows with a butcher's disregard for delicacy. 'I saw your picture in the papers the other day. Very handsome, I thought. Is it because of that stately face, I asked myself, that he sells so many books?'

Mohini smiled at the writer as if to say, Don't worry – this is just style. Take it on the chin, ride it. She felt the force of this man's youth in his wounded ashen look. Had he strayed into a lion's den? 'Whatever you might say, Jocelyn,' Mohini said, trying to befriend Sengupta, 'a photograph in a newspaper is a priceless bit of publicity for a writer.'

'Why not do a photograph in the nude then?'

The writer's jaws clenched to stop his mouth from dropping open.

'You're not being serious, Jocelyn. A carefully placed picture can be worth a thousand words.'

'But *you* don't believe in photographs. You've told me you never carry a camera. Anyway, Arun knows that I enjoyed his book tremendously. I think his next novel should continue where this one trailed off. Now admit it, Arun, it wasn't much of an ending, was it? The father dies, the little boy wanders into the slums of Calcutta. You're not very interested in telling stories, are you?'

The writer had begun to speak, when Jocelyn bellowed across the room, 'Maartiiin! It's time to take the lamb out and let it rest for a bit – where has the silly fellow gone?' she said, striding off to the kitchen door.

Whacka was nine days past his due date. Inducing drugs were on offer after two weeks; they would become a necessity when the baby was three weeks overdue. A heavy lunch of lamb and potatoes was being brought on to the table by the shuffling butler-cum-husband, and just as the young writer was beginning his careful explanation of why he had resisted pressure for a sequel, Jocelyn, wagging a finger, exclaimed, 'Wait a minute, I almost forgot the prawns,' and excused herself. She reached up to a blackened wok hanging on a hook. 'Priya,' she called.

Priya was talking to Jan, Leo's wife. 'So, I'm not sure what to do now,' she was saying. 'I'm in this fight with the head of the unit, who wants me to come back to work after three months of maternity leave, and I want six months off, and then I want to return three days a week.'

'So, have they made a decision?' asked Jan.

'No, they're forcing *me* to choose. But why should I? I don't want to put myself in a vulnerable position right now. It's a bit of a mess,' she said, as she moved over towards where Jocelyn seemed to be chopping some ginger. 'You mustn't do these prawns specially for me, Jocelyn. Look at that lovely lamb. I need more space in this damn stomach. I can hardly fit in more than a few morsels these days.'

'The prawns must be eaten. Shellfish bring on a birth. That's what you said you wanted on the phone. So I went and got these from the market yesterday. Don't you want them?'

'Hah, prawns I will eat, specially with ginger,' said Priya, shaking her head and slipping into Indian idiom.

'Walking up hills,' announced Jocelyn, 'seafood and sex.' She turned to the politely conversing writers. 'That's right, isn't it?'

'Well,' said Mohini, 'I've heard that shellfish is meant to bring on birth. The rest is news to me.'

'I can offer prawns,' said Jocelyn, 'and I propose, after lunch, a short expedition up the hill at the end of the road. The third thing is beyond my capacity.'

'I'd rather lie down and go to sleep after lunch,' said Priya.

'Walk, then sleep,' said Leo, lovingly. The sound of that voice addressing her sent a jolt through Priya's body. She moved to where her mother was sitting. How could he be so blasé? Every time she saw him she was reminded of scenes from the past that she was trying to forget. Something about him, it tended to be something physical, his fingers, his hands, his chin, the way he ruffled his hair, frightened and revolted her. At these moments she wished she could return to the innocence of their old brother–sister relationship.

Leo was reclining in the armchair next to the gas fire, his broad shoulders spilling out, his long fingers crossed in front of him. They were callused, rough, etched with grime. His dark curly hair was untidy, his black trousers were absurdly tight for his thick waist and his stout legs, and his shirt that had once been blue was now discoloured to a kind of dirty white, the collar and cuffs all frayed. He was chatting to Ben and Jan who were sitting on a two-seater sofa to one side of him. 'I became rather obsessed with the idea of making a soufflé.'

'Did you use a recipe?' asked Ben.

'No. You see, I'd learnt from watching Mum cook. I had this thought about the consistency of eggs. I read up about it, about the elasticity of the molecules. If you beat them they fill up with air and after a certain point they cease to expand. It's quite tricky to find the precise moment.'

'Exactly. So you have to get them to the point of soft peaks. I bet you did it by hand. Did you use a copper bowl?'

'I did. I found an old one in Mum's cupboard and polished it up. How did you know about copper?'

'Yes, but with a soufflé you have to mix the beaten eggs in with something else, and then all those beautiful air bubbles start to break up,' beamed Ben.

'So I wanted to find a way of stirring them into the mixture without bursting too many bubbles.'

'He spent hours on this problem,' said Jan. 'We had soufflés for three days.'

'I'm sorry,' Leo lied.

'I'm not complaining. They were delicious, except for the cheese one.'

'What happened to the cheese one?'

'It exploded in the oven.'

'You're joking.'

'Yellow slurry of melted cheese, like baby food splattered everywhere.'

Leo always had some kind of obsession. Once it was making a cornice just right, another time it was creating a kind of landscape using his new jigsaw to cut into an enormous canvas made of inch-thick MDF. First he did a huge painting of a section of a pond in Hackney Marshes, then he pasted it on to the MDF. Another time he brought the wreck of a vintage car into the front garden of their house in Hackney and it lay there for a whole year while Leo pored over ancient manuals and tinkered with the parts. He really thought he could make it work. According to him, he managed to get the engine running once. 'Maybe it's just that I like to see if I can find a way of working things out. I've always wanted to penetrate the logic of objects. Their raison d'être. It's like if you're walking through a desert, how are you going to find some water to drink? There must be a way. It's just a matter of looking.'

Bundled in sweaters, scarves and coats, like characters in a picture book, the lunch party – minus Sengupta, the writer, who had left precipitately, and Martin Batstone, who was working his way through the washing-up – ambled up the path to the top of Primrose Hill, their breath condensing into clouds of vapour in front of them. Priya remembered when, as a child of five, she had gone to the Lodhi Gardens on a cold Delhi morning with her father, and her smoky breath had produced a host of naive questions. The crisp day in March, and the smell of smouldering leaves and candy floss, had brought her father back.

That afternoon, carrying her load up the hill, her mother at her side, Leo and Ben jousting playfully, Priya had thought how strange that this had become her world. Once upon a time, she was a girl going to nursery in Delhi, then going to school in the seaside city of Bombay, and then she was a teenager at an American boarding school in a hill station, standing in a forest in the shadow of the Garhwal Himalayas, and now she was climbing up a hill in the middle of this city she called her home. She fancied that the air grew thinner as they climbed, and the rooftop vista expanded. 'Sometimes I wonder/If I'm ever gonna make it home again . . .' she sang to herself as she turned to look back at her extended adopted family, straggling up the path, the late afternoon light on their foreheads; the words felt right. Inside her, the demon baby was finally still, his head locked in her pelvis. After all those months of kicking and bumping, he was refusing to budge, tucked in for the fight. A person whom she had already started to love and whom she was aching to see. How could there be a happier time of waiting?

'You know,' said Priya to her mother, 'Ben and I have discussed leaving England. We've been thinking of going to live in Europe. He's done a course in teaching English as a foreign language. I was going to try and get a correspondent's job.'

'But I always thought he wanted to come and live in India,' said Mohini.

'Oh, he's always wanting to do that, but it's more like a dream. He's very rooted to his work here and yet he pretends it's me who doesn't want to leave this city.'

Mohini turned her serene eyes to look at her daughter, scanning her face for any effect her words might have. 'Anyway, now would be an impossible time to leave. For obvious reasons. And you do have a fondness for this city. It feels like your home, doesn't it?' They walked up a few more steps. 'It's changed so much since I came here in the fifties.'

A green kite drifted above the hill. A woman shouted for her dog. 'Joey!' she cried. 'Joeeey!'

'I remember', continued Mohini, 'some years ago now when you came to Poona on your own. On the evening before you left you seemed very sad.'

'It was the first time I truly realized that India was no longer my home. I felt so empty because I hadn't fixed myself here either. I had no sense that I wanted to stay here, although I was enjoying my life in London. But, yes, after that time, and you wrote me such a beautiful letter about it, I began to think, not of England, but of this city as my home, and I also began to think of parts of it as mine, my places. This place is one of my favourites. I love coming up here and looking out at the spread of buildings.'

'You feel this city has accepted you?'

'Absolutely. I came here as a seventeen-year-old and it took me in. The truth is, I know the weather's horrible, all grey and dark and depressing and all. I thought I'd get used to it, but in a way you never get used to it. But then you get a bright cold day like this. Everything becomes so sharp. Sometimes – it's funny – but when I look out of the window and it's raining again, I can almost find the rain comforting. I think to myself, I can stay indoors and do my work or I can get into bed and read a book.' There was a pause in which Priya thought, I have the best mother in the world. She seems to know what I'm thinking, even though we don't see each other much. I always talk so selfishly about myself, and she never seems to mind. They had stopped on the path, Priya panting with the weight of the foetus and her heavy lunch, her mother looking down the slope towards the zoo. The low slant of the falling sun lit up patches of her sari that showed through the overcoat and the shawl wrapped round her shoulders. Gazing at her mother's fine features, Priya wondered how many of them would be passed on to her baby. The dark eyebrows, the oval face, the opalescent eyes, the tiny birthmark on the flare of the right nostril, the oddly shaped, full lips. Mohini's was an unusual dark beauty, especially striking in this temperate country of pallid skins.

Mother and daughter walked the last few steps to the top of the hill in silence. There they stood staring out at the panorama of buildings, like a pack of cards fanned out on a table. They savoured the quiet before Jocelyn and party joined them. Mohini looked out to the blinking tip of Canary Wharf, skimmed her eye over the dome of St Paul's. It was impossible for her to stand here and not to meditate on the potential, the possibility of this place as a scene for her next novel, a location she could use for an epiphany. She tried to wipe these thoughts from her mind and just enjoy the moment as it was. A lifetime's battle against the writer's ineluctable desire to preserve experience. Then she saw an extraordinary thing.

A gleaming tower, whose wall of glass had been transformed by the angle of the dropping sun to the colour of blood. Parts of the building looked black, parts of it red. It was as if the blood of the workers in the building were flaming out incarnadine. The money god clashing with the fury of the sun. Mammon versus Surya. The City against Nature. Town against country. The concrete of capitalism burning in the late afternoon brilliance of this cloudless sky. It was a startling sight. There was an impulse to share it with her daughter, but when she looked round she saw Priya was some metres away, her head resting on her husband's shoulder. Jocelyn, Jan and Leo were in a separate little group talking and pointing.

Jocelyn came over to Priya and Ben. She stood next to Priya, looking benignly down at her bump. Then she placed her arm round Priya's waist and smiled her big, toothy nicotine smile.

Three years ago, Thursday night, Priya and Ben had retired to bed early. Ben had a week's paternity leave, and smiled as he remembered that for him there was no teaching tomorrow. It wasn't just being free from work anxieties that he was looking forward to – it was the anticipation of a new being in their lives. Someone you longed for, who was part of you, but whom you didn't yet know. With a lifetime ahead, a tabula rasa for pleasures and pains. What other relationship could compare? The one with your own mother perhaps, and yet that was the other way round. 'O my darling, "my new-found-land,"' he said as he caressed the hump of stretched skin. 'Come out when you're ready,' he whispered. Ben had always been sure that Priya would cope well with the birth. He used to tease her about having child-bearing hips, but it wasn't that: it was her flexibility of limb and her ability to express her emotions. Not like him. He would be too ashamed to shriek and cry. It would be like shitting out a huge boulder. He wouldn't have the belief. He studied Priya's face as it lay sideways on the pillow, her tangled tresses gleaming black. Hers was not a small face like her mother's. It was an angular handsome beauty of strong jaw and cheekbones, vivid dark eyes she had got from her father. She would be a good mother: he remembered thinking when he had kicked her out of the flat that there was no one else in the world he would rather have a baby with than Priya. Six years it had taken, six and a half years since they had first met in the autumn of '89 in Oxford, sometimes it felt like it would never happen, sometimes it felt like it was not worth waiting for. But now, kneeling between his lover's thighs, he felt a glow of contentment. Patience had borne its fruit. Fatherhood was waiting for him like a hot meal. They were ready now. They were strong. The bad years and the fighting behind them. When did they last have one of their horrible arguments? He tried not to remember.

'Come on Benny, I want you in me.'

'Are you sure it's okay?' he asked with a frown.

'It's meant to bring on the birth. Didn't you hear Jocelyn say that?'

'That's a myth. You sure it won't traumatize the baby?'

'Listen, I read in some book that sperm has some chemical in it that helps induce the birth, so stop dithering. I'm tired.' They still used the same mattress with its blood stain, its pee stain, its tea stain, its semen stain, each with its own spillage story. Ben lay horizontally across the bed with Priya's legs like the pillars of a viaduct arched over his thighs and waist. He turned on his side to face her, with one hand holding the inside of her thigh the way she liked it. He placed his other hand under her buttock. Smooth, effortless, into the cavern he went, thinking he mustn't slide too deep or be too abrupt in case he hurt his baby's head. Some days Priya's cunt felt spacious, some days tight, some days rough, like kissing a stubbled cheek. It depended on her mood and the time of the month. Today it was all largesse. On her back, one hand holding on to the side of her stomach, supporting her mound, he could just see her tweaking face as he pressed in further and her massaging fingers flew faster. He shifted a little. 'Just there,' she gasped. 'Stay there.' Careful not to lose what he was doing, he remained surprised at how he could plunge in without even taking aim, like a blinded archer finding his mark. There was something extraordinary about copulating so freely with a third person looking on. A foetus, with its eyes and nose so close to his trespassing engine. Ben was sure their baby was a girl and he had already started to call her Sacha. Sacha can't see, and anyway it's dark in there, but she can hear and smell, he thought. She must hear a kind of pounding round her head, a clanging of the blood as the vessels dilated and the muscles stiffened in her ears.

The third party is knocking at the door. Spying at us through the keyhole of my cock, thought Ben. A strange blunt animal getting ever closer to its head. Priya's stomach heaved. The mound rolled. Already distended, her belly stretched to a frightening drum-like tautness. But then Ben was lost in that moment of pleasurable physics from which no man can be disturbed or hindered. In the middle of his throes – ultra-intense, ultra-selfish, lasting the few seconds it takes for a thirsty man to drink a glass of water – Priya's voice could be heard. 'Just there,' she whispered, 'just there, just there.'

either side of his chin, cracks of light sneaking through the blind and finding his ever-present scars and scratches. Sudden sharp intakes of air, proving he is still alive. His dreams are impenetrable, unreadable, untellable – he yelps his name, 'Whacka! Whacka!', grumbles and snorts, rubs his nose with the backs of his fingers, makes slurping sounds on an imaginary teat and returns to his frothy breathing. His favourite tartan 'blanky' is wound round his body. He is lying crooked with his triangular head and black hair pushed against the bars of the cot. His pixie ears stick out. The broken railings of the cot have been secured by Ben with strips of cotton cloth on all four sides. Whacka is too big for a cot and has long been able to straddle and climb over the weak fence that surrounds him. On his right forearm, with the wrist facing up and the fingers curled, there is the scar, a scorpion's tail of stitches sewn together eight months ago when he fell on broken glass outside the Highbury pool. The worst of his many wounds. The one that had his parents worrying that he might never be able to use the fingers of his right hand. On his face now is the beatific mask of sleep. His skin is cool and gives off a gentle scent of cocoa butter. He is like a spring gathering energy into its coils, energy for twelve hours of frantic dynamo daytime frenzy.

3.29: The drizzle has turned into a more concerted shower. For an hour – the quietest hour in the cycle of day and night – the city almost sleeps. Apart from the solitary driver snagged at a red light, people are rarely to be seen. This is the hour when the weekday clubbers have straggled home, the sweepers are not yet out, the nightshift workers are still finishing, and the klaxons and sirens, even the birdsong, await their hours of toil. The tired tarmac, washed by the rain, lightened of its load, seems to expand and transpire the heat and smell of the previous day. It is good for any city, as it is for any man, to empty itself, to return to its bed, to contemplate its dark places, what it was that brought it – a huddle of wood and stone dwellings in a bend of the Thames – flickering into consciousness. How vast have been its accumulations, its consuming fires and how wide the arc of influence, the reach and return of its rippling waters, redirected, and swollen with corporeal detritus.

In the north of this wet place of the earth a triangle of humanity lies sleeping: man, woman, child, 26 Lynch Road, the basement bedrooms, with the rain falling outside and dreams spilling out of their brains. Intermittently Priya catches the sound of water falling on to wood, a dripping, louder than the rain, from a burst pipe Mick keeps promising to fix. A crack runs up the brickwork all the way along the right-hand side of the house, from just below Priya and Ben's basement window up to the roof. Inside the bedroom, stuffed with clothes and boxes, Priya lies with her pillow clasped between her arms and legs, a habit she has kept from when she was seven years old. In her head three voices speak: Roshan, her elder brother, Ben, and Whacka's Mary Poppins nanny with the pointed nose and the rockabilly haircut. The three of them are sitting round a kitchen table. Everyone is urging Priya to pick up the phone and get the head of Whacka's nursery to tell her what has happened. But Priya already knows what has happened and there is no use phoning anyone. She sees it all clearly. They are living in a flat in Poona. Whack is coming home from the nursery with Gloria, the nanny. They enter the lift on the ground floor. 'I wan my Daddy! I wan Daddy!' he demands.

Gloria replies in her prissy voice, 'Daddy will be home soon. First we must cook you your tea and if you're a good boy I might, *might*, give you a little chocolate ice cream.'

'I want my swaard!'

'You can have your sword when we get upstairs if you don't hit anyone with it and don't break anything.'

What is the point of a sword for a little boy if he doesn't attack people with it? The boy and his minder ascend to the fourth floor in the lift that Priya remembers from her cousin's apartment block in Poona, the lift with seahorses set in a frosted pane of glass. Dark wood and mirrors all round. Whacka jumps up and down, making the floor of the lift shudder.

'Stop that, stop it,' says Gloria in her sandpaper voice.

'Stop that. Stop it!' Whacka mimics.

Priya feels angry with herself for allowing Gloria to go on working for them. They should have sacked her earlier. Ben was right. Thank God she didn't invite her to Whacka's birthday party. The folding gate of the lift is pushed to one side, Gloria lets Whack out, he scoots to the right, towards the door of the flat. Someone is waiting for him on the other side of the door, someone with a baby in her arms. A small dark Tamil lady like the one who gave Rajiv Gandhi his fatal greeting in Sriperumbudur. And here is Whack letting out one of those battleground screams as he throws off his coat, and pushes open the glass doors. A red bag, like a gigantic boiled sweet has been placed on the other side of these transparent partition doors. Whacka runs towards it. Gloria is still dragging the buggy out of the lift.

'The bag!' Priya calls out. 'The bag, Whacka!' Why can't she find in herself the warning words – 'Don't touch the bag, darling' – not that she would have been able to stop him. Here he is demanding, 'Is it my present?'

The explosion comes, and Priya is watching what she cannot accommodate. She is a helpless bystander, as in a cinema where images cannot be torn from the screen. Swirling blood floods the corridor and rushes towards her. Glass doors bursting into a foam, a crashing wave of crystallized particles, a lethal spume. She searches into it for her son, hoping to see him flung out, but there is no sign of him, no sign of any part of him: an energy equal to his own, many times greater than his own, has swallowed him in its churning jaws. She looks and listens. His voice, his triangular head, his black mane, his floating arm, his wild kick, his gorgeous elfin ears. But all she sees is a picture in slow motion of the corridor teeming with shards of glass and blood. And then she is back round the kitchen table, back with the imploring voices asking her to phone Whacka's nursery in London. She wants to tell them what she knows – that Whack is gone, utterly extinguished, no parts of skin or bone or blood to salvage, or to weep over.

At last the phone rings. It is the nursery. A bomb has gone off. No one knows who is safe and who is injured. Priya wants to tell the teacher that it's not at the nursery that the bomb has gone off but outside her flat. She wants to tell her that all the children are safe except for her son. But what's the point? Who cares where the teacher has got her information? She'll soon find out the truth. The woman is babbling on about a letter she sent all the parents about health and safety guidelines. She wants to know if Priya can remember the contents of the letter or whether she still has a copy. Priya ends the call. 'I'll have a look for the letter and if I find it I'll send it on to you.'

Everyone round the table has hope stamped on their faces. Her brother and sister-in-law are there looking at her. And Ben, she won't be able to look at him ever again. Roshan asks, 'Is he sick? Is Whacka sick? What did the woman say?'

'She didn't say,' says Priya. 'She was banging on about some letter. I couldn't ask her. I didn't ask her about Whacka.' Was it something to do with her reports on Kashmir? The red bag meant for her. Poona, such a safe, quiet town. Why would they come here? Ben and she love taking Whacka for walks through the luscious rain-dripping gardens. Why doesn't she just shout at the old crone, 'Where's my son, damnit! What have you done to my son?' How can she, of all people, be embarrassed to ask this simple question?

Priya groaned in her sleep. She turned from her side on to her back, pushing the duvet off her hot torso. There was the sudden, happy realization of semi-consciousness in her London bed.

Once, when Whacka was a year old, she had left him in the car, strapped in his seat, and raced across the road to a kitchen shop on Upper Street to buy a peeler. She had locked the car from the outside and was keeping an eye on it from the shop window. There was a ditherer in the queue and it took her two minutes to get back. When she looked in through the window of the car Whacka was gone. Empty child seat, empty car. This was before Whack had known how to unbuckle or slip out of the belts of his child seat, so someone would have had to have taken him out of it. She remembered that feeling of the body becoming a hole through which everything has dropped out. A struggle even to scream, to run, where to? Peeler in hand. This only happens in films. Then she looked into the car once more and found him slipped down at the bottom of the steering-wheel, pretending he was driving. A blob of wonder-flesh. All it took was a second. She would never forget the feeling. Never again, she told herself, would she leave the child unattended. For what, a potato-peeler? How could she ever account to herself for that?

Five

A few minutes after Priya had eased herself back to sleep, her husband sat up in bed, woken by a child's crying. From across the street he could hear the engine of an idling car and a woman's voice bawling, 'I told you to get in the *fucking* car. I told you not to move from your . . .' Then a man's voice, trying to reason with her. Ben couldn't hear what he was saying, but soon there was the clunk of a door and the growl of the engine as the car sped away.

Two more hours of sleep. Then Whacka would come stomping in. You heard his footsteps first, then the door handle turning, then a quizzical look at his parents lying in their bed, a little run-up and then the biggest leap he could find straight into the midriff, ponging of his piss-sodden nappy: once he had landed on Ben's head, the nappy crushing into his eyes. Ben could hear Priya breathing about a foot away from his left ear. Every three or four breaths, she let out a whistling sigh. She smelt so lovely. Like a baby. That was something she had inherited from her mother and passed on to her son. Whatever time of day or night Priya's breath was without odour, and her skin gave off a smell like unsalted butter.

Dawn, birds calling, spring rain, wet buds. Ben wanted to linger in this half-asleep state, in the delicious comfort of bed and semi-oblivion. It was like falling softly through the boughs of a verdurous tree. He thought of Keats's 'glooms and winding mossy ways'. He remembered the morning when Whacka was born, walking Priya carefully down the snow-covered steps, driving her up Highgate Hill to the Whittington hospital, past empty pavements, both of them laughing with anxiety, him running off to buy her sandwiches, bacon, lettuce and tomato. She'd complained she was ravenously hungry: that's what made her shit when the baby was pushed out – he'd never told her. In his worst moments of anger he had thought of saying, 'There was a plump brown turd between your legs while you held Whack in your arms.' Proud he'd never told her, glad he didn't have to get out of his bed now, go to the hospital in the snow. But that morning he was so keen, so invigorated by the white outside. He was sure it was a good omen: snow on the day your baby is born. But he should have read the signs. A baby born on the Ides of March.

Priya turns towards Ben, she drops her arm on his stomach, warmth of her body, her smell, against his horrid wine-stained breath. A car passes, bumping over the uneven road, clanging the loose manhole cover. Birds again, a thin milky light slipping in through the curtains. Moonlight or dawn? The frying and hissing of rain. 'I cannot force your hand,' a phrase from Leo's letter, cuts like a lone ice-skater across this arena of impressions.

Waking at this early hour he felt his heart knock against his ribs, remembrances of past nights lying here waiting, not even waiting, just watching as the first leak of day sent fear crawling into his chest. His life, his job, his languishing book, his child, his marriage, his Helen fantasies. Fear of making decisions, of moving forward. Of having 'his hand forced'. He didn't want to have to make choices. He didn't want the images of them in Wales, of their sweaty lust. The new day's light ought to be a moment of hope, thought Ben, he remembered waking up early in India and going to look at the people praying and washing themselves by the river. But now it was as if the curtain of life would have to be drawn and the light rushing in would expose him for what he was. A coward. The great gash, the falsehood in their family would be clear for all to see. And it would be clear, too, that he, Ben Tennyson, was unable to deal with it. How ugly all bodies are when the clothes are shed. You look at the abyss, the risk of it, the pain of it, no Priya, maybe no Whacka, that's what Anouchka was saying: try and imagine what it might feel like without them. Life on your own. No one understands, no one understands the pain as the sufferer does. The horrendous emptying of strength, the disillusionment, the self-hatred, the lack of sleep, the cringing in your bed, alcohol, cigarettes, anything to change what only the passing of time can diminish, rolling over and over again with the past, inside, outside, different ways, backwards, forwards, reverse, obverse.

He had been so sure he had to go. At Haylesbury he had been taught to make a decision and stick to it. He had been so sure he hated her, that he could start again, peel off the scab. Yes, he had thought of Priya as a brown scab, a scarab: one day she would fall off and one day she would suffer for what she had done. But every morning after his epic nights of wakefulness she was still there. He had thought worse things about her than about anyone else in his life. Thoughts from which there was no return. Hate so certain, trust so broken. And everyone is going away and leaving you alone, and what if someone takes your baby, now you have no claim to him? How can I ever stop loving Whacka? 'I tried, but it didn't work,' he said to himself. Blood is not thicker than water. One night, in the middle of the night, he went into Whacka's room, as he usually did last thing, to stand over his sleeping body, to gaze at his beautiful face, a reflection of everything good he had made of himself, never to be taken away, a little bit of him set afloat in the world. The pleasure in seeing him and being with him and playing with him. He had always believed that was inviolable, and then he went in the middle of the night to look at him as usual, and Whacka had turned away, facing the wall, turned away from me, mine no more. Children are good at forgetting. From his classes Ben had experience of how resilient they could be.

She's done it before, she'll do it again. It's a repetition thing. Over and over we try to fight off the things we are afraid of, but they come back to haunt us. They stalk us, waiting for that careless moment, the moment to leap. Like a leopard of lust, the old impulse pounces silently on the brain to feed on all the peace you have collected there.

Every Thursday afternoon at four-thirty, he met Helen in her office. She would double-lock the door. He'd stand behind her and drag the black skirt up her thighs until, like a usurer's beard, the ball of hair was unsheathed. And there he pressed his hand, setting the finger free among the folds. He tries to hold the picture in his mind on this rainy morning, the morning his boy begins the fourth year of his life. But other thoughts crowd in. 'Go away, let me sleep! Let me sleep!' he pleads in his head. But no, he has to go back to the reasoning that has kept him here, kept him in this bed, night after night. At first, just after Leo's letter was found, he resolved to go, he slept upstairs, away from her, on a single mattress, away from the stench of the sheets: then, after nights of sweating and tossing, he came back down, forcing himself back down because, he thought to himself, Why should I be made to leave my own bed? He slept on the edge, far away from her.

There were trains rattling through this city. Wherever you slept, if you listened carefully enough to the sounds, you could hear the clattering of wheels – the weight of wheels in the brain – that's what the torture was like, wheels turning in the brain. Like the clever boy who, on seeing the approaching train, lies stock-still between the tracks and the train passes overhead. Round and round, like Satan . . .

> Round he throws his baleful eyes,
> That witness'd huge affliction and dismay
> Mixt with obdurate pride and steadfast hate.

Pain without boundaries, torture without end. He has been working on Milton with his A level group. They got stuck on the line 'hope never comes / That comes to all'. He let the class ponder it. He was relying on someone to spark. A dangerous ploy. But it worked. Emma – it would be Emma, with the mesmeric eyes, the one who had challenged his credentials, the one who made him feel stupid with her superb explanations – said, 'I think what he is saying is that Satan is in such a state of despair that he can't even hope for anything better, for any kind of change. Most of us are entitled to hope, however miserable our lives are, but because of where God has banished Satan to he doesn't have the luxury even of the most basic human right – to hope.'

He would weep sometimes, and it was a sweet release. But mostly there was a beating of the heart, like some relentless late-night visitor banging on a door. So he had to get up, walk, smoke a cigarette, drink the dregs of the whisky or the coffee. What could he have done to change things? How could he have been different? This must be slothfulness, a lack of strength, not enough *der Wille zur Macht*. Or maybe, it started earlier, with his father, his mother, his sister, his dead sister?

The thought of his class, his A level group, his next lesson with them, like a slip road carrying him away from his motor-way of bleakness. The way he had struggled to work, not believing he could make it through the first lesson, let alone registration, and how once he was in the building, once he got started on his lesson, his students, their faces, their lives, dragged him into action and even into laughter. And then, at the end of a day at school he felt something. Made it through another day without being admitted to hospital or strangling himself with his own sheet like poor Will, the chemistry teacher he had been so fond of. Two of his colleagues had committed suicide. If the thought of going home was no comfort, then there was some satisfaction in knowing one had made it through another day. That bit of Milton. That was something to hold on to.

By the time the penned-in Alsatian, four houses down, starts its ritual early morning barking, Ben has fallen asleep again.

He is standing on a tennis court in the kind of sunlight that makes flames invisible. A cooking contest is set to start between two Indian brothers, Anil and Sunil, both of whom are Ben's friends. At the request of the two brothers, Ben has booked courts 5 and 6 in Highbury Fields, the ones next to the road. It is to be a big public confrontation to which journalists, friends and relatives have been invited. Ben is excited. He wants to witness the outcome. He wants to be the judge. One of the brothers, Anil, has summoned him to his apartment. Anil is pacing about the room.

Ben is slouched on a vast white sofa. 'I'm not sure I understand this. You don't like this competitive stuff with Sunil, so why are you entering into this contest? It may be that he has lost his head with all the media attention, but why are you destroying yourself along with him?'

'Something is dragging me down there. It's as if my brother needs me. I shall certainly lose. Sunil's will-power is so strong. His technique is so good, whereas I run on inspiration. I feel so tired I can't even think what to cook.'

'Don't show. I'll go along and tell them you've declined to compete,' Ben says.

Head bowed, Anil strides up and down the polished floorboards of his empty white-walled flat. He has fine long eyelashes, beautiful bare feet, a sad smile. Ben imagines taking him to bed, kissing his shoulder. Short, tubby, languorous, with long graceful fingers. The way he stirs a sauce, the way he places his spoon and sprinkles herbs. A loner, a counter-intuitive thinker, an original. Sunil, his brother, is wiry, thin, ambitious, bristling with nervous energy. He needs to be talked to, noticed, loved. That afternoon he arrives in his silver XJS. Everyone, except Ben, wears shades. It makes him think this is some sort of Mafia set-up. Even as he sits in Anil's flat, Ben can see the heralded arrival of Sunil on the edge of the tennis courts. Anil is slumped in an armchair, his fingers meeting in front of a quizzical smile.

'Don't fight your brother. If you win, you'll gain nothing by it. He'll be even more resentful than before.' Ben can see Sunil unpacking large wooden stakes from the boot of his car. Is he going to build a fence? Linda, his beautiful wife, with short blonde hair, a lithe model's body, designer clothes, stands beside Sunil, ever solicitous, in gunmetal slacks and a perfectly tailored white shirt. Her tall slender shape, gleaming in the sun, looks more delectable than anything Sunil or Anil could cook up. Ben sees her get into the XJS and drive off. Where is she going? Why do they have a Jag and not me? What's so special about them? Dreams sometimes permit the pointless asides of waking thoughts.

★

Court 5 houses Sunil's entourage and on court 6 are Anil and his small band of admirers, sous-chefs from the restaurant, his manager, a TV producer. Ben is chatting to Sunil, trying to appear impartial. On Sunil's court there is a wigwam-shaped fire, logs of wood with a few pieces of charcoal thrown in. Nearby is a bag of hickory chips, imported from Vermont. Across the top of the fire is suspended an iron rod, with two tripods holding it up and a handle at one end to swivel the spit round. No sign of the fish or the piece of flesh Sunil is planning to roast. On a trestle table are two large stainless-steel bowls. Out of a box Sunil brings out bunches of parsley, thyme, coriander, basil and mint. A bag of pine kernels, some raisins, a large tin of salted anchovies, capers. Helpers bring a bowl of morels, dark and wet, to the table, another bowl filled with chicken livers, a bag of gnarled truffles. The trestle table wobbles. Sunil inspects a bucket with three live lobsters in it. The lobsters are put into a small cauldron of boiling water hanging over the fire. Soon he drags the amber lobsters from their rapid death and plunges them into a pot of iced water. Minutes later, he is cracking them open and folding the main segments in butter and parsley, in a bowl that has been lightly rubbed with fresh garlic. Pepper, salt. He doesn't bother with the claws, just the succulent bodies. The lobsters, flecked with green, pink and white, the afternoon light bouncing off their colours, suck in the bulk of the audience. There is no protective cordon here. A surgeon arrives on Sunil's court. He produces an operating table and sets up his implements next to the food. A uniformed nurse joins him. No sign of Linda.

Anil is doing his signature dishes. Dishes that are hugely successful at his restaurant, Argot. But things are going wrong, Ben hears him shout at someone, ingredients have been forgotten, temperatures are not high enough in these portable ovens.

'I hate open-air cooking,' he mutters. 'Where the hell are my tongs? Can someone tell me what's happening to this sauce? No fucking way, do it again.' There are perhaps 200 people gathered on the courts. Ben takes a breather and goes to sit on the grass with a cigarette and a bottle of beer. Damn, I've started smoking again, he thinks in his dream. How outlandish, how Indian this contest is, in such a British setting, with the toddlers from the Highbury two o'clock club playing in the background, their parents looking on with fascination.

Journalists and other members of the crowd concentrate themselves on Sunil's court. He is still laying out ingredients, some of them steaming hot, in neat rows on the trestle table, a rainbow of exquisite food, layer after layer. First the lobster, then comes a salad of mixed greens, rocket leaves and baby spinach, almonds roasted in cumin, thin slices of pancetta with croutons, then cod and capers, then wood pigeon, then fruit, mangoes and kiwis and strawberries and home-made hazelnut ice cream waiting in a bowl of ice. Ben's heart fills with envy at the plenitude of Sunil's banquet. He can't wait to sink his teeth into a chunk of lobster. The judges approach. Sunil is now lying on the operating table. The surgeon undresses him, and paints a brown line down the front of Sunil's chest.

The crowd draws close, thinking this an additional gimmick – Sunil sunbathing next to his food. But now injections are being administered, and a spray is applied to his chest. The nurse brings a mask to Sunil's face, and minutes later the doctor is slicing a vertical line down the front of Sunil's torso. He takes a large knife and bangs on the handle with the palm of his hand, cracking open Sunil's breastbone with the blade. The audience gasps as the surgeon carves neatly down to the belly button. Sunil pushes the surgeon away and with his own hands forces open the ribcage. Taking handfuls of food, layer by layer, from the table next to him Sunil stuffs it into the hollowed-out cavity of his chest. Ben senses a collective panic in the audience. Everyone wants to cry out, perhaps rush in, but they are transfixed by what Sunil is attempting to do.

The competition to end all competitions. All of a sudden, Ben understands the need for the spit. Self-immolation. It must be stopped. What is everyone doing standing round staring at this spectacle? Ben decides to call a halt to the proceedings. He makes to move forward, but he can't find the strength. He looks round and finds Anil amongst the crowd. He has given up on his own endeavours and is watching his brother with a faint smile. Everyone is watching Sunil. The competition is over. The show is all his. Ben feels how vulnerable, how desperate, how eager for recognition Sunil must be to have to put himself through this.

Now Sunil is stitching up the skin on his own body along the line of the shirt buttons. With each stitch, each plunge of the needle through his skin, he cries out in muted pain, like a soldier digging out shrapnel from his leg. Ben pushes through the crowd to Sunil's side and tries to hold his hand. The skin where his belly button was has split open, his face is turning blue. He looks up at Ben. 'This is not over,' he says.

'You've won,' whispers Ben. 'Let me get an ambulance to take you to hospital.'

'No,' says Sunil, 'don't spoil it, please, Ben. You're my friend. Stay here and see me through. It mustn't be stopped. I have made them swear no one will get in the way. Is the fire smoking yet?' He finishes his stitches by snipping a bit of thread below his torn navel. Where is Linda? Why isn't she here to stop him or to applaud his heroic effort? Ben supports his friend's shoulder, and begins to think of him as some sort of Prometheus. He will stay with him through his ordeal. He screams at the surgeon, 'What kind of doctor are you? What kind of heartless fool could let any man do this?' The surgeon shakes his head admonishingly at Ben. 'It was the gentleman's wish. He paid good money. We signed a contract. Insurance was arranged. It was all above board.'

To Ben it seems that Sunil may be dead. His eyes are closed, he has laid his head to one side, and his assistants are carrying him carefully to what might as well be his funeral pyre. The pall-bearers hold him above the hickory smoke. Water is drizzled on the flames. Sunil croaks, 'Don't forget the cold cream on my feet, and the champagne.' A thick ring of black rubber is placed round his neck. The unguent is applied to his feet, champagne is fetched, and Sunil asks for it to be sprinkled on his face. Ben obliges. TV crews are scampering towards them, asking for his last words, their lamps blaring, their presenters babbling. Everyone wants a piece of this farce and Sunil is lapping it up. His moment has come. Anil refuses to say a word to any of the journalists, but they click and chatter, surrounding him, vilifying him for allowing this spectacle to continue, accusing him of greed. Sunil is on the spit in the midst of the smoke, and the helpers are slowly cranking him round. Sunil, the lobster, the pigeon, the cod, the fruit, the nuts and the anchovies begin to roast, and the collective smell is awesome. It makes the crowd hungry despite itself, it makes Ben salivate, and now Sunil begins to groan piteously and some of the crowd start to trickle away down to the tennis hut and the café, where they munch sandwiches and sip tea from Styrofoam cups. Ben notices with shock that over on the far courts people are playing tennis as if nothing were happening.

Sunil's moans perplex the thinned-out crowd. Sometimes the moaning sounds like pleasure, sometimes like death howls. Ben holds his hand and waters his brow. Could it be that the smoke is preserving Sunil? Perhaps if he is kippered enough they can rush him to hospital and save his life. Ben speaks consoling words to his friend, like a priest administering the last rites. What are his final wishes? Ben asks. Sunil wants to talk about the old days when they were in the sixth form together, played pool for hours in the common room, then after graduation did the same at the Angel pool hall. A realization comes upon Ben. Sunil isn't going to die, certainly not in a hurry. And it is Ben whom he needs to keep him alive, Ben and his own brother.

As the hours go by, the journalists, the TV cameras and the last of the audience all leave the tennis courts. The light fades. Sunil is smoked to a dark brown colour like a slab of mackerel. The fire is almost out. Ben tries to lift Sunil away from it, but there is no one to help him. Anil is sitting about ten feet away, chain-smoking Camels. All the cooking paraphernalia has been removed. The courts are bare, the competition long since annulled. 'Where is everybody? Where is my prize?' Sunil asks.

A white froth spumes out of the side of his mouth, with bits of food in it. The cooked juices from his feast have started to leak from him. Ben continues to nurse him, bathing his head with wet towels, talking to him about their past, about his present, about anything that comes to mind. Then with a gigantic effort Sunil raises himself up and shouts to his brother, 'Get this mess sorted out, Anil.' And there, Ben realizes, is Sunil's elder brother right next to them. 'I've had it,' shouts Sunil. 'I'm bleeding out of my cock, I'm pissing blood, man. Kid, you tell them, eh? Tell Mum and Dad what happened. Tell them how well I did.' Sunil's voice is fading. Anil kneels down and holds his brother's head. He gives Ben instructions. 'Lay him down gently, bring honey and cloves, bring towels.

We must ease down his body temperature, not too fast, wrap him carefully, pour the honey on his wounds, not too fast, give him water, dehydration is the main problem. He should drink slowly, very slowly. He must vomit or shit out the foods. Neither must be too violent or he will burst, his organs will spill out in front of us. He can be saved. It can be done. Sunil, you will live, stop crying now.'

Ben remembers how once, when he was in Jaipur in India, he got a horrendous stomach bug. In the middle of the night he had to crawl from his bed to the veranda and there he exploded. Liquid shit running out of either orifice, like lava being expelled from the body. He had felt so weak it was a wonder he had not toppled over into his own puddles. Remembering the incident, he emerged now from sleep with the gradual realization that he was at home in his flat, lying in his double bed next to his honey-scented wife.

Who were those Indian men? He remembered the name Sunil, and felt as if he knew someone like that, someone so determined to win that he would be willing to destroy himself in the process. Did Sunil survive? He was proud of himself for nursing the Indian man so well. It must have been the fish he had eaten last night that brought on such a vivid dream. Strange conversation at the dinner party. The film producer with the bad leg who intimidated him. She said she liked intelligent men with a large vocabulary. She told him about how her back had given way and she hadn't been able to move for weeks. She had been in a brace, stuck in the middle of some huge project, and she had had to instruct people from her bed. That's what he would like to do now: stay in bed for the rest of his life and dole out orders to minions.

Six

Like a diver rising up from the deep, Priya was making her way to the surface of her familiar world. From her bloodstream came a nicotine-call. It would be so nice to slip out into the garden and have a fag, a misty, rainy March-morning roll-up. That first hit of the day. The one that makes existence bearable. Why had she denied herself? She and Ben had given up together three months ago. Since then, she had cheated and smoked a few times. She was clearly finding it harder than he was. He wasn't a real smoker. Even her dreams were full of friends egging her on to have a fag, or she had dreams in which she suffered memory loss, and was horrified to find herself with a smouldering Marlboro stuck between her fingers. And then the guilt, a sense of betrayal and guilt, of having let herself down, of having let Ben down.

There was this struggle of opposites inside Priya, between wanting the freedom to do what she liked and the knowledge that if she followed her instincts she often ended up with disillusionment and regret. Was it that the response to instinct didn't always lead to the promised pleasure? The thought of a cigarette, the desire for a cigarette, even the first cigarette, soon gave way to dejection. Only one in every ten cigarettes was enjoyable, the rest were like sucking an ash-coated lollipop with threads of tobacco in the middle. Thinking of cigarettes helped her to repair the loss of spatial awareness with which she woke these days. Emerging from sleep she had this half-waking sensation of rising up from the ocean bed without enough oxygen to get her safely to the surface. It was a feeling of panic that she had experienced most acutely during her first depression at the end of her second year at university.

There had been recurrent, but lesser, attacks – never as bad as the first time when she really thought she was going to suffocate without waking up. That was until last year, when she had once again caused a rupture in her relationship with Ben; torn up the trust they had pieced together in the preceding years. Since then the old panic had come back with renewed vengeance and stealth. It was like being in the centre of a void-whorl with nothing anywhere near to hold on to. Surrounded by an infinitude of watery space rushing away for ever and ever. She pressed her hand to the bedclothes. Why are so many things that I want to do so confused, so much pleasure indelibly mixed in with so much hurt?

Not being able to smoke was a loss. Of course there were benefits, but it was the loss that she felt most keenly. She'd been talking about this with their marriage counsellor, the divine Anouchka. 'It's the thought of never having another cigarette, or of never having another affair, never again lying in someone else's sheets, that makes me want to do it. It's almost as if something will erupt inside, I won't be able to survive, if I don't have that cigarette.' Why should she ask herself to give up these things? Why should *anyone* ask her to give up these things? But then she had begun to hate the smell of smoke on her clothes, she hated having to remember the smoker's paraphernalia, her nose stopped dripping, her sinuses unblocked, she fell ill less often. And what about the damage caused by her affairs, all the lies, the secrets? Like the setting sun they returned every day, with their reminders of crimes committed. The hurt caused. But always she went back to smoking because of the pleasure, the reluctance to *deny* herself the pleasure. On a perfect summer evening with the light streaming through cold beer in a bottle, what could be better, what could make you happier then a curlicue of cigarette smoke tingeing the air with its woody scent? Why shouldn't she? Wasn't that what life was about, taking and getting as much pleasure as you could from it? 'Have everything. Do everything,' Marcus used to say.

There was a story her mother told that had become part of family lore. Seven-year-old Priya and Mohini were sitting on a bed in their Bombay flat and reading a book. Priya asked, 'Mummy, what's the most important thing in life?'

Looking straight at her with her steel-grey eyes Mohini said, 'To be absolutely yourself. Absolutely true to the things you care about. Don't let anyone take that away from you.'

'Then why do you insist on me eating up my spinach when I've told you I hate it?' responded Priya.

There had been times in her life when Priya felt she was soaring. Nothing mattered except being absolutely yourself, absolutely articulate, absolutely wild, parties, drugs, men, travelling, disappearing for days into the home of someone she had never met before. She loved inspecting the insides of other people's lives. She wanted to see where the riff of experience would take her. She was a lotus-eater. Or at least that's how it seemed at the time, until the desolation angel began to beat its wings in her heart.

Like the time in Marcus' flat, where she had moved after Christmas 1994, just eight weeks after getting to know him. Marcus was a big tall man. Priya used to feel she could fit in his pocket. He was a studio manager at the Beeb with whom she had been working on and off that year. One night, a few months after she had first noticed him, a night when she had been expecting to stay late, she went down to the BBC club for a quick drink. Marcus was sitting in the basement bar on his own with a pint of Guinness and she stopped to say a polite hello. The polite hello lasted till one in the morning. By the end of that evening he'd broken into Priya's consciousness. She couldn't get him out of there. Three days later it was half-term and Ben left for a week in Snowdonia on a school trip. It was fated. She began to live in Marcus' pocket. They were together every night in bars, clubs and in his Camberwell flat. Marcus showed her parts of London, especially the clubs, that she had never seen. While Ben shivered in a Welsh dormitory full of smelly kids, she had Marcus in her mouth in front of a blazing fire, both of them loved up on Ecstasy.

She remembered his uproarious laugh, the goose-bump-thrill of their illicit kisses that made her think how boring her Friday evenings with Ben were. Go to a movie, sit in a desultory restaurant, argue afterwards. When Ben returned, she thought she would just slot the whole week's events away in a drawer, a secret file of madness, but everywhere she moved Marcus was dancing a dazzling sorcerer's steps in the corners of her brain. She was lying in bed, watching telly, on the way to work, and he was always there stealing into her thoughts. Soon she was having lunch with him, then it was after work, staying late in the bar having drinks together. Late one evening they had sex on the floor of the South Asia office. Within the space of two weeks they had spun round each other a dangerous web of lies and manic activity. Priya stayed away nights and told Ben she was at a friend's, without even checking that the friend would corroborate her deceit.

Late one night she asked Marcus, while they were walking down the street to his flat, his giant arm loosely slung round her shoulder, 'Don't you care that you're ruining my marriage?'

'We're all taking our chances,' he answered. 'In this world

you have to take everything you can or you'll be left behind. I want you, I like you, why should I stop myself? I want a part of it too. Why should I concern myself with Ben – he's thinking about his own problems. What about people like me who aren't married? Do married people care about us?' He was ruthless. She knew a woman had been in his bed the night after her, though he swore that it had only happened once; the woman freaked when she came across Priya's pants under the sheets. She went with him, thinking she could look after herself. Thinking rashly that it was time she and Ben should end. When Marcus had first asked her to move into his flat she had laughed at the suggestion. The day after Boxing Day, he called her at home. She and Ben were reading in bed. She went upstairs to talk to Marcus, having asked Ben to put the receiver down in the bedroom. He didn't. And so, on a freezing December morning she was standing in her denim jacket, clutching a duffel bag and a duvet box, waiting outside McDonald's for Marcus to come and pick her up. Marcus was leaving in a month's time to go out and string for the BBC in Zimbabwe and he asked her to go with him. What about her job? What about her husband? 'Just do it,' he said. 'I love you. We'll make children. Come with me.'

She didn't want to. She hadn't left Ben to get hitched to somebody else. It was about freedom. She must go and find a room to rent. She needed to be alone, to find herself. 'So what are you doing here?' Marcus asked when she told him. What was she doing in this flat with this guy she hardly knew, who was angry because she didn't want to throw up her job and come to Africa on a whim? Was he serious? She would never know.

Within hours of being in his flat she had developed a physical aversion to his voice. Priya recalled vividly hearing

Marcus on the phone the day she moved in with him. The way he laughed his uproarious laugh, that guffaw that had made her feel so cherished when they had first met. The way he laughed at her jokes. Now she noticed he was laughing in the same outrageous way with all the people who phoned. It made her sick. If she heard that hypocritical, empty laugh one more time she would be scraping at the plaster with her nails.

It was a bank holiday, and she was sitting in his small one-bedroom flat in Camberwell. She remembered her fit of uncontrollable shakes soon after arriving in his white-walled, white-carpeted ground-floor shoebox, the place she had found thrilling now seemed like an institution for the mentally ill. She was trying to read 'The Kiss', a short story by Chekhov, trying not to think of the way she had been torn from her sanity. Thrown out by Ben. No home, no friends she could talk to, stuck in an alien part of London with this huge gargoyle of a man, stuck in his pocket, listening to the endless waterfall of his laughter. Soon she found herself following him from room to room, as if she had forgotten that they were now living together. He turned on her. 'Stop following me round, man.' It was so sudden, so cruel, like throwing boiling oil at her face. How had she fallen to this level, trailing behind this callous hulk, without knowing what she was doing?

On this dank March morning, even the remembrance of being surrounded by those white walls in Camberwell, sitting with her duvet over her trembling knees, wearing Marcus' cream T-shirt, after their bath together, her bag close by, the humiliation of it made her shudder.

The first night away from home, sharing Marcus' futon, something happened after they had fucked. She couldn't get to sleep. She and Marcus had gone out to a local pasta place. As he played with bits of bacon and avocado, she was asking him some questions about a past lover, and he said, 'You know what, you're too nosy. I'm not going to tell you all that stuff. I've told you before, I don't like those questions. I hardly know you.' Then he laughed his stupid laugh. Even though Priya hated him now, there was some truth in what he had said. They didn't know each other. What did she think she was doing prying into his past? It was more obsession than love. She had crept out of the flat as he snored and gone for a fast walk down Camberwell Church Street.

Christmas '94. The second day in Marcus' flat. Burning cold outside. She started out in her denim jacket and came back after ten minutes because the wind was so bitter. Marcus had sucked her right into his big arms. Like marrow being gleefully swallowed out of a bone. The sweet shining slug she and her brother would fight over when they had mutton curry at home. She hated the thought of those arms round her. And those hours of Ecstasy-fuelled fucking. The great pride with which he went on and on and on shafting. How could desire and hate be so close together? Yes, she had desired him, loved the way he entered her and wrapped her in his arms, he was so big, she could lose herself in him. It was a daddy feeling. She had loved lying on his big chest. And it was also the strangeness of him, his blackness. She had wanted to know him, enchanted by his difference. When she slept with Ben it was so simple, so comfortable, like being with someone you had always known. There was no trying, no fuss, no showing-off, no endless gyration for climax.

By the time she had come back from her cold walk, four years ago on that late December day, she had fixed her mind on flight. The minute he was out of the flat she had packed in a flurry and rushed down to the minicab office, without worrying about where she might go. In the backseat of the taxi she was chuckling at the thought of his anger over her four-word note, 'Sorry, had to go', when she realized she was still wearing his cream T-shirt.

Seven

'Daddy, did I never saw you when you were small?'

Ben wipes the sleep from his eyes. Whacka is sitting astride his stomach. 'When I was small d'you know what day I loved most?' he responds.

'Why didn't I see you when you were small, Daddy?'

'Because when I was a baby you weren't yet born. But, when I was small, I loved my birthday.'

'Yes, but you . . . you . . . you never were as small as me.'

'Come here, crazy boy.' Whacka tries to fight free from Ben's arms.

'I wanna hug,' says Priya, joining in while Whacka attempts to strangle his father.

The alarm, set for six thirty, goes off.

'You're squashing me, I can't breathe. The monster's killing me,' shouts Ben.

Priya reaches over, stops the electronic bleeping. 'Hello!' she says. 'What day is it today? I think I've forgotten, can someone please tell me?'

'I don't know. What day is it?' asks Ben.

'Is Callum's paaarty and I going play at his house.'

Why is it always Callum's party or Callum's house, thinks Priya. 'No, it's not,' she says, shaking her head.

'It's not *Callum's* birthday,' echoes Ben.

Priya waves her arm. 'Look round you, Whacky Backy.'

'It *is* Callum party. It *is*.'

At the nursery the kids worship Callum, Whack most of all.

Callum is tall, he is handsome and he supports Man U. 'That's three good reasons to dislike him,' Ben would say to Priya.

'Callum get lots of presents,' says the boy, holding out his upturned hands, in a characteristic gesture, the fingers bent outwards.

Time to put a stop to this, otherwise I'll never get to work, thinks Ben. 'Whacka, little fellow, it's your birthday today. Look round the room. What can you see?'

'Clothes?' Hands turned outwards again.

'No, not clothes.'

'I spy window.'

'No, not window.'

'I see . . . I see pooh pooh!' says Whacka bursting into laughter.

A big sigh from his parents.

'Try again. We'll get there in the end,' Ben says.

'Maybe he's a retard,' whispers Priya.

'I'm not tired!'

'Who's gonna have a party later today?' she asks him.

'Me?'

'Yeeess!'

'Is Callum coming to my party?'

'Yeeess,' they say in unison. 'Callum definitely coming to your party.'

'Bloody Callum,' mouths Priya to Ben.

'Mary come?'

'Yes.'

'Richard come?'

'Yes, and they're bringing you a special present.'

'Is it a sard?'

'No more sards,' says Ben.

'I wanna sard! I wanna sard!'

'Don't tease him,' says Priya, laughing.

Whacka looks at them both, his black eyes narrowing, his bottom lip turning, his eyebrows furrowing. 'Nnnno! Nnnno! Nnnno!' Each negative howl is like an engine revving up and then exploding through its exhaust. The petulant ferocity of a minor Mussolini. He buries his head in the quilt.

Ben jumps out of bed, grabs a couple of the presents lying on the table. One is wrapped in gold paper, the other in glossy red. 'What's this I've found? Look, Whacka. Do you know whose these are?'

The big head comes up from the folds of the duvet, the wailing snaps to a halt, the square face uncrumples, still-glistening eyes dilate.

'Whose is that?'

'Shall we look at the wrapper and see?'

'I think there's something written on it. Oh, look, it says, "Happy Birthday, Arjun, from your Nani."'

The face brightens, spills into beaming anticipation.

'I wanna open it, I wanna . . .'

'Go on, open it, it's yours to open, darling,' says his mother.

The tearing of wrappers begins. Presents are strewn all over the bed. Ben wants Whacka to look in Maisy's house. Whacka wants to open the next one. Priya wants to get the batteries into the foot piano she has spread on the floor. A Batman costume appears. Whacka wants to put it on now. He leaps up and down on the bed. 'I box you, I box you down! I fight you down! I throw you in the bin.' Ben indulges him. Priya calls Whack to come and stamp on the piano keys. She pokes the plastic keys with her hands. Whacka jumps down on to the piano, starting a cacophony, stamping over and over on the same key. He gets a police siren going. Ben has fanned out the various pages of *Maisy's House*. 'Come and see Maisy in the shower, Whack. Look, Maisy on the toilet.' Whacka is too excited to pay attention. Priya turns a knob on the foot piano and it emits a whining 'Happy Birthday', then 'Jingle Bells'. She holds up some new clothes, including trousers and a jacket that she wants him to look at, but Whacka is shouting in imitation of some cartoon.

'I didn't know you'd bought him quite so many clothes,' Ben says.

'He needs new clothes. He's outgrown all the old ones.'

'What about the ones my sister gave you?'

'Ben, don't be silly, he needs some new clothes for the party.'

It's getting late. Ben runs the bath, puts on the radio, skips up to the kitchen, flicks the kettle switch, chucks bags in mugs, brings in the milk, leaves a mug of tea on Priya's bedside table. Fills a bottle with chocolate milk as a treat for Whack. Bath running, Humphrys blathering on about education: just because he has an organic farm he thinks he can come on all self-righteous and conscience-stricken about every damn issue. Not that the minister shouldn't be made to squirm. How much does he get away with because he's blind?

When Ben was teaching in his first job in Brent, the schools inspector told him that what the Tories had brought in with the Education Reform Act of 1988 would take at least ten years of counter-legislation to undo. Even if a Labour government were to come to power at the next election and had the will to make changes. Well, thinks Ben, they haven't done much.

'Priyaaa!' he calls climbing out of the water. 'Bath's ready.' Years ago she would never have thought of using his bath water.

'But, minister, you said in 1997, just before you were elected, that opted-out schools would remain as they are, and that you wouldn't bring them back into the hands of the local authority. Now you're saying that you expect that many of them will want to come back. Very understandably, the head teachers and parents at these schools are getting a bit worried.'

'I don't think they should be. What we have said, John – and you must try to represent the facts clearly to the listeners – what we have said is that we will give *parents* the choice through a school ballot.'

'But they've already made their choice through a vote. Why should they have to do it again?' The irritated interlocutor, the same voice of Middle England.

'What we are saying . . . Look, John, most of the day-to-day running of schools has been devolved to the schools anyway by the Local Management of Schools provision in the 1988 Act. Schools, the vast majority of which are not grant-maintained, are running themselves, making their own decisions. Under the local management of schools most head teachers are doing a very good job.'

'I'm not sure they think *you're* doing a very good job. Here's what the Secretary of the National Association of Head Teachers had to say . . .'

Ben gallops up the stairs to the living room where his desk is, and picks up his watch, his wallet, the brown leather briefcase Priya bought him in Italy years ago – he's never quite been able to get over the amount of money she spent on it. The leather has worn like a cowboy's saddle and he loves it now. He moves swiftly back to the kitchen, gulps tea, stuffs toast into his mouth and a banana in his trouser pocket. He makes for the front door, but bounds back down the stairs into the bedroom, kisses mother and child sitting cross-legged on the bed. Priya has Whack interested in Maisy – black-haired boy in Batman outfit, black-haired wife bent over him. Snap-shot of his family.

Whack wants him to stay – he wraps his arms round Ben's head and clings to his stomach with his wishbone-thin legs. They rub noses. Whacka says, 'You stay, Daddy.'

Ben pecks Priya on the cheek. The same feeling of regret mixed with fear that he has felt every day since that accursed revelation comes over him. Such moments of filial bliss – the marital succour he used to rely on before leaving the flat to join the whorl outside – are tarnished now. He wants to run back to the way it was.

The first two years of Whacka's life had been perfect for Ben. He had felt so creative, so powerful, so happy – say the word – he was so *happy*. But now there was always her betrayal following him like an unwanted shadow. The birthday morning had been okay, but no sooner did he kiss Priya, no sooner did she put her arm round him and tousle his hair, than he wanted to break down. He wanted to go into the bathroom and stay sitting there the whole day, crying for the way it used to be and for the way it could never be again. He felt smarting lashes to his soul on the way down the front stairs to the car.

Luckily, he was rushing. When a man is rushing, thoughts tumble in and out of the mind like clothes in the wash – first you see red, then orange, then green, then it's all gone, swallowed up by indecision that looks like haste, swallowed up by the street, the weather, the traffic, the leaking car, Rosa on the pavement, bustling to post her letter, milk bottles on the doorstep, Sam, the seven-foot giant from Guyana, standing in his customary position on the corner with his wide-brimmed hat and plastic bag.

★

Ben slammed the door and left home. He jostled in amongst the cars packed in to the Holloway Road like sheep. He'd bought this car, in an absurd, embarrassing colour, from a friend of Priya's mother. Cut-rate, but he remembered having to spend a day in strange Indian machinations, being sent up to Harrow to collect the keys, then the keys were not there, so he had to go to Marylebone High Street, where the Indian man owned an ancient hardware store. The man behaved as if he were doing Ben a favour. When he made a fuss about waiting, the Indian man said rather haughtily, 'This is not a Rolls Royce you're buying. This is a favour for Mrs Patnaik we are doing. You're getting this car for nothing. Four hundred pounds and you are asking for a service history.' Ben ended up in a back street in the far eastern reaches of the Central Line to pick up the car and found it bright orange, like the Holland football shirt. He was sure there was some mistake. He couldn't believe the man would sell him a car without warning him beforehand that it was orange. But it drove fine – a G-reg BMW with only 58,000 on the clock.

During Euro '96 he had people beeping him thinking him a supporter of the Dutch team. He loved the Dutch team and had been gutted when Gullit decided not to play in the '94 World Cup. Hard nuts in one of his English classes, 8MB, Chelsea supporters, were forever writing stories about Ruud-boy and Luca.

Radio Four was still droning on as he turned right off the Holloway Road into Liverpool Road at the familiar Beijing restaurant. They had once invited him to hand out some prizes to lucky eaters who had won fifty-pound vouchers. That was after he had written three restaurant reviews for the *Evening Standard*. 'Thought for the day' – Ben turned up the volume. A woman rabbi was comparing life to a football match in which a goal was scored in the dying minutes of extra time. Ben remembered Nayim's lob against Arsenal in the final of the Cup Winners' Cup – Tottenham's revenge. And Seaman, who made the mistake – there was always someone to be blamed – had left his wife and kid the weekend before. Ben listened to the woman rabbi's homily: 'What we witness on the football field is proof of the old adage that the game is never over until it is over. We may blunder, we may play badly, we may spurn chances, we may think we have lost ourselves to the devil, but it is always worth keeping with the endeavour, staying patient, there will always be another opportunity, sometimes when you least expect it. If you can go on working, if you can go on trying, the last-minute goal, against the odds, might happen for you too.'

But there was another lesson to be had from the analogy. 'What if we look at life from the losers' side?' the woman asked. 'The team that were draping their flag over the cup with minutes to go to their championship victory. The fruit of a season's hard toil lost in a few seconds – a moment of carelessness or misfortune. You may have thought you had done everything you needed to do, you may have thought all the hard work was over, you may have counted on those good deeds, those blessings, and those golden eggs, but it only takes a second for luck to be overturned, for a revolution to break out, for cities to be burnt. Is it ever right to condemn someone as finished, as no good, without room for hope or salvation? The losing side too must pick themselves up from their tears and their thrashings on the turf to go on living. And perhaps they will understand something more about the fragility of success and failure when they next encounter them. "Fortune gives us nothing which we can really own," said Seneca. "An hour, an instant of time, suffices for the overthrow of empires."'

Ben turned the radio off so he could think about what she had said. Fear entered his body. Inchoate fear of unknown things. It was as if his muscles might suddenly stop receiving messages from his brain. He would be unable to press his foot down on the brake. He would crash into that woman crossing the zebra. It was the same fear that had gripped him on the tennis court last week when John Welsh took the lead by four games to two. He had wished that their time was up and he could leave the score as it was. To ward off the panic he had slashed at the tennis balls, blasted his shots over the baseline, chucked away the set.

He passed the intersection with Islington Park Street, where Priya had knocked over a motorcyclist, sent him careering into the window of E. Wood, butcher. From an early age Ben had been protected – or was it that he had protected himself – from the experience of losing. At school he gave up playing sports at which he lost. He stuck to tennis because he was the best. From boarding school he had made it to Oxford, where he had played in the first team. In his finals, he had got the first he was aiming for. And then he had got Priya.

To the right of him, on a huge billboard, he was confronted by the grinning face of Leigh Perry, the writer who had beaten him to the *Enquirer* restaurant-reviewer job, wearing one of those trendy red waffle-stitched jumpers. Everywhere he looked he could see the awful face of Perry smiling out at him. On the television, in newspaper interviews, on the front cover of his new book, with 'his honest food, his roast chicken, cheese on toast, chocolate truffles made of melted Toblerone'. He thought of his own book languishing on his desk for weeks, stuck at recipe 32, or was it 33? The female rabbi was right. Ben was the loser, but he must stop thinking of what might have been. He had decided to stay with Priya and Whack. Leo and Jan would come to the birthday party. He was sure of that. He would stand and face them. Why should he fear them? It wasn't as if he had done anything wrong.

He hadn't been listening properly to Priya's instructions. She had made an arrangement with the shopkeeper who was to be there at eight with the rocking horse. But where was the Oxfam on Upper Street? He checked in his pocket for the piece of paper, found it and spread it out on the passenger seat. The traffic was stuck in the bottleneck into Upper Street. Five to eight. He was going to be later than usual arriving at school. Ben cursed and turned left down Parkfield Street, bringing a cyclist to a screeching, cursing halt. He shouldn't mess with his karma: one day he meant to cycle to school. He circled past the snooker hall and on to Upper Street. Why the fuck didn't Priya do this kind of job herself when she had so much time on her hands? Why did she have to organize such complicated plans in the first place? Now there was nowhere to park.

Eight

Sitting in the kitchen, looking through the tall windows, past a cherry tree coming into bloom, Priya studied the lawn, a source of endless argument and wasted money. Now that they had both given up looking after it, it didn't look so bad after all. Or at least no worse than when Ben was out there huffing, swearing, weeding and mowing.

Times like this, whiling away a half hour in her pyjamas – should she feel guilty? She didn't, or thought she didn't. Guilt was an emotion peculiarly suited to the English middle classes. That and tiredness. Whenever you asked somebody how they were, it was always, I'm so tired, I'm so exhausted. I'm whacked, wasted, knackered. Nobody in India would know the word 'knackered'. 'Take your knackered horse to the knacker's yard,' she said, laughing out loud at the sound of those words. How infected she had become with these English words. How often did she use the word 'tired' to describe her state of being? What about *guilt*? Did she feel any about Ben's having had to leave so early, with her sitting here drinking her oily espresso? Did she feel guilty about working part time, about not earning enough money? About staying in bed late and reading in cafés? Not very. Did she feel guilty about having hurt Ben? Yes. She should have destroyed Leo's letter. But then how long could she have lived with the secret? And she had wanted to keep a record of it. No. Guilt was not an emotion that had counted in her upbringing. Responsibility, pride, love, honesty above all – but not guilt. Unless you could do something about it. What could she do about what had happened with Leo? She couldn't rewind the tape and start again. It was stupid to ask her even to think about that side of it. She felt angry with their therapist Anouchka Bergman for making her dwell on that aspect. That's who Anouchka looked like! She looked like Marianne Faithfull. She wanted to ring Ben and tell him she had finally worked it out.

Or was it Faithfull's song 'Guilt' that had triggered the idea? She had remembered the song because Ben had been humming and whistling it earlier. That was one of the things that irritated her, his humming and whistling silly tunes like 'The Skye Boat Song' or 'The Red Flag' over and over again, or the *Eastenders* theme or Oasis's 'Cast No Shadow'. That and the anal way he insisted on keeping the toothpaste tube clean.

Sometimes she wished she hadn't been so led by monster impulses. A kind of anguish about not being able to govern her own destiny. That was the real difference between her and Ben. She believed that everyone is on their own. You can't blame someone else for your own unhappiness.

When she felt depressed, the presence of friends, or forcing herself to see them, could make her feel better, but whenever they tried to cheer her up she only felt worse. Other people's advice was no use at all. And when she was feeling high, she could be articulate, funny, charming, gregarious. It didn't matter that much who she was talking to, or even, sometimes, whether they were listening. It was the sound of her own voice, her own thoughts, that excited her.

Ben wanted explanations and accounts for everything. Every move had to be painstakingly analysed. He even vacillated over the use of words and phrases. This fogeyish, public school inability to decide on the right word reflected, she thought, a larger uncertainty about what direction to take. He could be offended if she didn't share in his everyday reveries. When, in a hurry, she'd phone him from work, he'd force her to listen to him going over his plan for the day. 'I could go to Sainsbury's first and then get Whacka and then go and get the jacket from Esther, but I've got a meeting at four, so, will I make it, I don't know . . . you know that watch I bought last month . . .' 'All right, Ben, I've got to go, I'm in a rush,' she would say, and would find him in a sulk when she got home. He was acutely aware of the way in which people ignored him. They didn't ask any questions, they didn't listen to his stories properly, they weren't interested in his job – she wasn't interested in his job either, didn't say hello and ask him about it at the end of the day, didn't acknowledge how hard he was working. Her eyes glazed over when he started telling her some story about a student or colleague. 'I'm your wife, if you want to tell me something just go ahead and tell me.' 'How do you think I feel when you answer the phone in the middle of a story I'm telling you? No one ever thinks about me. What I do, what I need. I killed myself over Angela's son's case and she didn't even say thank you.' She tried to tell him the way it was. People worry about themselves first.

Sometimes she imagined writing him a letter to explain. He really believed that what she had done had ruined his life. He really believed that if those bastards at the *Enquirer* had known his true worth, they would have given him the job. Even though he was better suited to being a teacher than a journalist. He was too small-minded, too accounting, too much like his father, eyeing up his stocks and shares each morning, adding up figures, keeping his punishing ledgers on the rights and wrongs of his friends' and colleagues' behaviour. She wanted to write to him to say that if you depend on other people to make you happy, you can never enjoy your life.

She looked at the time. 'Oh bugger! Come on, baba, we must get going.'

Ben parked illegally, half the car in a bus stop: a double-decker flashed its lights at him. He must stop here or be swept along with the traffic to the Angel. A green-corduroyed man was waiting for him in the shop. What does he have to worry about? Selling twenty objects a day, he can sit behind the counter and dream. Ben grabbed the rocking horse and dashed back into his orange car. That's what I should do, become a salesman in a charity shop selling second-hand toys. No more struggle. Sitting there reading novels and eating sweets in the dark bric-a-brac clutter.

He was late so he sneaked into the wide bus lane by Angel tube, raced down St John Street, swung right at The Peasant, cutting across at Skinner's and through narrow Bowling Green Lane into Farringdon Road, past the fucking *Enquirer*, its gleaming offices and high salaries, and down towards the river. The question he had been asked two years ago by the interview panel was there in his mind again.

He is sitting on the third floor of the *Enquirer*, with its shining plate-glass windows: the features editor, the editor, the managing editor sitting in a semi-circle in front of him, discussing the style and content of the 'Eating' page. This is the weekly section to which he will contribute restaurant reviews. The mood is one of bonhomie. Ben is talking about the recent interest in fusion cooking, giving them a sophisticated analysis about how the trend might develop. He is enthusing about his projected new book. He's considering a move to part-time teaching. He has more or less been offered the job. The editor is using phrases like 'when you do the piece on Monday'.

They made him wait three weeks. Three humiliating weeks, while his friends reassured him. Priya opened the letter. She tried to hide her disappointment. No one remembers the silver medallist. He recalled eventually getting the editor on the phone and wanting to kill this man who was offering his commiserations. 'We thought your pieces were wonderful, Ben. I'm sure you'll be snapped up by another paper. Leigh came in so late. It was unfortunate. You have a terrific future ahead of you.'

What was the deciding factor? Ben had asked. 'The deciding factor, I'm afraid, was that Leigh is a novelist with a big following and has a wonderful way with words. Still, it was a close call – that's why our decision took so long – but when it came down to it, although your knowledge of food was perhaps more assured, it was his descriptions, the ambience he conveyed, the sense of place and people, his sentence structure.'

Ben closed his eyes while he waited in the queue at a light on Farringdon Road. Two cars streaked past in the bus lane. This was his calming zone. Somehow the traffic always moved smoothly along this broad straight road. He let his eyes wander to the familiar windows and signs: Garbanni and Sons, the Eagle, the Good Cheese Company, Simply Sausages, Meat City, Kentucky Fried Chicken, Golf Accessories. One part of him had been snapped up by some bank or management consultants in the milk round at Oxford. He imagined himself in pinstripes, off to work in the City, and at the end of his day he would pop into that shop – Golf Accessories – to buy a new glove or some balls for his weekend foursome at the Rickmansworth club. He reminded himself that he had *chosen* to be an inner-city schoolteacher (he remembered Priya's mother telling him that *Time* magazine had called it the second most stressful job in the world), waving goodbye to Golf

Accessories and all that it stood for. Past the Blackfriars round-about and down the flyover on to the Embankment. His descent was greeted by a wall of grey buildings on one side, grey river on the other. Clouds sousing the light. He rolled down the window and ferreted his way into the left lane as a warm exhaust-filled gale blew at his face.

Every weekday Ben drove past the seats of power, along the Embankment – parallel to the Strand and Priya's gloomy office – under Hungerford bridge, rat-running through empty Great Scotland Yard to Whitehall, past Horse Guards Parade, protesters opposite Downing Street, the Houses of Parliament – Big Ben telling little Ben he had just enough time to get to his morning meeting – Westminster Abbey being scrubbed, past the Millbank Tower and the Tate, until, zooming across the junction at Vauxhall Bridge Road, he turned right into St George's Square.

Passing these places, screwing in and out of his short cuts, gave Ben a sense of importance. He wasn't just a school-teacher: he was part of a vast workforce. Sometimes as he travelled to school, he could imagine for a few seconds that he was a player in a company whose stage was at the centre of this great city. His first teaching job had sent him in the opposite direction, to the dreary north London suburb of Kingsbury. He had felt as if he were rocketing away from the sun, away from the heat and mix of the core. Teaching children who had never been south of the river, who hadn't the remotest idea even of the area where he lived. On that journey through Brent he would go past drive-in McDonald's, clapped-out carpet warehouses, sad Indian and Chinese take-aways, motorway junctions, the Neasden roundabout with its deserted museum and arts centre collecting the fumes of twenty-four-hour traffic.

But now, when he crossed the heart of London every day, he could feel the pulse of things: farmers marching, miners striking, anti-Gulf-War rallies, the flags outside the embassy after Brazil won the '94 World Cup. The City mile closed to traffic because of IRA bombs, forcing him to deviate from his old short cut through King Street and Queen Street. He could take several routes through the centre of London. He fancied himself a master of the London maze.

There were days when he got a sense on his journey to school of what he was missing: high-powered jobs, eighteenth-century central London houses, railings, old banks, the universities. Ben tortured himself with these thoughts. He led himself up an imaginary path – say, the academic career – until he reached a place like the one occupied by Priya's friend, Dan Kerrigan, the brilliant and handsome professor of English who had written four slim and erudite books. His name was often in the papers, and you could hear him on the radio, sometimes see him on late-night arts review programmes on television. Ben couldn't help also admiring his looks, his Hamlet-like penchant for elegant black clothes, his long hair, his quiet voice, his complex witticisms. Well-paid, respected, no kids. Why couldn't Ben have gone down that path? Or why couldn't he have ended up like Jehan, another of Priya's writer friends, with his beautiful, sultry psychoanalyst wife? The red gates of Tachbrook school came into view. The building was shaped like an ocean liner – not one of those forbidding Victorian piles, but a modern, late sixties structure of concrete and glass – set several metres below the level of the Thames on an old bomb-site.

'I wanna stay with you, Mummy,' Whacka whined.

'I am staying with you, babu. I'm just going to work for a

few hours and then Jocelyn will come and pick you up at lunch time and then we all meet here for your party.'

'I wanna have lunch with Callum and George at the naarsery.'

'Coat on, darling, where are your shoes? Don't you want to have lunch with Jocelyn at the Paris London Cafe?'

'Paris Lundun, Paris Lundun. I wanna go Paris Lundun, now, Mummy.'

'Do you think you can find your shoes for me?' Whack had an uncanny ability to remember where he had put things. He seemed behind other children of his age in identifying pictures in books and singing songs, but he had an excellent memory. Once he had dropped Priya's keys behind the sofa, and hidden her wallet in his lunch box inside his toys chest. The next day Priya was spinning round the flat, shouting for her keys. She phoned the nursery to tell them why she was going to be late picking Whacka up. The teacher called out to Whack while Priya was on the line, 'Mummy's lost her keys.' There was a silence, a space in which Priya could imagine Whack's little mouth shape a beautiful and silent O. Then Ferida, the teacher, asked again, 'Whacka, did you see Mummy's keys?' 'I put them in the sofa,' Priya heard him say in the background. 'And do you know where Mummy's wallet is?' 'In my Thomas the Tank lunch box, with the toys and her phone is also in my lunch box.'

Boy and mother begin running down the pavement of Lynch Road. Priya feels vague lower-back pain. Had it for days now. Getting old, like her mother, who has suffered from sciatica for ten years. Have I got his lunch box, his slippers? The cheque for Fran? My mobile? Damn, I've left my coat. 'Just coming, darling, you stay there.' Giant Sam is walking towards them, his huge angular jaw jutting out like a fist, from his craggy lips an extra-long cigarette dangling at an impossible angle.

'Sam, just make sure Whacka stays on the pavement,' Priya orders, 'I'm just running in to get my coat.'

'Goin' to the radio stashun? Where you broadcast to today? Africa?'

'No, India.' She dashes back, snatches her coat from the hooks by the door, wraps her favourite cashmere scarf round her neck, spots the box with the photos for Whack's birthday ceremony at school. Thank God I came back, she says to herself, picking up the shoebox and thinking this must be a lucky day. Down the four stairs.

Sam looks pensive. 'You got a cigarette?' he asks Priya.

'Sorry, Sam. I've given up. Thanks for looking after Whacka. Got to rush.' She strokes back her thick black hair.

'Aaright, aaright, goaan now or you go miss de bus.'

Boy and mother running down to the pedestrian crossing to catch the big red bus. The same crossing where Priya saw a Japanese tourist lying on the ground with blood on his lip and a strap torn off a rucksack in his hand. The Holloway Road, full of hidden highwaymen in olden times, still bristling with bandits. Priya scoops Whacka into her arms and scoots across, in front of braking cars. The bus pulls away seconds before they get to the stop. This was meant to be a relaxing morning. She remembers another disastrous happening from her dream last night. She pictures a scene in which she has run across the zebra to catch the bus and the trailing Whacka is hit by a car.

Boy and mother standing at the bus stop, breathing out, breathing in the fumes of juggernauts that have rumbled down the A1 from Leeds, Doncaster and Newark. 'Juggernaut' – that word comes from India flashes through the back of Priya's mind. She's going to be late to Whack's nursery but it doesn't matter, she tells herself, it's his birthday.

Ben hates being late, but why is *she* acting like him? Has she absorbed so many of his ways? 'Should we walk, darling? It's not very far.' The traffic is hardly moving and looking down the two-lane causeway Priya cannot see another bus approaching.

'I wanna cake the bus.'

'Do you wanna run a race on the pavement?'

'I wanna cake the bus.'

'You can walk on the wall.'

'Okay, Mummy, we race. You count five.'

Whacka scurries forward on the pavement. Twenty minutes to nine. Indian woman in a tartan scarf, unruly hair blowing, tagging a laughing toddler. Wriggling between the greys and blacks, the dull greens and beiges of overcoats that hurry mole-like, eyes cast down, faces set in the mindless concentration of a daily journey. No running, no playing, no laughing allowed. To notice anything would be a sin. At all costs keep your head down, stay in the tunnel of your own thoughts. Weave, duck, jog, walk, don't walk. Yourself to yourself.

Nine

At the school gates something miraculous happened. Ben became like a pilot who has just embarked on his walk through the airport corridors towards the cockpit. The passengers watch him pass in his smart uniform and cap, he gives a little nod to the customs officials, people step aside, he strides through a special gateway, carrying nothing more than a sleek valise, looking cool and rested, the odd greeting, the little flirtation with an air hostess, the confident step and stature of a person with responsibility.

Ben's troubles were left behind, his anxieties about being second best. He was an English teacher who knew his business in a place where he felt recognized and comfortable. As he turned his car into the red gates, slowing to a crawl and making sure that the kids knew he was there, he waved to one or two who called out, 'Hi, sir'. He had learnt over the years that it was just as well not to be too effusive to children outside school. Always let them acknowledge you first. Never give them the opportunity to be rude to you, or tease you or, worse, blank you. He remembered coming out of the chippy on Tachbrook Street with a colleague when he heard a voice at close range shout, 'Oi, Tennyson'. Caught unawares, he turned round; it was Patrick, a tall thin boy he had once taught, who had been banned from Stamford Bridge for chanting racist slogans. Ben moved towards him, before he realized fully who it was, because Patrick, older-looking now, was standing with his buddies, showing off to former classmates who were foolish enough to be still attending school. When Ben turned to greet him the boy just snarled and waved him away like a bad smell. 'Don't even try it, comin' to fuckin' talk to me.'

A nutter, Kashlul, stretched himself out in front of the car as Ben drove down the entrance ramp. Unperturbed, Ben waited for him to get out of the way. This place, which he had been coming to each morning for over five years, sometimes felt easier to enter than his own home. Often he arrived early, sat in the staffroom sipping tea with the other insomniacs. The minute he entered these portals his mind stopped jumping from thought to painful thought like a monkey chasing another from branch to branch. Once here, he was switched on: sort out the lessons, deal with the notes in my pigeonhole, quick cup of tea, chat with Brenda the tea lady, give out information, brief the student teacher, sort out cover, and avoid John Welsh, sidling up with a list of today's hot race tips and the details of his latest drinking spree or of imaginary money won at darts or snooker. Ben knew some staff saw him as an eccentric, a bit up himself, just because he had written a book. They made snide jokes about recipes and puddings.

When he'd started teaching nearly eight years ago, he'd tried hard, like a lot of young teachers, to get a job in a sixth-form or FE college. Fortunately, he'd failed to make it past the interviews, and had stayed in secondary. Now it was the eleven-year-olds of year 7 that he liked best. They arrived full of fear and anticipation. To watch them develop, to try to stem their cynicism, entice their minds to stay open – this had become the challenge.

His present year 10s had started with him in year 7. For three and a half years he had been their form tutor and their

English teacher. It had been the most satisfying experience of his teaching career. He remembered seeing this class in their first term on the first Monday morning, period 1, and how he had started off with a discussion about the previous week's news items. Slowly a routine had been built up that each of them would bring in a newspaper article with a story they had chosen to talk about. From these discussions he'd gained an affection for these kids, some of whom, like every teacher, he had begun by disliking.

With three minutes left to the start of the head's morning briefing, Ben arrived at the tea counter.

Brenda, bounteous or abusive in turn, was packing up. 'Don't you dare ask me fer anything, d'you 'ear? This counter closes at eight forty. Look at the clock on the wall, read my lips – there is no more service.'

'Brenda, may I have a cup of tea? Please don't give me a hard time. I've had a rough morning.'

'You bloomin' get 'ere on time if you want a cup of tea, or you do without.'

Ben stood quietly. He knew the tea would eventually materialize. In fact, she was readying a mug already. 'I'm gonner get me a big sign and put it up right 'ere. Where's that bugger Jonathan? I've asked him to do me a sign.'

'It usually takes him about three months to register anything, sweetheart.'

'Don't sweetheart me, you twerp. I'll clip you round the earhole. I'm old enough to be yer mother, you understand.'

'That's true. Now please can I have that tea.'

The mug is pushed towards him, plus a currant bun. 'Seventy-five pence. 'And it over, quick.'

'I'll give it you in the break, all right?'

'Take that sugar and get off the counter. You can give me a bleedin' 'and and all closing the shutters.'

The squat head rang her little bell. Words squelched out of her fat mouth. Every teacher always complains about the head – that's what heads have to live with – but this head, Lois Howl, was a bully. Ben had seen her treat kids brutally for even the smallest misdemeanours. She treated the staff no better, refusing to allow them to speak in meetings lest they voice objections to her decrees. And now that her incompetence was being exposed by a radical governor she was becoming more aggressive than ever.

Ben leaned over to Brenda, their elbows meeting on the edge of her counter. She whispered in his ear, 'Have you 'eard what she's done now? Looks like she wants to stop teachers wearing jeans to school.'

'Are you serious?'

Brenda spluttered into her hand and some of the blue-rinse brigade turned to stare at them. They never could work out what this relationship between Brenda and Ben was all about. Brenda was Ben's confidante and his entertainment in the smoking area. He was not a gossip, but he liked Brenda's take on school events. Only in the aftermath of discovering Leo's letter could he not face her saucy talk, and although he contemplated telling her what had happened, he felt too ashamed and hid from her. Brenda became sad, much sadder than she let on. Some months later, one of the inveterate smokers, Andrews, told him Brenda thought he didn't like her any more. So he went back into the smokers' den, and their friendship reflowered. Now he couldn't get through a day without his dose of Brenda.

'Where's your lover this morning? 'Aven't seen 'er anywhere,' asked Brenda.

'She's there in the corner,' Ben said pointing to a blonde nymph in a short tartan skirt.

'Stupid cow mooching up to that drunk Donald Scragg.'

'But he's your lord of the manor, free teas and sausage rolls any time of the day for him.'

'Yeah, and what's it you want – one day it's 'am, cheese and lettuce, no tomarters and lots of mustard, then tuna and mayo, no butter, then egg and crusty bread. And is it ready when you want it? "Please Brenda, can I have another cup of coffee, Brenda." You dir'y, ungrateful bugger,' she said pushing him by the shoulder.

Brenda lived in Ben's head as a Rubenesque cherub. She had scrubbed white skin. She was lardy, but her fatness was firm rather than fleshy. When she woke in the morning she had to have six Embassy filter-tips to start her up. In the smoker's compartment of the staffroom, the iron lung as it was called, she flicked through the *Daily Express*, burped and took her own blood-sugar level to see what food was needed for the day. She picked daintily at a packet of salt and vinegar crisps and wiped the bowl in which she made the egg mayonnaise with a piece of bread. That's all she consumed when she was at school. At 11.30 she went out to do a little shopping, popped into her flat a few streets down the road, gave her Jim his lunch, put her feet up for ten minutes, and then waddled back to school to serve the teachers' sandwiches.

Loud, vulgar, outrageous, Brenda was the mother Ben felt he had never had. Even in church she swore loudly when the priest kept the congregation waiting, or so one of the local Catholic members of staff complained to Ben. She had one drink a week, on a Friday night: a glass of sweet wine, with a rump steak. A flutter on the horses every Saturday, and on Sunday she went to bingo. Once a month the bingo ladies went on the town. Lately, they had made visits to a club called Mambo – Brenda proudly showed Ben her black and pink membership card – to watch third-rate gladiators strip to their thongs before getting the hall rocking with their grand finale: 'You shoulda seen the size of 'im, like a great big python 'e was, I never seen nuffink like it.' Ben would tease her about being immoral and she would say, 'Mind yer own business. I know your kind, posh gits sitting in your flat with yer glass of champagne.' Drugs was terrible, youth of today obviously was terrible, education was a sham, kids nowadays, women nowadays. 'I washed all me little ones' nappies in a bucket – there was no washing-machines in them days. Politicians nowadays, food nowadays. Smelly foreign muck. Pah! Nice piece of boiled bacon, cabbage, boiled spuds and sprouts, thas wha' I like. What d'you call it, peppers, and garlic, and them things, what are they called, chilli whatsits. You boy,' she would say pointing at Ben, 'you stink of garlic in the morning. My Jim likes all that stuff, chillis and all sorts, 'cos he was in the war. I cook it for him sometimes, but I won't touch the stuff meself, and I need to fumi-what's-it the 'ouse after 'e's done. The smell makes me come over all giddy,' she said flapping her hand in front of her nose as she smoked. 'I 'ave ter open all the winders wide.'

Ben and his friend Elaine from the science department, who was Brenda's surrogate daughter, liked to wind her up on the subject of food. 'Here, Brenda,' Elaine would say. 'Did you try any of them recipes from Ben's book?' Ben had given her a signed copy with an inscription that had pleased her – something corny, like, 'You make the sun shine every morning.' She had cooked one of Ben's curries for her Jim, who had not spat it out. The air round her counter was heavy with the scent of pickles and condiments: she had an array of very strong-smelling Patak's jars, as well as a dish of Branston, which was ladled on to sandwiches like chocolate sauce on ice cream by the teachers. There they were at the counter sullying their cheese and ham or tuna sandwiches with chunks of hot oily lime pickle, sweet mango chutney and mustard made from Colman's powder. And on the other side was Brenda, who made the best egg mayo sandwich this side of Tower Hamlets. At 9.30 each morning Bert the milkman, in his blue overalls, hobbled behind the counter with his plastic tray of milk bottles, his eye twinkling, his ruddy cheek readied for his morning kiss from Brenda. Ben liked it that these pockets of working-class life had withstood the invasion in Pimlico of the rich with their pieds-à-terre, the politicians, the yuppy-hoorays with their Space Wagons, the embassies and the hotels.

Whacka's nursery is on one of the roads that climb up the steep bank from Junction Road to Dartmouth Park Hill. Priya and son, both of them breathless from racing each other up the hill, arrive at the front door of Tree House. Fran Talkington, the owner and head teacher, a one-time Buddhist, now a devotee of the Montessori method, takes the birthday box with the photos and toys from Priya.

Whacka, hidden behind a pillar, waits for his morning call from Fran. 'Where is Whacka?' she asks. 'I see, you haven't brought him with you today?' Whacka's black eyes peep round the corner and Fran pretends she hasn't seen his ears poking out. 'All right then, we'll have to do without the special birthday cake we got for Whacka today. Never mind, we'll do it another day.' On cue he jumps out from behind the pillar.

While Priya chats with Fran, Whacka puts his juice on the table, takes his Thomas lunch box to the fridge and changes his shoes for a pair of lollipop-red and lurid green slippers, a confection of fleece and Velcro. He pulls at Priya's hand and they both stumble downstairs to Whacka's classroom.

'Hi Arjun,' says Ferida in her Bombay lilt – one of the few people in the world who calls him by his real name. 'What's this you've brought with you? A box of sweets?'

Whacka looks blank. 'I've got a na-na,' he shouts, waving the overripe fruit in the air. He puts it in the fruit bowl and takes his place at a table with two classmates, William and Milly. 'Cold hands,' he says to Ferida, who is crouching by the table.

'Feel *my* hands,' she says, covering his hands with hers. 'Should I blow on them to make them warmer? Like this.'

William giggles. He puts on a green apron with a crab on its shiny lurex front. Hiding between her father's legs, the wailing Amy comes in through the door; her Malaysian dad is in designer specs and a smart jacket.

'Good morning, Amy,' says Ferida, turning round. 'What are we going to do today? Should we show your Daddy some cutting?'

Amy holds on to the end of her father's jacket, shaking her head, turning away. She knows she is going to be abandoned by her father, she knows her weeping is to no avail. Dad looks pained. Amy stares at Whacka, intrigued by his cheeriness.

'Hi,' says Priya to Raj, Amy's dad, who smiles feebly, turning his mouth upwards in an expression of resignation. Amy has been like this for the past month.

'Hello, Amy,' says Priya. Amy shrinks from Priya's glistening hair. 'Have you seen my necklace?' she asks, dropping down into a crouch. She holds out her *Mangalsutra* to distract the crying girl. It doesn't work. Amy wails all the more loudly.

In the far corner William, a dark-haired boy dressed in blue trousers and a neat red jumper, is now pouring water from a plastic jug into four plastic cups. His eyes are full of intent. He has the concentration of an alchemist working with his crucibles.

Whacka runs over to the other teacher, Linda, the one with the chain-smoker's voice, who is sitting cross-legged on the floor, engaged with Adam in a game involving toy animals.

'I wanna book. I wanna read Pingu!' Whacka demands.

'Did you put your juice and fruit away?' asks Linda.

He nods. The door swings open. In come Milo and Maya. Close behind is Whacka's soulmate, Callum. The parents gently lead their children through the door. Ferida taps Whacka on the shoulder. He runs to the window and answers with a wave and a smile his departing mother's flying kiss thrown to him from the street.

As Priya eased herself down Cathcart Hill, she thought of all the nurseries she and Ben had visited. At seven months, they'd sent Whacka to a private nursery, the Nightingale, a concrete bunker at the back of a disused hospital on the Holloway Road. It was only two streets away from home. There Whacka had wedged himself in the lap of a large black woman who had four children of her own.

'Sometimes,' she thought aloud as she passed the tacky outlets on Junction Road – Goodwoods, Payless, the cat shelter, CashCity – 'I wish I could send him to the kind of schools I went to in Delhi and Bombay. But then those schools were so strict, so restricting. Whacka wouldn't last there.'

When he was one Priya had taken Whacka into work and left him at the Bush House nursery. She liked having him near her, but found it difficult to concentrate on her work. A couple of months later she found a mother who wanted to share a nanny through the *Lady* magazine. Gloria Twitchin, rockabilly freak, took them for a merry ride with money and time, and spent most of her days on the phone to friends and family arranging her wedding. Whacka spent his days being scolded and forbidden by Gloria. That was probably at the root of my dream last night, thought Priya. After weeks of agonizing, when Whacka was nearly two, they finally got rid of Gloria.

Next they sent Whacka to Boulders, a co-operative nursery with lots of parental involvement and open-ended playtime, where he had only lasted two weeks. Within days he was breaking things, hitting other children, pouring water and sand everywhere. The nursery asked Priya to sit in for the first couple of hours in the day. But when she'd stayed she became frustrated by the lack of structure. No one seemed sure what was going to happen next. Once again, she and Ben had to sit down and discuss. They decided that Whacka must have some form of discipline. Routine was needed, otherwise he had tantrums. They began to insist on a rigid 7.30 p.m. bedtime. There should be less asking Whack what he wanted to do or eat, whether he wanted to go to the garden centre or the park. They settled on Tree House. Whack had been there for twelve months, and his behaviour had improved. He could now spend short amounts of time playing on his own.

Lois Howl tinkled her bell to call the morning briefing to a close. Ben was approached by the Refugee Unit Coordinator, a kindly man with a thankless job. He wanted to know if Ben could come to the meeting that evening. Ben made his legitimate excuses. A look of familiar weariness passed over Nigel's goateed face. His meetings were attended by four or five teachers and they only took place twice a term. Ben had been to one this year and thought it worthy but tedious.

Angela, head of Year 9, came up to him and asked for a progress report on Ayesha Romain. 'I don't know what to say. She's hardly ever here, and when she is, she only wants to talk about sex,' said Ben. 'She's such a waste of time. Everybody knows she spends most of the time preening in the corridors, like it's some sort of catwalk. Here's her typical contribution to the class. "You know this boy, yeah, you know what boys are like, yeah, all right listen up, yeah. Boys are only interested in one thing, yeah, dipping in and dipping out." Then all the boys start shouting "Hou, hou, hou" and flicking their fingers in the air. She is a chaos machine. They should hire her on *Jerry Springer*. There's no way to control her except by throwing her out.'

'She *loves* your lessons, Ben. Yours are the only classes she'll go to.'

'Angela, is that meant to be some sort of compliment? You *know* why no one else lets her talk. I'm forced to let her speak by popular demand. The class can't wait to see her stand up in her skin-tight clothes.'

The head of year guffawed. 'You love it, really. Soon as you can, do that report for me, will you?'

'I just gave you the report.'

'I need it in writing,' Angela said as she went out of the staffroom doors.

The pips had sounded for registration. Ben snatched up his folder and took the stairs two at a time to his classroom, number 14, on the C corridor.

Ten

'*I've* been in an aeroplane,' says Whacka.

'This is a Space Shuttle,' Milo informs him, holding the toy rocket in the air.

'I've been on it last night,' continues Whacka.

Linda, the teacher asks, 'Where did you go?'

Whacka looks blank, then he notices Callum approaching their toy-strewn mat and his face lights up. 'I'm having a Batman cake at my birtday.'

'You lucky boy,' says the teacher.

'I'm going to be five.'

'You're not five, you're thwee,' says Callum. 'I know, 'cause I'm coming to your party.'

Whacka shakes his head. 'I'm going to be five when my birtday comes.'

'You're not!' says Callum.

'Why don't we see if this lion wants a drink of water?' says Linda picking up a toy.

'Nnno! Nnno! Nnno! I *am* five. I *am* five! I don't wan you to come to my paarty,' cries Whacka.

Callum goes over to the low wooden shelves that line two walls. The shelves have been constructed so that the toddlers can get the activity trays on and off them on their own. Callum picks one up, a tray bearing a little cloth and a jar of some kind of ointment. He sits down at one of the four central tables. He pours some of the polishing liquid on to the cloth and begins to rub at a metal plate.

All around the room three- and four-year-olds are settling down to work. This is the Montessori system. Learning to toil from an early age. Salvation in self-reliance. The children choose something they want to do: threading, buckling, pouring, polishing, painting, rubbing, cutting, sticking, jigsaws or various other 'pozzles', as Whacka calls them. The teachers, Ferida and Linda, move from child to child, offering encouragement. Maya is working with a wooden jigsaw. Next to her, Georgia, her best friend, is sticking bits of pink tissue on to a piece of black sugar paper. William is on his own at a table persevering with his pouring. From time to time he stops working and stares in front of him with an expression of quietude. Milly is moving little coloured glass buttons from one receptacle to another. 'Look, Fewida, I did it. I finished the jewels,' she shouts.

'Good girl, Milly. If you've finished with that take it back to the shelf and choose something else.'

In the corner next to a yellow bookshelf there is a small yellow sofa on which Amy has settled down to look at a book. William takes off his apron and hangs it in the cupboard. Then he carries his tray and cups back to their place on the shelf. He chooses another activity – threading – and settles down to work.

'Fewida, look! Bossom fell down!' says Georgia.

'Don't worry, put on a little more glue,' says the teacher, pressing Georgia's pink flower back into place.

Maya has changed activities. She is using a fruit-shaped stencil to draw on sugar paper. Georgia looks over her friend's shoulder to admire her work. Then she goes back to seeing if she can add another piece of coloured tissue to her impressive card.

Whacka is engaged in his favourite activity, cutting paper into little shapes that he puts into an envelope and takes home to show his bemused parents. He chops a few pieces then he sticks his finger in his nose, digging. Then three fingers go into his mouth. He walks over to the shelf, committing the cardinal Montessori sin of not taking his activity tray back to the shelves, goes to a large red bucket, pours water into a small washing-up bowl. Linda is watching him. 'Whacka, can you take your cutting back to the shelf, please.'

'I wanna juice,' he says.

'It's not drink time yet. You need to take your cutting tray back to where it should be, on the shelf.'

'I will cake it. I *wull* caaaake it!'

Neighbouring Milly stares at him.

'Whacka, be a good boy, take it back to the shelf. Let's do it together.'

William comes and stands next to Milly, joining in the gawping game. They sense an imminent confrontation.

'I *will* cake it back. First I wanna drink!' He says this as if Linda has not understood the import of his order.

'You can have a drink, Arjun, after you put your tray away,' Ferida intervenes.

'I donna wanna do it. I donna wanna cake it back. I wull cake it back *after* my drink,' pleads Whacka, moving towards the drinks table.

Ferida fixes him with her eye. She doesn't want to have to restrain him. William starts putting the bits of paper back on Whacka's tray. 'See, Arjun, William is doing it. Shall we help him? Good boy, William.'

Whacka glowers at William, stomps forward, takes charge of his own tray. Linda helps him put the pencils in the holder, the pieces of card back on to the tray, the safety scissors back in their box. 'Good boy, Whacka. When we've finished with our tray we must put it back where we found it.'

'Well done, Arjun!' adds Ferida.

Whacka stows away his tray, turns to her, hands upturned, fingers spread out, and says, 'Then other chidden won't be able to get the tray they want, will they?'

'That's exactly right,' his teacher says.

'I wan my drink now.'

'Get your beaker and have a few sips,' Ferida shouts. 'Anyone who wants to go to the toilet, line up by the door.'

On a Northern Line train at Archway, Priya shot towards an empty seat. She was heading for King's Cross. Londoners on their way to work were listening to Walkmans, reading papers and books, some had their eyes closed. In the crush by the door of the compartment people had to stand, bodies touching, like moths massed in a hollow. A snowdrift of silence when the train stopped between stations. Priya remembered an Italian friend at Oxford saying that when she first came to London, and was on the way in from Heathrow at nine in the morning the silence on the tube convinced her that someone famous had died. Priya could not forget an incident with Ben's father, when the three of them were walking down Chancery Lane and all she could hear, amidst the lunch-hour crowds of accountants and lawyers, were the thousands of steel-capped brogues beating out an anti-rhythm of humanity on the concrete. She had been explaining something to Richard, something to do with race. Abruptly, Richard turned to her. 'Do keep your voice down, Priya,' he said. She wished she had responded with something hurtful. Afterwards, Ben had tried to defend him. Things had changed since then. At least now he was able to see a little more of the kind of man his father really was. 'I'd like to cut his balls off and pestle them in a mortar. Jumped-up college porter. One of those old dogs from Keble.'

Some mornings on the tube Priya just sat looking round her, but today she had bits to read. She wanted to consider how she was going to put together her radio report on the Southall Black Sisters. It was their twentieth anniversary, and she wanted the package to portray the range of work they had been doing. She wondered whether to give the report a personal edge, since she had once, during her time at Oxford, had dealings with the managing committee of SBS. When she had first got involved with them during the Rushdie affair, she had wanted to be part of a group that was taking a stance against the race-relations brigade, the people who'd been happy to use Rushdie's writings about racism in Britain in their training programmes but were turning their pens against him after the fatwa was pronounced.

A man came and stood in front of her. Singaporean, she guessed. He was wearing a double-breasted light grey pin-striped suit. Absurdly over-sized. He had a square jaw, wet, reddish lips. Combed-back jet-black hair, a folded broadsheet tucked under one arm. He stood with feet wide apart, as if making room for a mastiff dick, boys only. Her friend Arif had always had a thing about gay Singaporean fat cats. He had gone off to be a banker in New York. Priya hated the arrogance that money seemed to bring. Arif was married now, had stuffed his wife in a million-dollar house and bought his sex from rent-boys on cocaine-driven weekends in Frankfurt and London. The Singaporean's boxy head had a zit-marked face, with thin black eyes, neat lashes and brows – there was something both puppet-like and sneering about his gaze. Perhaps I could have been a novelist, she thought, laughing inwardly. From an early age she had sworn never to get stuck in front of a typewriter like her mother. She wanted to be always on the move. The Singaporean had a tiny World Aids Day ribbon pinned to the lapel of his open overcoat.

She changed to the Piccadilly Line at King's Cross and got on to a westbound train. At Russell Square, a suave square Raj-type got on, sporting Harris tweeds and a brown felt hat. Priya, in novelist mode now, made notes in her head. Stubby but delicately balanced fingers. Sits slightly forward on the seat, so as not to crease his clothes. Bulldog face, well-polished black shoes, trousers with turn-ups, half-moon gold-rimmed specs, reads the paper with his arms spread wide, licks his thumb as he turns pages, flaring nostrils, big uppity nose, small cock, peanut cock, fat creased up like a scarf round his neck, smug gold band on his wedding finger.

A green-blazered schoolgirl said to her friend, 'D'you know what Jermaine asked me today? He said, "Why do you think boys have nipples?"' Both girls burst out laughing, whispering answers to each other that Priya wished she could hear. She tried to think of a reason. An image flew into her head. She was lying on the cool grass outside the Welsh cottage. They were both naked. They had both come. If it had been Ben, he would have moved away to his side, leaving her to her own thoughts, but Leo was kissing her nipples, nipping her nipples, snuffling her like a puppy. Smiling all the while. 'Your skin is so soft, like a petal,' he had said, his cheek coasting over her belly. She yearned to be touched by those slow, expert fingers again. And yet, when she saw him now there was revulsion. Caught up in these reveries, she almost missed her stop. Gathering her things, she pushed through the standing com-muters to reach the closing doors, slipping through, just in time. As the train began to move she had an uneasy feeling of having left something behind. She jogged alongside the compartment and there, through the window, she saw her scarf lying on the seat. She wanted to bang on the glass. 'Fuck!' she shouted. That had been a gift from Ben's mother. A Buchanan tartan, she loved the soft cashmere. Its bright red and sunny yellow had kept her warm through so many winter days. She sank on to a vacant platform seat and held her face in her hands.

She couldn't help thinking she was being punished for allowing herself to remember Wales. In the convent she had attended in Bombay they were always telling her that if you thought something bad, God could hear you. She had been so taken up by her clever observations. She felt empty, stupid, angry, sad. Within seconds her morning lay in pieces like a smashed milk bottle. This day that she had been so determined to enjoy: starting with the chocolate croissant, the sweet, bitter hit of the Italian coffee – she remembered them now as she did the colours of the scarf, dissolving in this swamp of stampeding commuters sucked in and out of the caverns of this city. A train stopped and disgorged its rush-hour load. All these people had a purpose, a motive, their lives were simple, happy. Three kids, a house in Finchley, cross the little bridge from the tube station to your quiet street, your car and dog, your two holidays a year. Where could she place herself in all that?

Everything seemed sullied by the loss of the scarf. But it wasn't just the scarf. Black tides enveloped her. Tears came. She hoped no one would try to console her. Perhaps she had been too proud. She was wrong to go on thinking that Ben had to be attacked for estranging her. It was time to admit something, something about the pain she had caused him, the hurt she had caused herself, the guilt even. She felt, almost as if for the first time, Ben's humiliation. All for what? Just because she couldn't find in herself the strength, no, not the strength, the weakness, the vulnerability, the humility, to say she had been wrong. That what she had done had not, even if it had been pleasurable, had not been worth the suffering it has caused him, caused her. Why did she have to go on inflicting her uncertainties on Ben? Stop now, she told herself. There was so much kindness and loyalty in him, and he loved Whacka so fiercely. She had stretched that love too far. Somehow, unimaginably, he had had the strength to stay, but she must find a way to make it up to him. She hoped it wasn't too late.

Year 7 pupils shoved each other through the open door of C14. Ben was writing on the whiteboard. The ones who were talking fell silent when they saw him. For two months since the beginning of term Ben had worked with them on the 'magic door routine'. 'When you pass through it', he would repeat, 'it's as if you've entered a magic world. In this "enchanted" place there is no talking until you've got yourself ready for the lesson and the teacher has taken the register. If you fail, you'll spend fifteen minutes at the beginning of the lesson standing behind your chair.'

Today it was Alex and Melanie who had to stand. When the children had taken their coats off, Ben asked them to turn to page 21 of the class reader, *Underground to Canada* by Barbara Smucker. 'We'll read up to the end of chapter 3, then I would like you to imagine that you're the central character, Julilly. Let's remind ourselves of what has happened to Julilly so far. Put your hands up. Rachel.'

'She has been captured by the slave driver.'

'Good. And what's happened to her mother?' asked Ben. 'Sit down, Melanie.'

'His mother has been left behind on the plantation,' answered Robert.

'*His* mother?'

'Sorry, sir, her mother. But, sir, Julilly has her little brother with her.'

'That's right. Can anyone remember his name?'

'Christopher.'

'Well done, Clarence. What I would like you all to do after we finish reading the next bit, which will tell us about what happens to Julilly and her brother and where they're taken, is to imagine that you are Julilly and are writing a letter to your mother about the journey. Try to include as many details as you can from the text. Sit down now, Alex. Let's start from the top of page 21. Angelica, will you read the first two paragraphs?'

Priya emerged into the gloom on the corner of High Holborn and Kingsway. Opposite her was the church with the Corinthian columns that said, 'Enter, Rest, Pray.' She let the office-goers carry her past Africa House with its stone lions guarding the door. So much of her recent life had been spent walking down this causeway. She had watched with horror the new-age bars and coffee houses sprouting along it, the Starbucks and Coffee Republics, the Tino's, Gino's and Amicis, the Soup Operas, Pitcher and Pianos. She hated these places for their bright lights, their fake cheeriness. Not one coffee she had ever drunk on this road lived up to Ben's Sunday morning brew.

What she loved about walking down Kingsway was the names of the buildings and streets: a trail of imperial pomp and self-satisfaction. She remembered when she had been on probation as a news presenter. She used to speak to herself all the way to Bush House, 'Must keep my concentration on the script in front of me. One of my problems is that I tend to get distracted by the small things, a fly buzzing round the studio, the clock's second hand, the glass of water. Mustn't panic if I'm talking and a voice comes over the cans.' She had hated the headphones she was forced to wear, they gave her a sense of claustrophobia, as if she were underwater. Her first report had been on the law of provocation. Kiranjit Ahluwalia's case. The Southall Black Sisters had been behind that case.

Resounding footsteps on the pavement like clip-clopping horses, all out of kilter. Men in suits, carrying briefcases and workaholic looks. Amidst this crowd of stripey-shirted gents and neat-skirted females, Priya walked and talked at a deliberately moderate pace. Her soft-lipped soliloquizing raised little alarm. It was not the dramatic, soothsaying variety of the drunks and bag ladies, though there were times, on a quiet street, when she allowed herself to be expressive with her hands. Priya found it difficult to think silently. She liked to hear her thoughts. She liked to test them out idiomatically, to play the game of talking, as if to a confidant, cajoling, advising, warning, disputing, deciding and decoding.

'Must remember', she said, as she dodged flapping sandwich wrappers and rolling coffee cups, 'to keep up the pace in my voice. When the speed drops, I sound like a bee droning. That Lewis, the voice-trainer, god, he was bloody good, he must have smoked 100,000 cigarettes to make his voice so resonant. What was it that Lewis used to say? "Smile, sound upbeat when you start. Don't try to imagine a million listeners out there. Imagine you're talking to one person, someone you know. Fix your voice on that person." How do you sound upbeat when the news is sad? Killings, fires, hostages, coups. That's what we all want to hear about. Other people's disaster stories. "Pretend you're talking to a friend," Lewis had said, "but don't hype your voice up too much, or you'll sound like one of those ludicrous Capital or Radio 1 presenters who are always enthusing and chuckling with false glee."'

When she had first moved to London, Priya used to be woken by those Radio 1 voices. She remembered burying herself under the hot duvet while the DJ described yet another doomed love story in tear-jerking cadences over schmoozy lilting music. Late into the morning, twisting and turning on her single bed, she used to imagine that one day her voice would be really famous, like that of Sue MacGregor or Valerie Singleton, or even the schoolmarmy Charlotte Green.

As she walked from Holborn towards the Aldwych and the great dome of Bush House, she played a familiar game – anticipating street and building names: Twyford Place, the Catholic church, Remnant Street, Imperial Buildings, Victory House, Queens House, Sardinia Street, the Peacock Theatre, Portugal Street, St Catherine's House. Where her marriage certificate lay. What were the legal issues in relation to Whacka? Could Leo ever have a case for custody? Her mind back-flipped to the question that had been haunting her in bed last night. Would Leo and Jan come to Whacka's party? A figure curled up on a cardboard mat lay sleeping in the doorway of St Catherine's House: matted hair, several layers of ragged clothes, newspaper stuffed into his shirt and trousers, broken shoes.

Priya read the inscription on the front of Bush House: 'To the Friendship of English Speaking Peoples.' She was proud to be part of this hub of swirling voices and myriad languages transmitted across the world. In a small village in India, a group huddled round a portable transistor was listening to the news in Hindi or Urdu, spoken by someone who, at the end of their working day, took the tube to a Spartan flat in Turnpike Lane. Priya pushed through the revolving doors of Bush

House as, she thought, through those magic roundabouts of childhood, on which we all swing round and round and then, one day, walk out into the other side of the adult world.

Reception was ablaze with gold. At first, Priya thought it was the sun slanting in through some high windows, but it was a manufactured aura: spotlights, cleverly hidden behind statues and pillars. Flaxen beams reflected on the walls and ceiling.

In the seventh-floor offices of the South Asian Languages Section she dropped her bag and sat down at her desk. These fusty rooms reminded her of bureaucratic offices in India, with piles of paper stacked beneath desks and heaped on shelves. She was surrounded by brown carpet, tapes, computer screens, and constant news reports fed out through the speakers in the corners. People were pushing themselves round on their wheely-chairs. Half the desks were empty.

'Priya, what are you doing here today?' asked Clare, one of the production assistants.

'Just finishing my package for this evening's programme.'

'Keep your head down. Adam is desperately looking for a presenter. Shamsher's got a horrendous cold and couldn't come in.'

'He'll have to do it himself then,' Priya said.

'You know he hates presenting.'

'I've got twenty kids coming to a party. There's no way I can do it.'

Just you try and make me feel bad about not presenting today, Priya thought, when I've done four weeks on the trot. You're the head of the unit, the man with the big salary. Let's see you do your job. 'I'm going to disappear into one of the self-op studios,' Priya said quietly to Clare. 'I'll phone you from downstairs to pick up the package when I've finished.'

Eleven

Period 2. Ben stood silent and tall in front of his own class, 10BT. Arms folded and feet parted he looked straight into the centre of the desks and voices, with an expression of calm resistance. One of the girls asked him, 'What are we doing today, sir?' His face registered the disturbance, but he didn't answer.

There had been nights early on in his teaching career when he had lain in bed imagining a special power he might employ to bring a class to attention. He dreamed of a small device he could surreptitiously operate, a little button like the one television weathermen hide in their fists, which would, like thirty cattle prods in unison, administer a short electrical current to the haunches of his students, springing them into robotic compliance.

Steve Lack, the teacher Ben was training to take over 10BT from the following week, had been surprised when Ben told him that he should stand at the front of the class and think of absorbing the noise. Though the son of a vicar, Steve nevertheless looked at Ben as if he were some sort of religious freak. Ben reminded himself to tell Steve not to take the register at the start of the lesson. The jokers always used the calling out of names to imitate or interrupt the teacher. And he must remember to make a seating plan for Steve.

Ben turned his gaze on Raz, who was a mixture of Turkish Cypriot and East End, with a large nest of curly black locks.

She was still chattering away to Lucy, a mixture of Caribbean father, long disappeared, and white middle-class mother who taught women's studies at Roehampton.

'Char,' said Raz to Lucy, 'you know what a chief the boy is, he said he was gonna not listen to the teacher, and then Dean who was standin' there, yeah, just came up and boxed him one straight in the eye.'

'He never! The boy's crazy.'

'And listen to this, yeah, after he got boxed, the other geezer stan's up and 'e's wobblin', yeah, 'e's wobblin' like a jellyfish and yeah . . .' Ben couldn't contain a wry smile. The rest of the class were enjoying this too.

Lucy screwed up an eye. Both girls were drama queens. 'What a chief!' she said, trying to disguise her middle-class drawl. She was strikingly tall and attractive girl who had come late to Tachbrook from a private school she had loathed. At the beginning of year 9 Lucy had been diagnosed with cancer. Once, Ben and Raz had gone together in his orange BMW to visit her in hospital after a bout of chemotherapy. Ben remembered how he had gone through a red light on Oxford Street and Raz had screamed with delight. Lucy had lost all her hair, which brought out the beautiful shape of her head.

A raised eyebrow from Lucy at Raz signalled that Mr T. was waiting for them to stop talking. Raz looked over to where Ben was standing, 'Go on, sir, we're ready,' she said.

'Today you're going to be starting work on your autobiographies. We've spent a lot of time telling stories and listening to each other's stories in the last two lessons, now I want you to take your time and think and write. In silence.' A collective sigh from the class, which Ben pretended not to notice. 'You did that very well last week. I was really pleased to hear from Mrs Benson that you behaved yourselves on the day I was away. I want to congratulate Kofi especially, for being so sensible.' Kofi beamed.

'Kofi, my son,' said Leroy, leaning over to pat him on the back. Everyone loved Kofi. He was a soft-spoken, shy boy. Once, in year 7, when Ben had taken the class ice-skating to the Streatham rink, Kofi had fallen over and bumped his smooth close-cropped head on the ice. That was before the fissure opened up in my life, thought Ben.

Kofi was the cement in the class. Most classes split along roughly racial lines round years 8 and 9. The black boys sat together, the Bengali girls sat together, so did the white boys, the Chinese girls, the middle-class boys. The danger was that these separate groups became self-sufficient splinters. It took a lad like Kofi, both shy and charming, to bring the various parts together.

'I'll give you a couple of minutes to settle down. There's paper on my table if anyone wants some.' Ben spoke quickly and quietly. 'Make sure you've got everything you need in the next two minutes. If there are any general questions ask them now. But, please, don't ask me whether you have to write the date and title. Try to paint a picture with your words. Remember the work we did on adjectives. We'll talk about how to edit your first draft in the next lesson. Let the ideas and thoughts come naturally. Close your eyes if you want to. Put your head down if you feel distracted. Try to find the images you want.'

'All right, sir,' said Raz, 'have you finished now? Can we get started?' You couldn't mess with Raz. If a boy in the class tried to tease her she would turn round and give him a fat kick in the backside. There were some who were genuinely scared of her. Ben remembered gibbering Luke who came to him after school one day. 'Please, help me sir, please sir. Raz and Josie are going to beat me up. I'm serious. They're waiting for me outside school, sir. You've got to talk to them, sir. They think I grassed them up to Mr Bogle for smoking a spliff, but I never.'

So lost in his own thoughts was Ben that he had hardly noticed how quietly the class was working. He got out a sheet of blank paper to draw up a seating plan to give to Steve in the break. He didn't have to look up – he knew where they all sat. Luke, in the fourth row on the right side of the classroom, was half Brazilian. Combat 18's youth brigade, who handed out leaflets at the tube station, had persuaded him to attend one of their meetings, after which he had come to Ben full of innocent questions. 'Is it true that the Indians and the blacks are taking all the jobs in Britain? Isn't that why there is so much unemployment? I just want to know, sir, if – just say – if all the black and Asian people who were not born here were sent back to their countries, wouldn't that mean that all the unemployed would be able to get back their jobs? What do you think, sir? Do you not think they have a point, sir?' So when he came to Ben shaking with terror that the fearsome Raz and her gang were going to pulverize him, Ben couldn't help laughing. Where are your Combat 18 friends now? he wanted to say.

A tough customer, Miss Raiza Mushit. She insisted her name was pronounced and spelt M.U. shit. Not Murshid or Majeed, which were surnames Ben had come across before. 'When people ask me to spell my name on the phone, I say straight out, "M.U. shit, got it?"' About a year ago she had started refusing to work. Ben did not relish taking her on. Her indignation frightened his insides. He had been more at ease confronting the bully of the class, Zechariah Waters.

★

SEATING PLAN FOR 10BT IN C14

DOOR

Jin	Kofi
Leroy	~~Zechariah~~
John	~~Dean~~
Farhana	Salma

Annabel	Vanessa	Ann	Lisa
	Hebbah	~~Christine~~	Yan-Quing
Emma	Raz	Lucy	

Tennyson/Lack

WHITEBOARD

Ilie	Luke
Zadie	Ainsley
	Naushad
Charlie	Daniel

Ben didn't know it at the time, but Raz's Cypriot father had split from his wife and moved to Manchester to set up some sort of business. Raz's mother was a set designer. Raz wore trendy outfits, vivid oranges and beautiful greens, flash trainers, which belied the difficult job of having to divide her time between Manchester and Bow. Sometimes it seems best that teachers don't know about the traumas their students have to face, thought Ben, as he filled in Raz, Lucy and Kofi's name on the class map.

What a relief that Tachbrook didn't have a uniform. What a relief not to worry about having to scold children for wearing a bit of jewellery or the wrong-colour shirt. Tachbrook was cool, it didn't have provincial hang-ups. It was more than a local school, it took children from all over London. Yes, there was bullying, name-calling. But when the lessons were over and the girls and boys funnelled out of the narrow corridors down the broad staircases – one or two shimmying down the red handrails – and into the super-wide glass and concrete concourse of this seventies-airport-terminal building, you could hear a jazz of voices; a disparate mass of London youth, each voice jostling for space. Everywhere you looked there was a person carrying a story from some far corner of the world. It could be scary when it was raining and there was no door open to the playground. Sometimes a fight started, and there would be this surge of children, rushing down the concourse like a stack of football supporters slipping down the terraces when a goal is scored.

Along the sides of the concourse there were benches built into the walls, and Ben thought about being one of the students sitting on one of those benches eating his peanut-butter sandwiches with a group of friends – like Jack, who came to meet him by the school gates every Thursday when he was on break duty. Little piggy Jack was always there with his friend Prakash, the weird Indian kid who was into heavy metal, to greet Ben in the sun or more often in the rain which spangled Jack's spectacles. Jack liked to ask him: 'Sir, why do you eat something different every week? Last week it was tuna, this week it's cheese. It's not good for you. You should eat the same sandwich every day.' That was Priya's fault, Ben pondered. His dad did eat the same sandwich every day. After meeting Priya he could never be that kind of person.

He felt a sudden lightness about Whacka. What did it matter where he came from? So many people can never have children of their own. In the middle of this silence in which his students were writing he thought, I love my boy. No one can take that away. Where had this feeling come from? Was it that he found himself attracted to the jumble, to the mix of kids, to the mix of voices, to the different sandwich every day? Wires untangled in his brain, as if for the first time in months, even years. He felt that life might hold something interesting in it again, something worth getting up for. Don't question it, don't examine it, he told himself, let the feeling float by like a barge. In the past year, he had assumed life had to be all endurance, all suffering, emotions fizzing in test tubes.

Across the middle of the nursery floor, cutting through the circle of children, there is a thick green arc painted on the parquet. Ferida gets a candle, set inside a small, round orange holder. She places it in the centre of the circle of children, in the lip of the green arc. The toddlers fall silent in anticipation of a ceremony they know and love. Ferida, perched on a small chair in her tight black trousers, has Whacka sitting next to her. He looks dazed, eyes tilting towards the ceiling. Priya's shoebox with the birthday notes and photographs is in Ferida's

lap. Linda, who is holding Milo, sits cross-legged at the opposite side of the circle. Ferida smiles at the children. There is a
palpable buzz round the room. Ferida enjoys these birthday
rituals. At the birth of her half-English son, now four, who has
just started school, she was disowned by her Muslim parents.
'For them I might as well have been dead,' she had said to her
friend. It made birthdays doubly important for her. She needed
to compensate for the sadness that separation from her parents
had brought.

Ferida was born in the Muslim hospital in south Bombay.
How odd that she should be sitting here now, a Bori Muslim,
carrying out a Montessori-style ceremony – an Italian professor's way of celebrating a birthday – in a north London
nursery. The world has come full circle for this boy's mother
and me, she thought. Arjun, like my son, is half-Indian.

'Now children,' said Ferida in her nasal voice. 'We've all
seen the ceremony that is about to happen, but can anyone
remember what it's all about?'

Hands go up: Milly, Jack, Milo.

'Milo, you tell us.'

'It's . . . the sun . . . the sun will go to the earth.'

'Good try, Milo, but I think it's the other way round, isn't
it?'

'Birthday, Fewida – is Whacka's birthday.'

'Yes, Milly.' Ferida nods. 'So, it's the earth that goes round
the sun, isn't it?' Most of the toddlers stare blankly, a few
nod their heads. 'Today is Arjun Tennyson's birthday.' The
children look puzzled, so she uses the name they all know.
'Stand up, Whacka. Come on, come forward.' From the floor
next to her Ferida takes a coloured globe and places the plastic
blow-up orb in Whacka's slender fingers. She helps him hold
it up for all the children to see. Whacka still has his befuddled

expression. 'This is the map of the world. Now, Whacka, you know what to do, don't you?'

'I know! I know!' several children shout. Linda puts her finger to her lips.

Ferida wears her calm-but-strict look. 'Right, I'm going to remind you all. In the middle you can see the candle burning brightly. Everyone listen very carefully.'

'Is hot,' says Jack.

'If you touch it will burn,' says Callum.

'That's right, Callum. The candle is like the sun. The sun is very, very hot. Let us say that this candle', she says, pointing to the amber holder, 'is the sun. Orange like the sun, hot like the sun, bright like the sun. So, Whacka, what is the candle?'

Hands shoot up in the audience.

Whack comes out of his daze, tries to think, people are whispering all round him, 'Sun . . . sun . . . sun.'

'Yes, the candle is the sun and you're carrying this ball in your hand – which is the . . . ?'

'Is a ball. Is a football!' says Whacka.

'No, Arjun, it's not a football, it's a globe. It's the map of the world. It's the earth. The earth goes round the sun once a year. So if you're three years old, how many times will the earth go round the sun?'

Puzzled faces. No hands.

'Three times,' says William.

'That's excellent, William. One, two, three,' says the teacher, drawing circles with her arm. 'The earth goes round the sun once a year. So you, Whacka, will carry the earth and walk round the sun. Walk along the green line.' She hoists herself up and trundles Whacka along the green line meant to represent the earth's orbit. 'Walk very slowly on the line, Arjun, because it takes the earth a very long time to go round the sun. One whole year.' Ferida goes back to her seat. Whacka has got to the middle of his orbit. 'Stop now, Whacka, stay there. So, as some of you know, today, the fifteenth of March, which is also called the Ides of March, is Whacka's birthday. To show you how long ago he was born and how long it took him to get to his third birthday, I'm going to ask him to walk, three times, up and down the green line. Let's start.'

Ferida speaks slowly. As she speaks, she feels the nudge of a very early memory: her Muslim primary school at the bottom of Colaba Causeway in Bombay. She can't think why it has come to her. Perhaps it's because this boy's mother is also from Bombay. His black hair, especially the way it streaks his forehead, like tar on a freshly laid road, his large ears and his dark eyes, so fiery black, like boys she used to play with in school, not like her son Arshan's pale brown eyes. She wants to clasp the boy to her bosom.

'So Whacka has begun his journey – with the earth in his hands, he's going round the sun. Stay on the green line, Whacka. He hasn't been born yet. His mummy and daddy are waiting for him to arrive. Where will he come from? From inside his mummy's tummy, of course. Everyone is waiting for the big day. Whacka was a few days late but eventually he is born. Here he is,' she says, holding up a picture of the baby Whacka. 'Eight pounds and seven ounces. Quite a heavy baby. His mother says it was a very cold day. Snow was falling. It was all white outside the Whittington Hospital. How many of you were born at the Whittington Hospital?'

'I was,' shouts Georgia.

'I was too,' shouts Milly, and other children join in with their raised hands.

Ferida shifts her well-padded behind, too big for the tiny chair. The movement sends her back again to that childhood memory of her primary school. She sees herself bouncing up and down, like Tigger, her four-year-old's favourite Winnie the Pooh character. She sees herself as a small girl in Bombay, dancing in front of a big mirror, pig-tails hopping with delight, her *abba* and *ammi* standing there in their traditional clothes looking proud. She was one of the best actors in the class. She always stood first in the end-of-year rankings. Bombay was a quieter city then. Her parents enjoyed peace. The only riot was in the heart of their happy daughter. There they stood: her father looking old, with his beard and cap, her mother, with her younger, plump face. Ferida was like a little bird flying from its nest, like one of the fluttering sparrows tweeting on the tree outside her window, but her parents would always be there to catch her, feed her, console her when she fell – when she cried that her friends in the building wouldn't play with her, or her brother wouldn't share his toys, or when she didn't get the part of Cinderella. How could they have cut themselves off from Arshan and her? Four years and she had not heard a single word from them. At first, she vowed never to contact them. Later, it was more like disbelief. This image she had of them standing there, at the door of the classroom, watching her frolic, she wanted them to be standing here, now, as she conducted this ceremony for this other Bombay woman's boy. To see how well she looked after these children. And how all their parents praised her hard work. Could she ever experience that uncaged feeling again if they weren't there to catch her? A tear pricked the corner of her right eye. She wiped it away and carried on.

'His grandma, Mohini, came all the way from India.' Ferida paraphrases from the notes that Priya has carefully prepared. 'Here she is,' says Ferida holding up a picture of Priya's mother. A stately photo of the novelist in a blue and white sari, the end of which she is using to cover her head. 'This is Whacka's granny at a ceremony she performed at their flat one month after Whacka was born. Look, children, she is holding a silver dish in her hands and there is a little flame burning – that's called a *diya*.' The children crane their heads and one or two of them come up close to meet Mrs Patnaik's serene smile.

'Can't see, can't see,' cries Milly, trying to push Callum out of her way.

'Don't worry, everyone will be able to see. Here are Whacka's daddy and mummy. And this, I think, must be Whacka's other granny and grandpa,' says Ferida, squinting at a picture of Ben's parents, Richard and Mary. 'They're also at the ceremony when Whacka was one month old. Now, children, everyone sit down. No, we're not going to pass the pictures round because they can get spoilt and they are very precious pictures. Whacka, can you take a step forward from the line. Good boy. Exactly three years ago, Arjun, whom you all call Whacka, was born.'

But Ferida wants to give herself up to the invasion of memories from her own childhood. The children seem tired and hot. Both Milo and Linda appear to be falling asleep. Linda's eyes, directed at Whacka, have a blank sheen. Ferida remembers how she used to run through a long room in a white dress that had a lacy pattern on the front. She must have been four years old then. She loved that dress. She wanted to wear it to school every day. And then once, when they were on Chowpatty beach . . . Early evening . . . She recalls pink clouds in the sky. She had on her white dress and something happened, something awful happened. She can't remember what.

'When Whacka was three months old, he managed to roll off the table where his mother had placed him and he fell on to the wooden floor. Look, you can still see the tiny scar on his chin. At six months, he started to crawl, but he was still waking his mummy and daddy in the middle of the night. At eight months, he stood up and walked. Now here's a picture of Whacka when he was one year old.' The photo showed Whacka sitting in a bouncy chair suspended from the door frame. 'So, Arjun, you have reached the end of the green line, the earth has gone round the sun one time. Whacka is one year old. Now the earth starts moving very slowly round the sun again and Whack is growing older. Walk slowly, Arjun, so I can tell them something about when you were one and a half.' Ferida glances once more at Priya's notes. 'Let's see how slowly you can walk? That's better. So, children, his favourite nursery rhyme was "Frère Jacques", and that's how he got his nickname, because he used to say, "Whacka, sing Whacka, Mummy!" Now which one of you can sing "Frère Jacques"? Go on, let's all try to sing it together.'

The children sing and Ferida remembers her favourite nursery rhyme, '*Ha, ha, ha, ha, dolly re . . . kevi mari dolly tu*'. Her mother would sing it to her in Gujarati. Even when she went to college at sixteen she liked her mother to stroke her head and lull her to sleep in the afternoons. Then she remembers what happened to the dress. It caught on something, a nail perhaps. She was running to get a snack from one of the brightly lit food stalls along the beach. The dress tore. She remembers howling, she remembers her mother scolding her, she remembers her father picking her up and patting her back. He had to cover her up with a shawl because the dress was so badly ripped. How can it be that her *abba* and *ammi* have never seen Arshan? How can they bear it?

'Frère Jacques' comes to an end and Ferida grabs a tissue to blow her nose. She glances at the clock and decides to quicken the pace. 'So, now, put up your hands if anyone knows what are the first sounds babies make.'

'Da-da, ma-ma' – voices from all over the room. Someone shouts, 'Pooh, pooh.' Everyone laughs.

Ferida puts on her serious face and holds a finger to her lips. Her Bombay accent intensifies. 'Whacka's first word was "na-na". Afterwards he used words like "koklate" and "minished". You all know what "na-na" and "koklate" are, but do you know what "minished" is? No, it's not an ice cream. Whacka was trying to say "finished". "Koklate" is for chocolate, and "na-na" for banana. Now he is two. Here is another picture of him at his birthday party with the cake and the candles. And now Whacka is carrying the earth round the sun again. One more year is passing and Whacka is going – small steps, Arjun – from two to three. At two he came to us at Tree House. His favourite foods are fish fingers and olives, and his worst food is tomatoes, which he calls "natos". And now the earth has gone round the sun three times and finally Whacka has reached his third birthday, fifteenth March. So let's all stand up and sing "Happy Birthday" to Whacka. Arjun's mother, Priya, has left some sweets and Fran has brought a cake. After "Happy Birthday", everybody can have a small slice before we go out to play in the garden.'

Whacka stood in the middle of the circle, voices sounding on all sides of him. He couldn't help but join in. And when they were all clapping he clapped a little too. How could they ever know the painful knots tied at his making?

Twelve

Ben's English class worked in silence on their autobiographies. He smiled at Raz in the first row. She looked back, showing him her pen poised over the paper and whispered, 'What?' Which was short for, 'What're you looking at?'

Leroy put up his hand. 'Can we use swearing in our story, sir?'

'Yes,' said Ben, 'if it's appropriate to the speech pattern.'

Leroy gave him his baffled look. 'Aaaright then, wickeeed. I know what I'm going to do.'

Ben wrote the boy's name on the seating plan. Leroy's mother, Mrs Dobson, a large strong-minded lady from south London, had turned up some months ago at reception, demanding to see Ben and Mr Bogle, the head of year 10. It was a matter of the utmost urgency, she said. She was holding a videotape in her hand. Ben was summoned to Bogle's office. Mrs Dobson's face was set in a grimace. Leroy, a bulky, square-headed, raucous boy, was sitting beside her. She held out the video to Ben. 'Mr Tennyson, do you have any idea where this came from?' Ben shook his head. 'This filthy thing comes from somewhere in this school and I'm going to find out where it came from. I walk into my house yesterday evening, and what do I see on the screen? These two Indian men engaged in . . . I don't know how to describe it . . . Perverted filth, that's all I can say. I could not believe my eyes when I saw what these men were doing.' Ben was frightened that he would not be able to control for long the laughter he was containing in his gut. 'This is a pornographic video!' she shouted. 'I found my son and my daughter, Leroy's sister Jessica, sitting in front of the television watching this Sikh man, turban and all, doing . . . even a dog wouldn't do what he was doing to these women.' Every time she came near to describing the actual scene she became so puffed up with indignation she couldn't get the words out.

Ben looked at Leroy and then at Bogle, the mild-mannered, pot-bellied head of year who was smiling his usual meaningless smile.

Leroy admitted that it was Jin-Man's video. Jin, who sat behind Leroy in the class, was summoned. Poor Jin who had never done a thing wrong in his life, even though his wastrel father spent his day in and out of the local betting shop. Ben was surprised, but not by the boys watching porn – he remembered Leroy having started one of his stories with the description of how as a three-year-old he had been whipped for pretending to have sex with his teddy after seeing such an act performed on television.

The boys were dismissed, and the mother partly placated by Trevor Bogle. He had a way of speaking that leapt up and over-emphasized the last few words of every sentence. Ben recalled how Bogle, a man with an old-fashioned sense of decency and an old-fashioned Caribbean accent, had come running after him, finger held up in one hand and video in the other. 'Tennyson,' he said, 'what are we to do with this video? I don't want to have it in my office. Would you like to keep it in your locker? Or should I ask the boy to destroy it in front of us? That's the best thing.'

The Chinese boy and Leroy were recalled to the office. 'Crush this tape,' ordered Bogle, still wearing that silly smile.

'How, sir?' asked Jin. The head of year placed the tape on the floor. 'Stamp on it,' Bogle said. Ben spluttered with laughter as the bemused boy laid waste to the tape as if it were a giant insect about to bite him. When he got home Priya said, 'You're crazy. Why didn't you just say, "I'll keep it." We could have watched the Sikh and the Sikhani on all fours.'

Emerging from his reverie, Ben noticed Vanessa whispering to Annabel in Cantonese. He filled in their names on the class map. Vanessa looked at him and scowled. Thin, angular, sharp-tongued girl. Vanessa's dad had started a takeaway in Hackney, and she and her brother lived above it with their father. Her mother had left them for another man when Vanessa was eight. Ben forgave her being a motor-mouth because she had helped her friend, Annabel, stand up to her own violent father. Vanessa and Annabel, a round-faced pudgy girl with short glossy hair, conversed in a mêlée of staccato London English mixed in with a smattering of Cantonese.

Looking round the class to check his seating plan, Ben wondered how many of these kids had been hit. Sometimes there were tell-tale signs: flinching when the teacher talked to you and looking petrified when sitting next to your parents at open evenings. Many of the school's worst-behaved kids were the ones who were being slapped at home. Politicians and the public had this notion that if only parents disciplined their children when punishment was needed, there would be better behaviour in the classroom and fewer crimes on the street. Ben's experience at school had taught him the opposite. What children seemed to want, and this could only be satisfied by spending time with them, was attention.

The bell rang for break. 'Leave the class quickly,' ordered Ben. 'We'll continue where you've left off when we come back.'

On the way out, Hebbah came up holding a piece of writing in her hand. 'Could you please read this, sir.'

'Not now,' Ben said. 'I'll look at it at the beginning of the next lesson.'

'Please, sir, just quickly.'

Ben sat down at his regular table in the staffroom. There was no sign of Steve. He took a bite from one of Brenda's rolls and, having nothing better to do, glanced at Hebbah's work.

My So Called Friend

Christine had specail powers she could hynotheis you and command you to do something and you would do it, abit like a dog, sit you sit, roll over you roll over. Christine had problems in her life I guess thats why she was really open with me. She would tell me everything about her life I was a bit like an agony aunt but I wouldn't give her good advice because I have never been through it my self. you would not believe the things she would tell me. She would have these mood swings, one day she is really happy and hyper the next she would be writing love letters to her mother who lived in Dahomie. Her mother left her when she was really young but she still loves her. She would write these letters at the back of her English book science book and her own book which she kept like a diary. In this diary she wrote every thing she felt and what has happened to her day by day. one time she showed me it when she and I was out of school, looking for something to do, anything just to get out of school. school was like our worst enemy we would not go near it with out a reason. Anyway the bit she showed me was a bit about how she felt about her mother being away from her, how much she missed her. the one bit I remember so well when she showed me her diary, it said 'I wish I had a mother like my friend Hebbah lucky bitch'. straight away when I read that I knew that she was jealous of me. There was one time when me and Christine were talking about life making our minds run wild. She said that she wanted to be a fashion designer for the rich and famous and I wanted to design people's houses. I realy used to hate her sometimes she would put me down – like for example she would say that I want to be an interior designer then she would say why didn't you take art or graphic media to do GCSE and then you can go to college and do what you want to do but now you can't be a designer so I would choose office work if I was you. Suddenly blood would just shoot to my stomach and anger would rush to my fist I would start having images of me just punching her in the mouth and telling her to stick her office work were it belongs and she should be the one, sorting out her life, but of course I didn't. Instead I would just say, you don't need art to be a interior designer bang we would start a fight, not a cat fight but an argument blah, blah, blah thats what she sounded like when she would talk to me.

Now the other thing which I really did hate about her is that she is, and I must say it, she is a slut. Boys thats all she thinks about, she would boast about it like today I'm going to meet Danny or Richard or who ever and then she would bring up the big question 'So Hebbah who are you going out with'. That same feeling happened again full of anger but instead I dream about me hanging her by her neck and laughing in her face. Rage was running all round my body. Christine was a girl who made you think like a devil.

There is one thing that once happend to me and Christine. It wasn't an incident that happend it was a chat we had that made me feel sorry for her. It was during the summer time me and Christine were in Hyde Park sitting on the bench like we used to when we bunked off school. Christine turned to me like as if the 12 oclock strick on big ben.

'Hebbah, what is it like having a mother? Do you love her?'

'I love her, but she can be a pain sometimes'

'I wish I had a mother, my dad, I just can not talk to him about things. Hebbah'

'Yeah'

'I want to tell you something about my life I need someone to talk to'

'Well tell me, thats if you want to'

'When I was in Dahomie I used to go to school there. One day I had to stay behind to help out with my teacher, he was a man. You can say I had a crush on him but not that much, not enough to enjoy him raping me'

My mouth dropped as if a piece of heavy metal had just landed at the bottom half of my lip. My heart started to beat faster like I have just run a marathon. I just did not know what to say, I could not say sorry. I just did not know what to say.

'I see your surprised'

'So Christine who did you tell this to, including me.'

'I told my other friend who still lives in the Dahomie'

'and what did she say, you did tell someone else didn't you?'

Me and Christine sat there in Hyde Park. The sun was shining in her face. You could still see the memory haunted her. her eyes were wide open as if she couldn't believe it her self. I can not imagine what she must have been through.

I did the most stupidest things in year 9, missing school, not doing my coursework, not caring about what my parents might say. Lying to them. If I had one wish it would be going back to year 7 and changing everything about my self and maybe change my friends. I would work hard, working my way up to full A grade be what ever I want to be. Like I said it is only a wish a wish that could never come true. I partly blame Christine for this but at the same time blame myself. Some of the dreams I had were unbelievable At one time I wanted to fly a plane in the airforce. The other thing I wanted to be was a lawyer, what a dream. Now I'm in year 10 trying to keep up with some of my work but coping. All my dreams have flown away, away from reality, but still in my heart I want to be a lawyer. In ten years time I could see myself with a bunch of kids gathering round me like little birds calling for their mother asking for food. No independence. My friend said I should not put my self down and aim for what I want to *do, but it is not that easy. In my heart and mind everything is black and I just want to scream and cry.*

I guess I just have to carry on with my life and do the best I can even thought I can not be a lawyer.

Ben was surrounded by his colleagues' animated conversation, like an audience gathered together in the interval of a play. He let the collective cackle wash over him. There was a cup of coffee in his hand and half an egg-mayonnaise roll in the other. He had lost his appetite. He took a sip of coffee and closed his eyes.

Hebbah's story had reminded him of his own anger. Perhaps he should be like her and want to punch Priya. He identified intensely with Hebbah's regret. Like Hebbah's dreams of being a lawyer, he had had dreams of a perfect family, of being a famous writer, a TV presenter, a household name. Dreams of the mixing of cultures. Love, respect, trust, all those clichés that Priya had trashed. The bell sounded, and the swirling voices broke back into his head.

Back in with 10BT Ben found that Salma the Bangladeshi girl who had joined the class in year 9 had been left out of his seating plan. Salma was a scrawny girl with an adult's face. About three months after she had arrived, Salma cornered Ben after school. She started complaining in Bengali. Ben was sympathetic when her friend Farhana who was translating explained that Salma was being bullied by Ann. But it was all Ben's fault, Salma said. It was because he gave all his attention to his favourite students. She said she knew that he spoke a bit of Hindi and that he had been to India, but he made no attempts to talk to her. She said he just looked through her and left her just to get on with her work. By the end of this tirade Salma was hyperventilating. Ben tried to calm her down by saying he would do what he could to change things, and that he was glad she was being honest with him. Salma's face turned blue and she looked faint. Farhana reminded Ben that Salma was asthmatic. They carried her into the deputy head's office and an ambulance was called. By the time the yellow and green paramedics arrived on a motorbike Salma seemed to have lost consciousness. The paramedics put her on oxygen and revived her.

On the seating plan Ben wrote 'asthmatic' in brackets under Salma's name. Remembering the incident, Ben went over to her table to check what work she had done. She had written two pages in Bengali and was busy using Farhana to translate the story into English. She looked up and smiled at Ben. She was so small and frail, the size of an average nine-year-old.

In the same class as girls who had been born in Beijing and Bangladesh there was also the ponytailed prodigy from Newington Green, Daniel Lock, and Charlie, the Oasis fan from Manor House, whose father was a Dickens enthusiast. At the back sat the half-Brazilian boy, Luke, whose mother had worked in Bush House and had been a passing acquaintance of Priya's. The same boy who had attended Combat 18 youth meetings after being repeatedly terrorized by the Electric Avenue rude-boy, Zechariah Waters. There had also been Dean, the handsome, lithe pathological liar, whose deceit ended in a piteous scene: his single-parent mother, a woman who had changed from size 10 to size 16 in the time Ben had been teaching her son, shed tears of shame at Ben's reports, which caused the fourteen-year-old boy to break down alongside his mother. Dean was like a leopard: fast, strong, graceful. Girls queued up for a taste of him.

Both he and Zechariah had been removed from Ben's class.

Tired of the trouble Dean was getting into, his mother sent him to live with his aunt in Barbados, and to attend her old school to see what the cane and slipper might do for this slippery character. Four months later the rogue was back, surrounded in the corridors by his acolytes. On Dean's return, Ben persuaded Bogle to give the boy a fresh start in a new class.

And where had Zechariah ended up? Expelled, like his brother. Ben's diagrammatic representation of 10BT should have no room for him and Christine. They seemed to have been erased from everybody's map; they had fallen through a gap in the law, which nominally required all under-sixteens to attend full-time education. Zechariah joined the thousands of teenagers who frequent shopping malls and free-base on the ramps of housing estates, spinning like bullets through strip-lit barrels of concrete, not knowing what to do with their young bodies except to abuse, rob or destroy. Someone told him Zechariah had been seen helping in his mum's patty shop in a side alley off Brixton market. Ben hoped so. He would never forget the day when, for Christmas '97, he had made a special effort and written a card with a personal message to every kid in his class. When he gave the card to the normally arrogant Zechariah he rocked his chair back and lay horizontal on the desk behind him, almost toppling over. A happy smile spread across his huge mouth. Holding the card up in the air, he said loudly, 'You know what? You are the first teacher in this school who has ever given me a card.' From the start boys like him are reviled in the staffroom, thought Ben, and it sometimes feels like they have no choice but to live up to their reputation.

Once, Dean, who had been Zech's close friend, had stood up in a personal and social education lesson, in which the class were discussing the stereotypical behaviour of boys and girls, and told them a story. Zech and he were going home one evening, a little later than usual because Mr Tennyson had just kept them in for detention and given them one of his usual lectures about doing their homework and using their brains. They were sitting on the top of a double-decker when Zech had said to Dean that he thought that what Mr T. had said was right. He did have the brains and he could work hard and do well at school and surprise the teachers with his good behaviour. Sometimes he really wanted to do it and maybe he and Dean should try it.

'So why do you think it didn't happen?' Ben had asked.

'Is like . . . is like, there are two of us in all of us, sir. But it's almost as if that other one, the other Zechariah, the part of him that could've ended up with a job and car and kids was living in some far-off place, you get me? When we was on the top of that bus, maybe 'cause it was a clear day or sometin', Zech almost get in touch with this other part of himself, you know what I'm sayin'? And then later on, he forgets all that and become the Zechariah we all know. You get me, sir?'

'True,' had said Raz. 'I get it. That's really true. It's like, I can feel sometimes that Zechariah was really a nice guy. In fact, I could almost find him funny, but then he went back to being like shouting and bullying and that. Dean's got a point, you know. We are two people, many of us. I feel like that too, sometimes. I wanna go home and do my homework, finish my coursework and all that, but somethin' takes over when I do get home and I end up goin' my friend's house or sitting and talkin' on the phone to Lucy for hours.'

What got to Ben about Dean's story was how near Zechariah had been to making contact with that other part of himself and allowing it to work for a while. But that's the struggle, he thought. How do we keep in touch with that other part of ourselves, the part that wants to go home, forget about the past and get on with that East/West cookbook, instead of the one that skulks with a whisky and a joint in front of the telly?

Ben felt guilty about his role in forcing Zech out of the school. Zechariah was like a hapless lizard flailing about in a sea of uncontrollable impulses of aggression and self-destruction, but every now and then, on the top deck of a London bus, boys like him saw a glimmer of something outside the turbulence, a possibility of dry land, a patch of green almost within their reach.

Late one night, in his comfortable bed, Ben had seen himself caught in a riot in Broadwater Farm. Lying on the floor with legs jackknifing round him; cartoon figures of violent black youth and truncheon-carrying 'pigs' ready to crush his genitals. Then, out of the bricks and bottles and flames, Zechariah's grin looms over him. Those devilish flashing teeth, rolling eyes; the look he liked to scare teachers with. 'You know it. Mr T.!' And then what does he do: help Ben off the ground or step on his face?

Ben checked his class plan. A quick glance at the clock told him there were fourteen minutes to go to lunch and the other half of his egg-mayonnaise roll. He'd have to rush through the remaining students.

He'd missed off Ilie, with the globe head and the cauliflower ears, whose Moroccan father was a tennis fan and had named him after his Romanian idol. You had to handle him carefully, because Ilie could come out with the most virulent sexist remarks. Ben counted the names on the register to see who he had forgotten. Ann. She had arrived in year 7 as a pretty, biddable student with neat handwriting, sensible shoes and tidily ponytailed hair. Every weekend now she was out on the town with Leroy, John and Dean and looking sick on Monday from having overdosed on morning-after pills. Her father still thought she should go to Oxford. And John Nwosu. No sign of mother, and his father lived with a succession of women and didn't want John around. He had no choice but to stay with a volatile aunt, and every so often Ben had to take him for a walk and let John complain about his aunty saying that he stank, that his clothes were second-hand, that he was a tramp.

Lisa: working-class south London girl with no desire for academic grades. Her main ambition seemed to be to go out with a black boy. Ainsley: kind boy whose mother had to separate from her drunken, violent husband. He once complained to Ben that a teacher in a fit of rage had told him to 'grow a few inches', Yan-Quing came late and, unusually, was from mainland China rather than Hong Kong. She and Salma were friends. Ben gave her *Wild Swans*, which she took six months to read, and when the dog-eared copy finally came back, her verdict was that there was nothing in the book she didn't already know. She and Vanessa had got As in Maths GCSE in year 9, two years before the rest of their class sat the exam.

Was that everyone? Three missing. Zadie Child. Inveterate Luton supporter. Tomboyish good looks, spent all her time with her boring, fleece-clad father. Lazy, but she passed all her subjects easily. Big friend of Ainsley and Naushad, another slouch who lived in an old council block right in the heart of Covent Garden. His aged father was very ill.

Emma: friend of Lucy and Raz, strawberry-cheeked airhead blonde, wore clubbing gear to school. Not interested in work.

Will get good grades anyway. Mother worried about dyslexia because Emma made a few spelling errors.

Sitting in the airconditioned self-op studio on the sixth floor of the World Service building, Priya began recording the links for her report. 'Twenty years ago this month, in a small house on a quiet street in west London, three Asian women banded together to start an organization called Southall Black Sisters. The organization grew out of the collective fear experienced by the Asian community in Southall, during violent disturbances in the late seventies, fomented by the National Front, which culminated in the murder of Blair Peach, a schoolteacher from New Zealand. The aim of Southall Black Sisters was to support women in the Asian and Afro-Caribbean communities who were suffering from domestic violence and its related problems: homelessness, loss of benefits, difficulties with immigration status. I asked Sadaf Fidwi, one of the founding members of the group, about her background and the ways in which it had contributed to the work she was doing.'

Priya switched to Sadaf talking about the strong influence her mother had had on her and about how, as a student, Sadaf had walked around clutching a copy of *A Portrait of the Artist as a Young Man* and chanting to herself, 'I shall not submit.' Using her stopwatch to time the insert, Priya found a pause at thirty-seven seconds where she could cut the tape. She had let Sadaf go on for three and a half minutes when she had interviewed her in the Southall office. Priya knew the house well. She had spent time there, coming down from Oxford to help organize a march by women supporting the publication of *The Satanic Verses*. Sadaf was a small woman with a round face who held herself with dignity. She was the most radical

153

of the main players in the organization. Priya had listened carefully to all the answers in the original interview. Like a lot of thinkers on the left, Sadaf tried to avoid talking too much about her personal history. Priya thought of her as fearless – Sadaf would rather resign from working parties than accept a consensus view. There were very stressful situations to deal with at SBS headquarters; others would lose their temper, but Sadaf never raised her voice. I suppose, thought Priya, where there is no fear there is no anger.

Priya had two tapes, one with her recorded links, the other with the inserts, which she needed to cut down to their correct length. When she'd finished, she could go and have half an hour's peace before she returned home to Whacka and Jocelyn.

Had Ben been right to invite Leo and Jan? Would they come to Whacka's party? She could find no answers to these questions so she pushed them away.

The first six months at Bush House she had hated putting radio packages together. She was happy coming up with the ideas and asking the questions, but when it came to writing the links and cutting the interviews into clips she wasted energy worrying about what was lost and what she could cram into her three-minute reports. Her senior producer would complain that her links were too long, too literary.

She had tried to slip in a bit of colour and imagery into her reports, until one day the producer blew up. He said he was sick of having to monitor every bit of writing she did, and when the hell was she going to learn to write properly for radio. From that day on she cut out any extraneous word or phrase from her links. She began to appreciate that it was the clear statement of essentials that caught the attention of the listener.

'In the past two decades SBS have mobilized some of the

most public and poignant campaigns in defence of women jailed for murdering their violent spouses. When Kiranjit Ahluwalia had her sentence reduced from murder to manslaughter and was released from prison in 1992, it was the Southall Black Sisters that she thanked first of all.'

Here the link ended and Sadaf came back on. 'When Kiranjit came out of prison and saw we were so few, she said, "How do you do it from such a small place?"' The cuts from links to inserts should follow the progress of the story. 'This is no everyday nine-to-five job,' continued Sadaf. 'The phones ring constantly, the offices are cramped, more than a thousand women a year ring for help and advice. We have four fully paid members who work non-stop during the day answering the phones. We have to find other times, weekends and evenings, to complete all the paperwork and admin.'

With her next link Priya introduced an academic from Birkbeck. 'In 1979, there were clashes in Southall between anti-racist groups – gathered there to protest against neo-Nazi marches through this most famous of Indian communities in Britain – and the neo-Nazi demonstrators. Mira Remington-Smith, professor of gender studies at Birkbeck College, followed those events closely: "As usual, it was the death of someone like Blair Peach, a white schoolteacher, that made the media and society sit up in their seats. At the same time, and as part of a trend of general unrest and protest, black women's groups, especially from second-generation immigrants, were springing up in many cities in Great Britain, but SBS never drowned in what was then fashionable identity politics."' She had Smith go on for twenty-nine seconds before she was able to find a suitable pause.

Priya remembered visiting London for the first time at the age of sixteen, with her mother, and hearing the name Blair

Peach. They were at a friend's house in Fulham. An argument broke out, and she was confused as to what it was about. There was a lot of talk about who had killed Peach. The killer, some said, was known to be a policeman. At about this time a skinhead on the King's Road was pointed out to her, and she had thought she could sit him down on a bench, share a cigarette and reason with him. That was just before she was called a 'Paki'.

She was in a phone box, one of the old-style red ones, in a little recess off the Fulham Road. There were two teenagers horsing round outside, waiting for her to finish. It was dark, and she was having a long, difficult conversation with her American boyfriend Ralph. The girls kept peering in. One shouted, 'It's a Paki!' and they both cracked up. She remembered going back to her room and lying on the bed, face down, thinking herself silly for being so upset. The girls had laughed at her as if she were a weird animal in a cage.

With the next link she introduced a dissenting voice. A Tory Ealing councillor complained that SBS were draining council funds, that their politics were extreme and not representative of the way in which most people in the community lived. Priya put his comments to Sadaf. 'We have often been under fire from all sides, not just from the racists and the Tories, but from members of our own community. Death threats, bricks thrown through the window, even shotgun fire – but the most difficult thing for us to deal with is that we are sometimes reviled by members of left-wing groups for fuelling racial stereotypes.'

Nearly ten years ago, Priya had taken part in the SBS march outside the Houses of Parliament to protest against the burning of *The Satanic Verses*. The hatred on the faces of some of the Muslim men who had come to demonstrate against

Rushdie's book and were trying to push through the police cordon to attack the women had frightened her. 'Get back to your kitchens, you whores!' they had shouted. 'You stink, you're traitors!' Those men could have overpowered the police, broken through the thin wall of blue uniforms. Throughout Sadaf, in a defiant, feet-apart stance, shouted out slogans through her grey megaphone.

Thirteen

Ben was big on responsibility. There was a right way to live, a right way to behave. And moderation was important; keeping one's emotions contained. Be controlled, be vigilant, his dad used to remind him.

He would have liked to have sex with Helen, but it wasn't the correct thing to do. He worried that his impulse was spiked with the desire to get even with Priya. And what would be wrong with that? Was there some sort of eternal damnation waiting for him if he transgressed the vows of marriage? Why did his fantasies torture him so? Was he scared of appearing to be the wrong-doer? At Haylesbury he might sneak off with his friends to smoke a cigarette, but when it came to taking drugs he always declined.

He didn't feel his marriage could support the strain of more infidelity. He was jeopardizing so much in these imagined encounters with Helen, and yet, his brain was bombarded with carnal pictures: his hand meandering under her skirt, his head in her breasts, lingering in the bowl of her thighs. These images collided with the reality of his work. Helen and he had a close professional relationship. Ben had been successfully teaching one of the troublesome classes in her year. She looked to him for words of advice on how to handle the difficult kids. She listened to his complaints and did her best to amuse him with her anecdotes. Helen performed a light dance round his plodding moods. She had a way of introducing a subject just as they were saying goodbye, some morsel of information, some snippet she had forgotten to relate, that forced him to stay for a few more sentences.

So when she turned up in his classroom five minutes into the lunch break in a smart blue skirt, the shape of her breasts pressing against her black top, locks from her streaked bob falling in front of her blue eyes, part of him wanted to close the door and act like an animal. He wanted to bite her cheek. He wanted to fox her in a hole, stand up close and sniff her skin. Just once, he wanted her hands on his face, their breaths entwined, her fingers in his hair. He thought of her as a delicious confection. A lustrous sweet in its cellophane twist. Every day he got a chance to examine the way the light bounced off her translucent curves, imagine the sound of the wrapper crinkling open, the first touch of the effulgent lozenge meeting his lips, the ripples secreted on his tongue, the way it would last for ever.

This lunchtime he had a rash on the tip of his penis. He wanted to sink it in a basin of icy water. Had he contracted some venereal disease from a filthy toilet bowl? A punishment for his philandering thoughts? Helen stood next to him for some time, as was her way, eyelashes fluttering. He had an urge to complain. 'I've had this pain like a needle shooting up the eye of my cock. Do you think I should visit the doctor?'

'Mr Tennyson, have you forgotten our little meeting with Marlon's father?' Helen said, in her mock-mothering tone.

'No,' Ben lied, 'but I was hoping to get a sandwich before the meeting starts.'

'You can share mine. By the way, Mr Gibbs, Marlon's father, turned up during period 5 on Friday. He was not a happy man. I said you were teaching and he should make an appointment for Monday. You're free after lunch just in case the meeting goes over time, aren't you? I've arranged for someone to take your register. I warn you, he's a tricky customer.'

'Let's try and keep it short,' Ben said as they walked down the wide staircase. 'I'll see you upstairs in five minutes.' On entering the staffroom he was hailed by John Welsh, who had his mouth full of baked potato, beans and chilli pickle. The man who bragged about having been a lady-puller in his day. 'Before you came to Tachbrook,' he would tell Ben, 'I tell you, that was some time we used to have. A different woman every week. Ask Sam.' Sam Ganpath, a teacher from Birmingham, would come over in his double-breasted blazer and his stripey tie and pat Ben on the shoulder. 'Tell him what it was like, Sam,' Welsh would say.

'Those were the days, my friend, John and I, we were some pair. A different woman every week. Anyway, I've left all that behind. It's the family life for me now,' Ganpath would wax on. 'A bottle of wine, a video, *University Challenge* on a Wednesday, delicious meal with the wife. Last Wednesday Josie and I had a great bottle of Bordeaux, crusty French bread and a Pont-l'Évêque in perfect condition. You know that cheese, Ben. You're a man of culture. I'm like you now. I want to enjoy all the gentle pleasures. No more complications with women, that's why I don't stay late on Fridays. Tell you what, we're having one of our wine-tastings this Sunday. If you feel like it, Ben, come along.'

'He won't come,' said Welsh. 'He's too grand for us. Famous cookery writer, hobnobbing with the literati. What's happened to that newspaper column you were doing?' Welsh sniggered. 'When's the new book coming out? I've told my friends all about you. I bought three copies of your last book, you know. Hardbacks. Bloody expensive they were too.'

Pair of hucksters, thought Ben. What Welsh really liked to do was sit in the pub and drink nine pints of Foster's, checking carefully to see that everybody was buying their round. He always made sure his turn came right at the end of the session and whenever anyone who had already bought a round left early Welsh would say, 'You're not leaving, are you? It's my round next, I was just going to get you a drink.' In the friendly kickabouts the staff had at the end of the week Ganpath spent most of his time like a crab, dribbling the ball from one side of the penalty area to the other. After football John and Ganpath got their rocks off playing snooker or darts. Jingling the pound-coin winnings they had wheedled out of younger colleagues.

The worst of it, Ben thought as he picked up a coffee for Helen from Brenda's counter, was that the last time they had played tennis he had allowed himself to be defeated by Welsh, who had spent the rest of the week calling out to Ben in the staffroom to remind everyone of his victory. He had told the story of their match to anyone who could be nailed to a chair for long enough to listen. He must have played Welsh at least fifty times, and this was only the third or fourth time he had lost. He couldn't wait to get his revenge. Plate in hand, John came up to Brenda's counter where Ben was lingering. 'Shame you can't play tennis today. You've got that kids' party to go to. I was really looking forward to a game.'

'It's not a kids' party, it's my son's birthday,' said Ben. A horrible thought entered his mind. Suppose Welsh knew something about his and Priya's troubles, suppose Welsh had managed to find out about Leo? It couldn't possibly have happened, but what if it should? 'It's probably going to rain anyway,' said Ben, turning conciliatory. Life was full of these damn suppositions that rocked the heart. You could spend hours with a completely absurd 'what if', churning it up until a 'worst fear' became a probability, until you might end up pleading your innocence to someone who had no idea what you were talking about. And what if Leo and Jan turned up at the party? What if there was a scene in front of everyone?

'Just grey skies,' said Welsh. 'I might play with Sam. He's a bit crap, though. I've got this brilliant weekend lined up. This friend of mine, who is a secretary to Michael Meacher – I've told you about Bob, haven't I – has invited us to his house in the country. He's got an amazing wine cellar. Anyway, it was a good game we had last time. Down to the wire. I think I've retrieved my form on the forehand.' Whilst Welsh spoke he swung his right hand through the air triumphantly. 'You're going to find it very hard to beat me next time.'

If I smack your face with my racquet, Ben thought, you might learn how to hit a forehand. Welsh had no strokes at all. He pushed and chopped and looped at the ball. His swing was an ugly, primitive thing. But he was quick on his feet, which made him difficult to beat unless you attacked him with depth. He could volley and smash well, although his serve was putrid. He was one of those players who had started young and was still playing the game like a jack-rabbit eleven-year-old: scurrying around the court, blocking everything back, rushing the net, using a stratospheric ball to buy time. His lobs were so high they made you laugh enough to miss your smash.

Ben's game was classical. He had been coached, in a club in Amersham, to hit the ball flat and hard. He got into position quickly, met the ball early and volleyed with panache. What he hated was the high arcing topspin shot that forced him to pedal to the back of the court. He was impatient to win the point and get ahead, which he usually did. But if he wasn't leading, uncertainty crept into his shots; his forearm stiffened and he became disgusted with his errors. Ben's game was built on confidence. John Welsh's grunt, run and retrieve was aimed at destroying that confidence.

As he climbed the stairs to Helen's office, Ben thought, it serves me right for having laughed at John's lobs. One should never ridicule one's opponent. 'Why is competition so unpleasant?' he said as he entered Helen's office. 'Why do I waste my time playing these three-hour tennis matches against John when I should be going home and writing my book?'

'What's happened now?'

'I was two sets up and coasting to victory in the third when I chuckled at one of John's twenty-second lobs. I hadn't missed any before that, but I fluffed this easy one, and from there on my game fell apart. Even so, I had so many chances in the third and fifth set.'

'Same old thing. Welsh winding you up.'

'Yes, but why do I care so much? I've beaten him so many times, and yet the few times he beats me I can't get to sleep at night thinking about how I should have held my composure.'

'I don't understand about competition. I can't understand why it matters so much.'

'You're like one of those non-smokers who doesn't know why people make a fuss about giving up.'

There was a knock on the door.

'Damn,' whispered Helen, 'looks like they're early.'

Priya labelled her tape with the date and title. From that Rushdie march in 1989 she remembered the sneers on the faces of some of the policemen who were meant to be protecting the marchers. Sadaf Fidwi had told her about the policeman sitting in his heated car during the troubles in Southall, drawing

National Front logos with his finger on the steamed-up windscreen.

Ten years on from that demonstration, these interviews reminded Priya of how much she had changed since the time when she was actively involved in politics. She felt ashamed of her liberal acceptance. 'I've become a domesticated animal now. All dinner-party talk with objective BBC points of view.' It was her time with the cynical Marcus that had pushed her inwards and away from the struggle. In the short spell she had known him he had torn the fight out of her like a protestor being pulled from a crowd. She remembered going on an anti-capitalism march with her friend Julia. Forming body-barricades across roads in the City, being handcuffed, the revulsion on the faces of the policemen who dragged them into the van. She had fallen into the belly of chaos, almost losing her job, almost losing Ben.

She imagined herself in a flat on her own on the eighteenth floor of a tower block, painting the thin walls yellow to give herself the illusion of light. She remembered the time when she sat on the steps of the dance floor at the Ministry of Sound. Marcus was holding her from behind, blowing small torrents of cool air round her burning ears. Not doing anything, just holding her with his wet fingers. That was the moment. Sitting on the edge of that storm of flickering bodies, mists descending from the ceiling, strobes freezing sepulchral fingers, like dead branches of trees caught in flashes of lightning, music rising in thunderous crescendos, and nothing, nothing mattered in the passing hours except her body. When she tried to describe this feeling of joy during their therapy sessions, Anouchka said it sounded like a return to the womb. She was right. With the help of the drug, the music, the maelstrom of bodies, Marcus's black hands, she felt she was in a cocooned embrace of maternal flesh. Shut out was every sorrow, every need, every anxiety that she might normally experience. Of course, it was the thrill and illusion of the drug, but why did that matter? For one night she felt she was walking along on a cliff beside the sea. She could dive into the water below and allow herself to be borne away on successive waves of sound and light. The rapture and liberation were like nothing she had ever known before. And it was never the same again. Could anything else ever match up? The hours of chilling out, until one in the afternoon, that she spent drinking tea off Leicester Square with Marcus. They couldn't stop talking about their mothers, their fathers, their lovers. And it was all the truth. You couldn't hide from yourself if you tried. It was there that she had discovered his ruthless side.

Twice he had written to her from Africa. She tore up the frivolous letters. She never wanted to see him or hear his voice again, never wanted to hear that booming laugh. At their last meeting they'd sat in a booth at the back of some dingy bar near Marble Arch. He was holding her hand and insisting that she come with him to Zimbabwe. She tried to kiss him, just one more time. But he had gone cold on her. He could tell this was the end.

A colleague at the World Service told her that Marcus had married an Australian journalist. They had ended up living in a suburb of Melbourne. One day, Priya thought, he would slip into their bedroom late at night with a pair of somebody else's knickers in his coat pocket. But who was she to judge Marcus? Perhaps he was enjoying his married life with one child in a semi-detached bungalow in Melbourne. Perhaps he needed a sporty Australian chick to keep up with his hours of self-satisfied humping.

Priya carried the tapes out of the self-op studio. The Bush

House elevator sucked her down to the lobby. Marcus, or was it the Ecstasy, had sucked the marrow out of her bones. It had taken her months to recover. At the reception desk she phoned Clare and asked her to pick up the SBS report. She walked out of the building slowly, soaking in the pleasure of this unusually short visit. Outside she spied a shaft of sunlight at the entrance to India Place and made her way towards it. There was always in her this urge for the sun. Ben got his peace from snowflakes – but a cathedral of spring sunlight made Priya feel whole again. When she had first come to this country, the weather had been new, exciting. She made it through her first winter enjoying the gradual onset of cold dank days, bulb-lit afternoons when she would take to her bed with Dostoevsky. She had laughed when told about the Indian student who had been bedridden for months until his illness was diagnosed as lack of sunshine. The amusement faded when, with each successive year, the darkness of winter gathered round her: lights on all day, parks closed at four, impossible to go out for a walk without being lashed by rain or wind.

Priya stood in her pool of light. She willed the brief, bright rays to cut some warmth into her body. Three years ago, on this same date, there had been snow in London. In the afternoon the sun had shone hard in the opal sky. She liked that weather. Ice and sun. Sun and snow. She remembered the sight of tissue-pink cherry blossom against the white lawns. New-born Whacka swaddled in her mother's cashmere shawl was being carried along the cleansed pavements of Highgate and Holloway. But now a wind scudded down the corridor of India Place and Montreal Place and the sun clouded over. She wished it would be confidently hot for days on end . . . like . . . like that time on a summer's afternoon when she lay on the grass, listening to lambs' bleating in the Welsh valley.

A Saturday morning in Wales. Almost four years ago – June '95. Before confusion had slipped into her bed. Inside the Brecon Beacons holiday cottage were her husband, and their two closest friends, Leo and Jan, the other parts of the inseparable foursome. This was the third vacation they had spent together walking, cooking, eating, drinking, playing cards.

Priya remembered sitting on the lawn behind the rented house, gazing out at the treeless hills. The patches of burnt yellow, the long grass tipped with brown, the shorn grass scattered with buttercup yellow, a dark crag of shadow spread across the peak of Pen y Fan, a hilltop they had climbed from two directions. She lay down on the ground, resting the back of her head on her palms and thinking of the horror of her Christmas with Marcus and the depressing January and February days of coming home to find Ben mooching in front of the television, unable to speak. For three months their relationship had been mired in self-conscious doubt. Tortuous discussions about what to do next, what to think next, what to feel next, when the truth, for Priya, at least, was that she had lost the ability to sense clearly what she really wanted. She was afraid, she was not herself, she didn't know how or where to find her old self. Somehow they had survived the horrible arguments, dismal evenings. Then, at the end of March, Priya's brother had come to stay for a week. It took a third person's presence to make them look at each other properly, to hear each other, to feel the sexual charge again.

Why is it, reflected Priya, that a hopeful moment is so often followed by some awful happening? Is it because we drop our guard? Four years ago, staring out at those Welsh peaks, at the single tree a hundred yards in front of her that looked like a giant sprig of parsley, she was looking forward to the days ahead, returning to London, to her job, to her flat, to her husband, to the long evenings of summer light, the quiet nights when she could read till late. How had she managed to ruin all that? Perhaps she had forgotten the way that things can swerve, the way the clouds race in from the west and obscure the sun. She should have learnt from the past. She should have been vigilant.

The summer of '95. On the last evening of their holiday in Wales. The last night in the rented house. There was a lot of whisky and smoking of joints. There were recountings of past affairs, there was talk of first loves and teenage flings. Jan went to bed at round eleven, then half an hour later Ben, who had woken early that morning to clamber up some hillside with Leo, also disappeared to his bed. Not for the first time, she and Leo were left on their own. It was she who had suggested they go out for a walk in the moonlight.

There is something utterly irrational about our actions, thought Priya. Something disruptive and self-destructive that she wished she could understand. Or was this just a delusion, was she using Whacka's birthday as an excuse to go over the story of that last night in Wales, lure herself once more into the maze of retrospection, with its regrets and wrong turnings, its false hope of retrieval, its steps retraced, the 'should haves' and 'could haves' that do nothing except recycle pain? 'And now,' she said aloud, 'to make matters worse, Ben has gone and invited them to the party. I wish they had made some excuse not to come.'

Whilst thus occupied in her mind, Priya had strolled past India House, through Montreal Place, crossed over the Strand, walked down to Surrey Street and then through Temple Place. She went down the steps past the station to the Thames, where she looked across the bend towards the spot where they were constructing the London Eye. Her exposed neck was buffeted by a wind that appeared to ripple the surface of the grey river. She wanted to sit down somewhere before descending underground.

Fourteen

'Can I help?' asked Helen as she opened the door of her office to a thin, bespectacled man in a grey suit and narrow tie. Ben was sitting near her desk.

'Derek Lloyd,' the man said, resting his briefcase on the floor, 'parents liaison officer from the unit for raising achievement for Afro-Caribbean students. I've come to attend the meeting with Mr Gibbs.'

'We've met before,' said Helen, 'at Melanie Akinyemi's hearing. I wasn't expecting you today.'

'Mr Gibbs phoned me and requested that I attend the meeting. He feels, very strongly, that his son has suffered some injustice.'

Helen played it cool. 'Come in. I'm sorry, but no one informed me or Mr Tennyson that there would be this representation from the council. I'm not sure it's fair to Mr Tennyson that you should be here without representation from his side.'

'I don't mind having Mr Lloyd here,' said Ben, 'just as long as I know what his role is.'

The race officer spoke in an even-toned voice that unnerved Ben. 'I'm here as an observer and to take notes. Mr Gibbs is known to us at the unit. At the end, if I may, I will ask you both a series of questions.'

As Lloyd was speaking Gibbs and his son walked into the classroom adjoining Helen's office. The boy was a burly hulk with the gait of a giant bear, the father a smaller version of the son, shorter, more compact, looking like a prizefighter. Helen did the introductions. Gibbs made it a point to shake hands with her but not with Ben. The five of them sat down in a cramped circle, Ben's knees almost touching Marlon's father's.

Helen took charge. 'I understand, Mr Gibbs, that you're here because of an incident involving your son and Mr Tennyson. I should say that neither Mr Tennyson nor I were aware that Mr Lloyd was asked by you to come to the meeting, but we have agreed to him being here to observe and take notes. I think the best thing would be if we allow Mr Tennyson to tell us what happened with Marlon.'

Ben looked Gibbs in the eye. As he began, he tried to gauge what was going through the man's head. 'Last Thursday, period 5, just after lunch, I was asked to cover 11DH for English. I walked into the class and found the children unsettled. I asked everyone to be quiet so that I could explain the work they had been set. Most of them stopped talking, but there was a group of boys – Marlon was one – who were laughing loudly and play-wrestling.' Here Marlon started to shake his head. 'Marlon was holding one of the boys round the neck, I'm not sure of his name.'

'Jermaine,' Gibbs senior offered.

'Jermaine was calling out, "Stop, stop, stop. Sir, please tell him to stop." I asked Marlon to let go of the boy's neck, but he didn't pay me any attention.'

Once again Marlon started to shake his head and sigh. The father placated him. 'Let the man finish his story.' Then he returned to glaring at Ben. Sometimes parents came in to verify the stories their children had told them and, usually, after hearing the teacher out they went away satisfied. Ben was beginning to sense that this might not happen today.

'Having repeated my request,' Ben continued, 'I went up to Marlon and said, "If you don't let go, I'm going to have to throw you out of the class." At this point Marlon turned round to me and in a very aggressive voice shouted, "What?"'

Again the boy shook his head saying, 'No way, no way . . .' The father raised his hand.

'I asked Marlon to leave the class. He refused. I said if he didn't go outside I would have to get someone to take him out. Marlon replied rudely, "I'm not going. I didn't do anything." So I went out to look for another teacher, and unable to find one I came back to the class. Then I saw Mr Hensman, Marlon's form tutor, out in the corridor. I called out to him and explained what had happened. Mr Hensman asked Marlon to go and sit outside the staffroom. Marlon continued to protest. Mr Hensman had to ask him several times before he agreed. As he passed by me on his way out of the classroom Marlon said, "Watch, just watch."' Ben could see the father's face becoming more agitated. All this time Lloyd had his head down, scribbling notes on a small pad. Ben began to feel as if he were on trial.

Ben attempted to carry on with his story, but the father interrupted. 'Hold on a minute there. I came to the school on Friday, you weren't available.'

'I was teaching,' said Ben.

'I put it to you,' said the father, 'that what happened was that you went home, had time to think about it over the weekend and have concocted this story. My son said that he had been unfairly treated by the teacher.' He looked at Helen. 'My son came home to me and told me that he had been threatened with suspension. He phoned me in the middle of the day. In fact, when he left the class the second time, which Mr Tennyson here has omitted to mention.'

'That's because I haven't been allowed to finish what I was saying,' said Ben. A fire raged in him. He wanted to throw his chair down and storm out. But his years of teaching told him not to move. Thank God Helen was in the room.

'My son is not a liar. He was very upset with what happened. I asked him for the story in full detail.' Gibbs produced a sheet of paper from his jacket pocket. 'I wrote down all his points. I interviewed some of the boys in his class to check that he was telling the truth and I found that he was telling the truth. There was no wrestling going on in the class. There was no fighting. There was probably some noise in the class, yes, you couldn't control the children and you decided to take it out on my son.'

'So,' said Ben forcing himself concentrate on the man's face, 'you're calling me a liar. I've been teaching for nine years and I've never yet been doubted in this way by a parent. I wonder if we should call a halt to this meeting now and reconvene when the head teacher and my union representative are present.' He looked at Helen. She began to speak, but Ben interrupted her and said to the boy, 'Marlon, let me ask you this. Were you holding your friend by the neck?'

'I wasn't holding him by the neck. I had my hand round his shoulder.'

'So why did I ask you to stop then?'

'I don't know. I was talking, but so was everybody else.'

'In a court of law,' said Ben, 'it doesn't matter if a criminal says other people have done worse than him, he is still guilty.' This was a line Ben had learnt from an old teacher.

It brought an immediate response from the father. 'This is not a court of law. I know all these tricks. Why are you talking about a court of law and criminals with my son? How can you, a teacher, talk like that?'

'Look, this is not getting us anywhere,' said Helen. 'Mr Tennyson and Mr Gibbs, let's all calm down and think carefully about what we're saying and where it's going to lead us. We're here to find the best solution for Marlon. Mr Tennyson is not a liar and this is not a court of law. You are both right, but it might help you to know, Mr Gibbs, that the reason Marlon has not been suspended is that Mr Tennyson asked me not to. When I got the incident report, saying that he had sworn and shouted at Mr Tennyson, I went and found him and I told him that since the offence was serious, I was going to suspend him. Marlon is in year 11. It's the fifteenth of March. GCSEs are not far away. Mr Tennyson is a teacher of many years' experience. I have had a lot of dealings with him. It wouldn't make sense for him to lie about Marlon's behaviour. It sounds as if there has been some misunderstanding and the sooner we clear it up, the better for the sake of Marlon's education.'

'Marlon,' said Ben, 'when I asked you to stop, did you not turn to me and say, "What!"' He couldn't convey the impact of Marlon's growl. It had been a cross between a belligerent bark and an ejaculation of contempt. It was meant to make Ben jump out of his skin and it was meant for the whole class to witness. It came out of an ancient fury at the system and with teachers like Ben who thought they could walk in and subjugate Marlon. He was not to be controlled, he was to be hated, and if he was to be hated he would shove his own hate in your face before you had time to open your mouth.

Ben knew about the way that a lot of black boys both despised and ridiculed figures of authority. Policemen, teachers, social workers, were all people they believed would like to emasculate them. The previous Thursday had been a troublesome, exhausting day and when he had entered the class – irritated at having been asked to cover an absence in period 5, he was in no mood to tangle with unruly pupils. Usually he would avoid confrontation when he was doing a cover. It was best to have a laugh, chat to the students, ignore the troublemakers, who, if they didn't get any attention, tended to lose interest in annoying the teacher. But that Thursday, Marlon's affront caught him off guard.

'No. I didn't say it like that. I said, "What?"' said Marlon in a even voice.

'You didn't say it in a threatening tone?' Ben asked.

'No, I didn't,' Marlon repeated.

'And you weren't strangling your friend?'

'No, and he wasn't screaming the way you said.'

'I checked that with Jermaine,' said the father, nodding at Helen.

'Right, so when Mr Hensman asked you to sit outside his office, why didn't you stay there?' Ben continued. 'How come you walked back into my class without asking me?'

'He asked me to sit outside and then when he didn't come back and I didn't know why I had been sent out, I thought I better go back to my lesson and do the work.'

This brazen nonsense was so insulting to Ben that he couldn't think how to respond. 'You pointed at me in front of the whole class and said, "Watch, just watch, I'm going to get you . . . Watch."'

'I didn't say, "I'm going to get you,"' said Marlon with that look of contempt creeping back on to his face. 'I said "Watch", meaning, Look I'm going, I'm leaving.'

'Oh, is that what "watch" means?' said Ben with a barely disguised contempt of his own.

'Yes. What does it mean to you?'

'To me it sounded like some sort of threat. But now I see this whole thing is pointless. You're going to carry on with your story and not admit to what you did. I was hoping that your father would understand, especially since I asked for you not to be suspended, that I bore no personal grudge. I don't even teach you.'

'No one is saying that you had a personal grudge,' the father said, 'but what we are saying, what my son is saying, is that he feels picked on. There were many others who misbehaved, but you picked on Marlon. Maybe because of his size he looks threatening, so you misread his intentions.'

Once more Ben became enraged. He had been trapped into making several stupid statements. 'I did not misread his intentions. I'm not a fool.'

'No one is calling you a fool,' said the father, enjoying his victory.

'If I can intervene for a second,' said Helen, sitting up straight. 'I think I have the picture. There are two ways to try and resolve this whole thing. The first thing I need to know is: what do you want, Mr Gibbs?'

'I want my son to get back to his studies and I want no more of this talk about suspending. This is a minor incident that has been blown out of all proportion. I would like it to be sorted out.'

'What about you, Mr Tennyson?' Helen asked. Ben stayed silent. 'What would you like to happen now? Would it be all right by you, as we have already decided that Marlon is not to be suspended, for me to suggest that the situation ends here?' Ben could see how clever she was being in not mentioning the incident report on Marlon's file. 'As teachers, Mr Gibbs and Mr Lloyd, I'm sure you'll understand that we want Marlon to get the best education possible, but he must cooperate with all the staff in this school.'

'I've told him that on many occasions. I know my boy is

not a saint. I know that he has done wrong things in the past. But when he has done something bad he is brave enough to come home and tell me. This time he phoned me during the lesson to say how angry he was. I'm sure that this gentleman here realizes that we all make mistakes and I'm willing to forget the whole thing and move on as long as he doesn't get on his high horse and start talking about criminals and courts of law.'

Ben remembered it was Whacka's birthday. He wanted no more of this meeting. He decided to say not another word. Helen's tactics were obvious. She was taking a sensible, moderate position. Appeasement. He found the whole affair sad and demeaning. He wanted to cry out against the injustice of it. They were all so stupid, he felt so humiliated sitting there and swallowing the lies of this barrel-chested boy. And the father, with his waving hands, and his gift of the gab, helping him to be dishonest. Rolling along the primrose path to everlasting damnation. Well, let them, this was the day of his son's party and he wasn't going to let this devious duo spoil it. No, let them dance in a hellfire of their own making.

Helen went on for a bit and then the father delivered a pointless homily. 'I have always taught you,' he said to Marlon, 'if you suffer any injustice, to come and tell me, and to behave yourself and be respectful to the teachers.' With head bowed, Marlon assumed a look of repentance.

'Well, I'm glad we've been able to resolve this issue. Oh, Mr Lloyd, do you want to say anything?' Helen inquired.

'I did have some questions but you've answered them all,' said Lloyd, keeping his head bent over his notes as he spoke.

Oh really, thought Ben, you smug little notebook-toting jerk with your fat-cat salary for sitting there and saying nothing.

'Right then,' said Helen. 'I call this meeting to a close.'

Everyone stood up. Before Ben could back away, the honey-tongued Gibbs stuck out his bullying hand and he felt forced to shake it.

Back-tracking towards the car-clogged thoroughfare of the Strand Priya pondered, Why do we find ourselves returning over and over to painful incidents from the past? Is it because we never have access to the full story? 'Perhaps we are all strangers to ourselves,' she thought out loud, 'every time we rewind and revisit a section of our life, some unknown character trait or some hidden facet is accidentally uncovered, as when we're searching for something and cannot find it, but happen upon other valuable things that we had lost or forgotten about. After all, we are never the same person from this second to the next, so the way we view our past must also change.'

The sex with Leo had been intense, exciting, illicit, but she daren't bring that up in their sessions with Anouchka. The only place it was allowed to be told was in her head. That's why she needed to relive it, that's why it still flashed into her thoughts at night. Hard as Priya tried to resist the part of her that slipped these pictures of pleasure into her brain, it was a fight she rarely won.

She walked against the traffic towards Fleet Street. She ought to head home and start preparing for the party, but she hadn't planned to return before three. Let Jocelyn play with Whacka for a while. Responding to a pang of hunger – she had eaten nothing since breakfast – she said to herself, I'll have a cup of tea and a samosa and then head back.

She climbed up the black and white chequered stairs of the Hotel Strand Continental, past the dingy red-carpeted reception to the first floor. The large Polish woman who had been serving at the India Club for twenty years brought her a pot of tea. Priya ordered a plate of daal and bread for the sake of sentiment, telling herself it was auspicious to eat this food on her son's birthday. Good luck, or *sagan*, as her Parsee friend Shireen called it. Piping hot in a soup plate, speckled with roasted cumin and crisply fried onion, accompanied by two rotis and some slices of white bread, the daal was served just as in some railway station restaurant in India. She returned to her earlier thoughts and to the words exchanged between Leo and her the morning after their moonlit tryst in the field behind the house. Once again, she was sitting on the small apron of sloping lawn outside the stone cottage in Wales. Jan and Ben were asleep inside.

Leo had come and sat beside her. He wrapped his bent knees in his muscular arms. She hoped he wouldn't touch her. He didn't. He sat far enough away for her to know he had come to talk. He loved to talk. Some people are at home in the water, some in the mountains, some in the city, Leo was at home in a conversation. It didn't matter where or when, he could make you feel interesting. He could grow dialogue on the rockiest of soil.

'I never expected it to happen,' he said.

'I did.'

'Really? You didn't plan it, did you?' he asked.

'Of course I didn't. But I have thought about it. The four of us have always been so close. You've even joked about it,' she said.

'That's different. I wouldn't have if I'd thought there was any likelihood of something happening.'

For a while they sat on the hot grass in silence. Priya tried to imagine in a different life the two of them together. It wouldn't work. She didn't want it. She felt ashamed of herself for thinking about it. She wished Leo would leave her to her thoughts. She wasn't looking forward to their long drive home. She wished she could snap her fingers and be in her own kitchen. Would her face betray her when Ben woke? 'Look like the innocent flower, But be the serpent under't.'. Why did it have to be so fucking complicated? Why was there this overriding need for sexual fidelity between couples? Why couldn't she just throw the shame aside and go on living? Ben was her life partner. The Marcus episode had decided that for her. What had happened last night between her and Leo was an aberration. Betrayed by her body, she had entered the forbidden chamber, she had opened the sacred box and looked inside. Now she wanted to lock the room and throw the key away, or put the box back where it belonged. No one need know. And still her insides burned with remorse.

'Now what?' Leo asked in a muted voice.

'Now, nothing.' Priya was as puzzled as he was but she had to give him the impression that she had it all sorted. 'Now it's . . .' She wanted to say, 'Now it's over. I don't want to talk about it.' But it sounded too cruel.

'Did you enjoy it?'

'Wasn't it obvious?'

'I know I'm being a bit childish and maybe even stupid, but can we talk straight about this?'

'Are you crazy?' she whispered. 'They could walk out at any moment. Anyway, I don't think I ever want to talk to anybody about it. Can we agree to that? Will you be able to do that for me?'

'If that's what you want. Perhaps you're right. Let's leave the experience to be what it was. Let's not analyse it.'

'Yup. What happened last night happened in a time capsule. Let's bury it in this Welsh ground.'

★

Three months after the night on the Welsh hillside with Leo, Priya found herself making for his house in Hackney. She had phoned him from work at an hour when she knew Jan would be out. They met at two thirty on a dull early October afternoon. The sky was thick with cloud through which a weak pebble-grey light filtered ineffectually. It was cold in Leo's loft workshop: bare, unpolished floorboards, leather tool bags collected in the corner, bits of wood leant up against the wall, open trays with nails and screws of varying sizes, hammers and saws, a router lying naked under the strip lighting. Priya was shivering. She kept her coat tightly wrapped round her and stared at the steam rising from the mug of tea cradled in her hands.

'You know all those months ago in Wales you said we should talk about it and I said no. Well, I've changed my mind. I think . . .'

'What's made you change your mind?' Leo inquired as he crouched down and rested the small of his back against the wall, knitting his fingers under his chin.

Priya looked away. It was those fingers. They were alone in this house. The warmth of the tea eased through her shaking limbs. Dreaminess came over her. The same opiate-numbness that had overtaken her when they had gone out to look at the moon that night on the field behind the house. She had come here to tell Leo she was pregnant, and now intoxicated by a sudden desire she wanted to hold him in her mouth the way she had seized him under the tree in Wales. She wanted forgetfulness, the scream of abandonment with which she had flayed the Welsh night. The caress of his dextrous hands. She told herself she had come this far, why would it matter if she went there again, one more time? This would be the last.

Priya's tea was still warm when she retreated to her seat.

She took little sips to try and stop the cold returning. Do I have no control over myself? she thought. 'Do you mind if we go out for a walk, Leo? I need to get some blood circulating in my limbs.'

They entered London Fields. Leo seemed keen to get back to his work. He walked briskly, using long strides. Priya let him go and looked at the people sitting on the benches. Men in dark overcoats and sleazy jackets, smoking. She deserved this dismal fate. Like them, nowhere to go. No one to see, no one to love. A useless weight of flesh.

She caught up with him standing by a tree. 'I can't sleep,' she said hesitantly. 'I wish you had stopped me. I wish none of this had ever happened. I lie in bed for hours, wide awake, trying to think of a solution, trying to think of a way out. I keep thinking of ways that it could have been different.'

'I don't understand, Priya, you made the first move.'

'I *know*, I know. It's not right. I find it difficult to stop myself. Ben and me almost broke up last time. I don't want to lose him. I want to have a family with him.'

'But you *are* going to have a family with him. We're not talking about breaking up relationships. I know this is going to sound cruel, but I thought you could handle this. I thought I was the weak one. When you sounded so cool the next morning it gave me confidence. I felt I knew where we stood. Then you phone me the other day and now, once again, I'm not sure what's going on. I was surprised at how light I felt when we came back from Wales. It was as if this should have happened a long time ago. As if we should have got it over with and then maybe it wouldn't have been so complicated.'

'That's just it. I wish I could supply some answers. All I know is that here we are and I hate it. I feel jittery. My confident side has been obliterated, and I don't know how to find it again. I can't explain it and I can't make it go away. What happened today is my fault. I arranged to see you.'

'I don't understand why you're so down on yourself. We haven't committed a crime. You know I'm not going to tell anyone, least of all Jan. I'm as worried about that as you are.'

School kids spilled into the park. Bawling at each other. Girls in uniform, smoking. Priya was sure they were laughing at her. She felt glum and dishevelled.

'You and I,' said Leo, 'let's say we made a mistake, although I don't think it was a mistake. I don't like to call it that. We had an experience. I've learnt something from it. Perhaps we should avoid meeting on our own? Perhaps talking about it only makes it worse.'

'Leo, I'm three months pregnant.' She strode away towards a bench which was empty, not wanting to observe his reaction. She had promised herself to keep it a secret. But then why had she come to see him? As he made his way to sit next to her she noticed his jutting cheekbones and some fine sprigs of hair growing out of his lower chin.

'I don't know,' she said, anticipating his question. 'I'm not sure.'

'When did you . . . does Ben know?'

'He's delighted. That's all he knows.'

'What are you going to do?'

Suddenly the schoolchildren seemed less of a threat. 'I'm going to have the baby,' she said, looking straight out in front of her.

It had happened twice. The first time was in Wales on that summer night, the second time was in his workshop on that cold afternoon in Hackney. A long time ago. Almost four years. But Priya still felt as if she wanted that time snatched out of her life. She wanted to go back there and tear a piece out of their holiday in Wales. Just that bit. That one night. The Hackney thing was a pathetic flail. It hardly mattered. She went up to Leo where he was crouching. She started to kiss his neck and whispered something she couldn't even bear to recall. It was his hands she wanted more than anything else. She took them from out of her hair and laid them in her shirt. The way he had held her on that hillside in Wales. She wanted that again. That's what she had recalled this morning on the tube when she overheard the schoolgirl telling her friend a joke. She was kneeling on the bare floorboards. Leo was kissing her breasts, teasing her nipples with his nose. She was in the jaws of the moment, wanting it to last. But like an elastic band stretched too far, something broke inside her. It was the shift of position, perhaps the unbuttoning of his shirt. She began to notice the crinkles of flesh on the sides of his stomach, the protruding plait of ugly navel, the long neck with its Adam's nodule poking at his taut skin, the sound of spit in his mouth. The hands that had made her ecstatic seemed now like the talons of some scavenging bird scratching a way into her trousers; a hawk's cold claws ferreting out her vagina. She had pulled herself free. Embarrassed, at how quickly revulsion had overtaken desire.

There were those moments during sex, she thought as she sat at the ugly Formica table in the India Club, spooning daal and roti into her mouth, when the mind wanders away and watches what you and the other person are doing. Out-of-body experiences that normally last for a second or two. She remembered her encounter at boarding school in India with Ralph, the trembling American boy who took so long to get hard. In the middle of it she had thought it was like being bashed with a wooden board, like a *dhobi* beating clean his wash. This is not me, this is not him, this is just two bodies slapping.

In Wales it had been helpfully dark, and she'd been helpfully drunk and stoned. They'd done it in a field. She'd been able to give herself over to the pleasure. But in the milky light of that Hackney afternoon, in the strip-lit surroundings of Leo's workshop, she had seen the way his teeth were tinged with blackness, and the chin with its strands of hair. She had thought of Leo as some sort of goat she had to get away from. Bestiality wouldn't have been worse. It was never like that with Ben. Sure, there had been complaints, times she felt uninspired, fucks that were briefer than a spring shower. But never with Ben had she had that experience of revulsion.

And now, as she paid the Pole for the tea and bread and daal her mind wheeled round again and she was thinking that same useless impossible thought: if only she could erase the consequences of that one night. Her friend Jean, in whom she had confided, would say to her, 'Everyone has their big regrets, mistakes they want to rectify. You have to move on to the next thing.'

She would try, but once again she would see herself walking round London Fields with the dead leaves scattered in the dank grass. She remembered a thin black woman pushing a pram and smoking a cigarette and a Turkish schoolgirl sitting across her boyfriend's thighs, one arm slung round his neck. Such sights could sometimes give her a lift – but that day she had felt so impoverished. Meeting Leo had made it worse. She envied his hardheadedness, the ability he seemed to possess to exclude unwanted thoughts from his mind.

How much more brave and complicated had been Ben's reaction. He had been fiercely loyal to Whacka, fiercely loyal to the idea of his family, enraged by her repeated attempts to ruin their marriage. And yet, their relationship was still going. Today they were celebrating their child's birthday. Somehow, she must put all these thoughts of the past away and enjoy the present.

Fifteen

'You were close to losing it there,' said Helen, filing papers away in her cabinet.

'I know, I'm sorry,' Ben said.

'What a bastard!' Helen gasped. 'I need a cigarette after that.'

'You did really well.'

'Once you kept quiet and let me take over.'

'Let's get out of this building. Get some fresh air,' said Ben.

'Tell you what. I'll phone Susie and say I have to leave early to pick up the kids. You and I could do with a coffee. Let the deputies deal with it if there's any trouble after school.'

'Weren't you going to stay for a drink?'

'I can come back.'

'I mustn't be too long. I've got to get home for Whack's party by four.'

'You've got time. It's only twenty-five past two.'

'I'll move my car and see you in the café.'

Seated in the Jolly Pepper Ben waited for Helen to arrive, two frothing cappuccinos ready on their table. He felt fortunate in this friendship. The sexual contortions that he had imagined earlier had evaporated from his mind. Her company was one of the few confidently safe spaces in his life. He felt happily impelled or even compelled to tell her his thoughts. Often before they were due to meet he would counsel himself, 'I must let her talk. I must allow her to tell her story. I spoke too much last time.'

But when they were together she cleverly manoeuvred the conversation so that, hardly realizing it, he became absorbed in the telling of his own stories or explanations. She was good at spurring him on, but also at bringing his generalized explorations to bear on something solid in their lives. She wanted examples of what he was talking about and he tried to avoid the details. It was a habit he had learned from his mother. His parents must be getting ready to leave their Amersham home. Mary putting Whacka's present in the boot, then Richard checking that all the doors and windows were locked and the petrol gauge was pointing to full. They would arrive half an hour before the party, in time to be served a cup of tea, hand over their neatly wrapped gift and step out of the way of their daughter-in-law's chaotic arrangements.

Jocelyn, Leo's mother, not *his* mother, would help Priya with the party preparations. It had been a long time before he had allowed himself to pronounce Leo's name. At first he had hated everybody connected with that man, but Jocelyn wasn't to blame for what had happened. Priya depended on her, and Jocelyn had always been keen to look after Whacka. What if she knew? What if she had known all along? That old dread took hold of him again. Fear of being humiliated, of being cuckolded, of proving his father right. Perhaps everyone knew and it was only he who was living in a dream of ignorance.

No wonder Jocelyn had been pleased to be made Whacka's godmother. It was a way of keeping watch. Why else should she care so much? It was as if he had seen only three sides of the square. Then he concentrated on the technique he had learnt from Anouchka. 'Step back. See the wood for the trees. Take a look at the choices you have made,' she would advise.

He'd never had any thought of losing Whacka. A long time

ago he had decided not to be the man his father wanted: the same sandwich every day, the safe job in the City, the white middle-class Christian wife, the clean suburban dwelling. He had chosen to go to India, he had chosen Priya, chosen to stick with her. Whacka was his son. He didn't want to have a blood test. It would change nothing about the way he felt. He sensed that Anouchka admired him for it and he was sure that one day, when Whacka was old enough to be told, he too would admire his father. And then he fought off the conventional side of his upbringing, the side that made him feel like a sissy for having stayed – afraid to prove his father right about the Indian girl, to live with the stigma and loneliness of separation.

Helen breezed in through the chrome and glass, slicing his paranoia with her smile. The Moroccan behind the counter greeted her with a lustful dip of the eyes. She sank down opposite Ben. He noticed she had reapplied her lipstick. Once, not long ago, after a pub session, he had been walking beside her when he felt his dick palpitate. A few minutes later, he realized with amazement that it was stirring itself, peeping out of his open flies, into the night air between his thigh-length coat and the crotch of his trousers. In his drunken state, having checked to see that his coat was done up, he had let his aerated penis rub its restive head on the inside of the baggy garment. He had carried on walking for a little, letting Helen talk, his eye glistening with amusement and illicit arousal, as he enjoyed the hardness grow and slide against the lining of his big coat. Helen and he had become such close friends that he had almost been tempted to tell her his story. Sometimes he alluded to a family secret he was not at liberty to divulge.

Drizzle was spotting the pavements. The sky was larger now and held out promise of a season of sunlight like a vast bedsheet spreading itself out to dry. Helen wiped the drops of rain from her cheeks, leaving them ruddy and glowing.

'I'm hungry,' she said. 'I feel like something sweet.'

'Go on, it's my treat,' he said.

'Will you have a cake?'

'I'd better not. There's going to be so much food at the party. And I can never cook unless I am a little hungry. I might have another coffee. I had a bad night.'

'What are you cooking for the party?'

'Get your cake, then I'll tell you.'

He still had to boil the rice and layer it with the spiced lamb for his biryani. Last time he had overdone the rosewater, and the dish had been inedibly fragrant. He must underplay the flavours. Underplay everything – that ought to be a rule for life, he thought to himself. He mustn't, as he was wont to do, moan about the slow progress of his East/West book to Helen.

She returned with her brownie. He was determined to engage her in a question of his own. 'How's Steven's work going?'

'Seems okay. He doesn't talk to me about it much these days. He writes away, especially late into the night.'

'No more attempts to throw the laptop out of the window?'

'He was on the radio the other day,' she said, raising her eyebrows.

'Really. Which programme?' Helen always portrayed Steven as a loser.

'On *PM*.'

'What was he talking about?'

'Some health and safety issue. He's managed to get funding for this pressure group he's set up. He sounded good on the radio. He puts on his public school articulate voice,' said Helen, spooning chocolate into her mouth.

'Which school did he go to?'

'St Paul's. I've told you that.'

'You said he was good at tennis.'

'He used to play twice a week until a few years ago, when he did his knee in.'

'I should ask him to play.'

'He won't.'

'Why? Does he hate me?'

'Of course not. He's too obsessed with his work to hate anybody. No, he knows about you, he's looked at your book. He even cooked a curry from it. A milky chicken thing.'

'That's a Persian recipe. He ought to have ended up with some job in a merchant bank if he went to St Paul's.'

'But he did work for a big firm of City solicitors before he found his social conscience. Try this, it's not sweet,' said Helen holding out a fork heaped with luscious cake.

Ben swooped. 'And where did you first meet?' he asked, forcing her to go on talking.

'Haven't I told you this before? I was enrolled on a foundation course at the Royal College of Art. This was almost twelve years ago. He came in to give an evening lecture on copyright law. I was fascinated by his face. He was clearly young, passionate about his work, but he had this wrinkled face, like W. H. Auden. You know that joke about Auden, when someone saw his face and said, "Imagine what his balls must look like."'

Ben barely laughed. She was trying to deflect him. 'So, go on with the story,' he said.

'I stayed behind to talk to Steven. He offered me a cigarette, I didn't expect it to be a roll-up. I was so impressed with the way he smoked. And then the way he handed me the beautifully made cigarette. I fell in love immediately. Took him home on my motorbike.'

'You rode a motorbike?'

'Yes, I had a bike and a leather jacket,' she said, blowing smoke out of her nostrils.

'And then?'

'We started going out after that.'

'So what made you get married to him?'

'It just seemed like the obvious thing to do. Grammar-school girl looking for upper-class boy with a social conscience.'

How can you just get married like that? Ben thought. Especially someone as lovely as Helen. He wanted to ask about the romance part but he knew the answer to that. Two children, Steven working on his book for years. He wanted sex whenever he could get it. She was often too tired, sometimes too tired to say no. He lived for his work. She liked Steven, she relied on him in some ways, but theirs was a long-life, low-voltage relationship.

'You know what?' asked Helen.

'What?'

'I don't think you've told me how you met Priya.'

'I'm sure I have.'

'You've told me lots about your marriage and your relationship in the past couple of years, but you've never told me how you met.'

'What time is it?' he asked.

She laughed. 'It's almost three.'

'Let's go before the kids come out of school.'

The rain had stopped, but the sky had turned sombre. As they left the café, the trees were dripping water all round them and there was the distant rumble of thunder, or was it the noise of airplanes descending through the fug?

Helen and Ben strolled down Claverton Street past the Peabody estates built at the turn of the century. Two grimy tower blocks loomed. One of them had licks of charred black climbing up the walls where fire had gutted a flat. They walked along the snarling traffic on Grosvenor Road – so loud they could barely hear each other – crossing to the riverside opposite the flats of Dolphin Square. Here, next to a Shell petrol station, was the unlikely tennis court where Ben played his regular games with John Welsh. Adjoining the court was a patch of lawn with a couple of benches and flowerbeds. A wall separated the benches from a houseboat and the water. The boat owners, a young couple with a newborn baby, would wave to Ben and John and throw back the wayward tennis balls that occasionally bounced on to their deck.

It was to one of these benches that Helen and Ben repaired. His gaze was drawn to the white stacks of Battersea Power Station, which he liked to think of as giant leeks soaring into the sky.

'So, tell me,' said Helen as they sat down.

'Okay.' The water looked cold. Ben imagined falling into it. There must be discarded bicycles, and worse, in there. Ducks were picking their way over the mud flats. The murky river flowed gently on. 'I was in Oxford. I had just come back from my year teaching in India. I decided to go up to Keble a week early because I wanted to acclimatize myself to college life again and to try to get into the mood to study hard for my final year. The college streets were all empty. I remember feeling sad, lonely. Couldn't read. Couldn't study. Though, come to think of it, I did go to the library every day to read the Greek tragedies, which is probably what made me a bit morbid.

'On the second or third day I met this girl at the Bodleian. I just loved being in the reading room; the sense that all these scholars before me had sat in this same place poring over the texts. It was in the tearoom that I met this girl, Leone, from St Catherine's College. She was the daughter of the headmaster of a comprehensive in Wiltshire. Like me, she had a dislike for Oxford toffs. St Catherine's was a college I had never visited. It was designed by a Danish architect, Arne Jacobsen, lots of glass, a bit like Tachbrook, though smaller, and much more stylish and clean, like something Scandinavian. The front of the building has long flat pools of water running underneath the college rooms. When you were in Leone's room, you felt as if you were floating on water, because the window side was floor-to-ceiling glass and underneath were white and pink lilies staring up at you from the pools.'

Helen smiled at him indulgently. It was almost as if she were saying, I know you're enjoying this so I won't spoil your reverie.

'I loved being in that college and talking to Leone. It was as if I was still somewhere different, not back in Oxford.'

'You're keeping me guessing as to how this is going to get to Priya.'

'The central quad at Catz was full of autumnal trees and the sun was shining as if we were in some New England college in the fall. I had just come back from India and landed in the middle of a different kind of Indian summer. I'd forgotten how beautiful England could be.' Ben was thinking, What if I'd taken that turn, stayed with Leone? 'That was before all the students piled into town.'

'I wondered then whether I was in love with Leone. We spent so much time together. We were so similar. We used to listen to this tape together. A compilation of classic American stand-up comics. It had a bit of Woody Allen, Lenny Bruce, it had a recording of Woody Guthrie talking and singing "This land is your land". We became obsessed with that song. I suppose when we heard that song together I did love her. Like a sister maybe.'

'What did she look like, this Leone?' Helen asked in a slightly challenging way.

'Well, she was thin-faced, far too thin, kind of bony, kind of plain, very rosy cheeks. She blushed a lot. I thought she was attractive but not in any obvious way.'

'So, did you sleep with her?'

'I think she wanted to. I was so withholding. We were both withholding. I always left when things started hotting up. But I remember we cooked together in this tiny kitchen. She showed me the joys of simple Italian food, a lovely tomato sauce, fresh basil, pesto – I'd never come across it before. I remember thinking sex has to be very good to beat the experience of ground-up basil and pine nuts. That's what we did instead of sex. Oh and a wonderful red salsa with crinkled new potatoes, which I still have the recipe for. Why didn't I think of using that in *East/West*? Sorry, do you have a pen? I must just jot that down while I remember.'

'I'll remind you when we get to your car.' Helen gave him a look that said, You *are* a weird man. 'Ben, are you going to tell me about meeting Priya or not?'

'On the last day – I think it might have been the Sunday before term started and people had been pouring into the colleges. It was so depressing, undergraduates with college scarves being motored up by mummies and daddies in their Volvos and Mercedes. I just wanted to cling to Leone and our world. It was only a short time we had been together. That Sunday night before term began I remember we had dinner in a Greek dive in town and came back to Leone's room rather drunk on Retsina. I lay down on the carpet. It must have been past eleven. She turned out the light, brought out a bottle of vodka, put Woody Guthrie on, and I remember feeling this was either the end or the beginning of something. I hate the end of things. I just wanted the evening to carry on like that for the rest of my life. The strange thing was, I had come early to Oxford to ready myself for the beginning of term, and now as it was only hours away I felt everything good was going to be ruined by the stupid bright young things, with their dangling scarves and their jingling eunuchoid backsides, descending on the lecture halls; and the silences in tutorials while we fiddled with our pens rather than offering any opinions. Leone lay down on the carpet next to me. We were both self-conscious creatures. I think we may even have been touching each other when the door burst open, and this Indian woman wearing a denim skirt storms in. Leone jumped up, switched on the light and the two of them started hugging and giggling. Who was she? How dare she just barge in and ruin our perfect evening? She kept whispering in Leone's ear, "Who's this? Should I leave? Why don't I come back later?" As if I couldn't hear what she was saying. Leone goes all embarrassed, her cheeks turn blotchy red. I was so angry I could hardly speak. And I was disconcerted, because a, this woman was Indian; b, Leone suddenly seemed to have lost interest in me.'

'How awful,' said Helen, laughing.

'I know. I can laugh now, but at the time I was livid. I wanted this usurper to get lost. Then I developed this stabbing pain in my kidneys. I don't know whether it was anxiety or shock but it was really serious. I couldn't move. The Indian woman – I don't think she'd been introduced to me yet – had started holding forth in a megalomaniac way about some job interview that had gone really well. Leone started making tea. Tea! Three minutes ago we were about to take our clothes off and now I was stuck, my arse on the carpet, unable to move for the pain in my stomach and back! When I told them I couldn't move Leone couldn't help laughing; of course Priya joined in and the two of them just couldn't stop. They were in hysterics.

'Priya didn't even know me and she was doubled up. Leone alternated between fits of giggles and shows of concern, but every time she started to ask me where it was hurting she would relapse into wild laughing. I asked them both to leave the room and I lay there thinking, Never ever will I speak to these two women again. How could I ever have thought of going out with that scarecrow? And the rude Indian girl – how unmannerly Indians can be, I thought. And all the time I could hear Priya's voice in between her giggling. "Come on, Li, the poor guy is in a lot of pain. What are we going to do – he shouldn't be in your room at this time of night. Just say he's your brother. But what will the porters think? They'll think he's done his back in having sex with you." That's when I became paranoid and started yelling. I started doing this loud groaning thing,' said Ben. 'Shouting for them to call an ambulance. I have this wild-tempered side.'

'I can't imagine it,' said Helen.

'One or two college students had been brought out into the corridor by my shouts. I don't know whether the pain was that bad or whether I just wanted some attention. I could hear other students telling them to be quiet. Priya went to her room and produced a tube of Deep Heat and Leone gave me some painkillers, covered me in a blanket and put a pillow under my head. She decided she would sleep in Priya's room on the other side of the quad.'

'I think I can guess what happened next,' said Helen, getting up from the bench. They started to walk slowly back to where Ben's car was parked.

'The next morning I was a bit better. I left early and returned to Keble, thanking God for its dingy red-brick ugliness and the thick slices of bacon they served for breakfast. I had to spend the morning of the first day of term at the doctor's.

'I remember later Priya saying to me that it was the sight of this bespectacled Englishman lying on the floor of her friend's room, immobilized, the unlikelihood of Leone and him sharing this intimate moment, that made her laugh. I think she thought Leone was gay. Maybe she was.'

'Do you still see Leone?' Helen asked.

'No, she and Priya fell out, but that's another story. I kept to my resolve to study hard. I was in the library every morning after lectures and there I bumped into Leone once or twice, but I never saw Priya and had no wish to see her. I would sometimes go to sleep thinking about that night. My missed chance of sex with Leone. Then one night a good three months later I was in my room on the fourth floor of this dreary Keble building. It was late and I was quite drunk. Lying awake in bed, I couldn't go to sleep and I found myself reflecting on the incident and I started laughing. It's strange how you think of the same thing a hundred times over, reexperiencing the humiliation, rearranging things, *l'esprit de l'escalier*, as my housemaster would say, and then on the 101st time it dawns on you. I suddenly saw the funny side of it and started chuckling. There I was lying in my bed looking at the scene through the eyes of an observer. Me on the floor, the shy schoolteacher's daughter lying beside me, when this strangely dressed Indian woman with her mop of black hair and a denim skirt storms in. I became intrigued just trying to visualize Priya standing there that evening. All I could see was this long denim skirt with a sexy bum in it and black hair with a streak of premature silver and grey running through the front.'

★

Priya headed back up Kingsway towards Holborn tube station, walking fast, her head wrapped in a memory, not noticing the streets or the buildings or the people any more. She remembered sitting next to Ben in the back seat of their car, the orange BMW, as Leo drove the four of them back to London. She had felt a pain, a tenderness round the walls of her vagina. The folly of the previous night flickered through her head like the brutal cars on the M4: flash of the beautiful green hills of Wales, flash of Leo's and her naked bodies stark under the moonlit tree, the one that looked like a giant parsley sprig, flash of her letting out her wild cries of animal pleasure. What if Ben had woken and heard her? What if he had looked out of the window and seen their interlocked bodies like crooked stumps of lust on the unsheltered hillside? One-night stand, zipless fuck. There, that pain again, and now, the sensation of something seeping like lava from a cracked rock, burning its way down to the seat of her pants. What about diseases? What about protection? Another flash from the distant past. The night she had fucked Ben after fucking Marcus earlier in the evening. Once upon a time all that had seemed part of the necessary excess of existence. In the orange car she had felt regretful, sullied; disgusted with the strength of her lust.

There was silence except for Ben's occasional whistling. 'Imagine', and then the opening bars of the *Eastenders* theme again. Perhaps, she thought, what vexes us most about our partners is also what we would miss most about them were they to die. I hate Ben's whistling, but were he to leave me I would be sitting there in the emptiness and crying my eyes out for its return. Flash. Flash. Flash. Car. Car. Car. Speeding to her doom on the M4.

★

Priya raced down the left-hand side of the deep escalator at Holborn. She had a birthday party to set up. There was an entertainer coming, she had to lay out the tea. She was glad to have done the party bags yesterday. She remembered the time she had walked into the kitchen and found Ben, a fag in one hand, an ashtray full of butts on the table, and Leo's letter in the other hand. It was 1998, April, a month after Whacka's second birthday. She had emerged from her winter of depression. She and Ben had spent a blissful holiday with Whacka in Portugal. He was enjoying his cooking. They had given dinners. There was enough money to pay babysitters and go out at least once a week. That evening, she had come home late from work and was looking forward to her glasses of red wine and Ben's cooking.

When she entered there was the smell of burning coming from the garden. Priya moved to the window to see what it was when Ben said, 'What am I supposed to make of this?' Holding up the letter. Leo's letter to her, written after their meeting in Hackney, in which he had renounced any claim to Whacka. She had kept it in the pages of her *Bhagavad Gita*.

She went to the cabinet and got out two tumblers and the half bottle of whisky. She thought of snatching the letter from his hand and flushing it down the toilet. She scanned her brain for a ruse. But perhaps she had not wanted to make up a story. Perhaps she had kept the letter so that one day it might be found. She couldn't even remember the words Leo had used. Just that he would never interfere or seek to make any claims to the child.

'I would like to know, what the "secret" is,' said Ben, speaking like a prosecutor.

She had tried to lie. She said they had had a kiss many years ago and that she had felt very guilty about it.

'I want to hear the truth, Priya,' he said as if he might forgive her.

She had been carrying round this family secret for close on three years; at times she'd thought she wouldn't survive the corrosion of holding it in. The only friend she had talked to, Jean, thought that she should tell Ben, whatever his reaction might be and now, now she just wanted it out. She didn't care how he reacted. She knew by looking at Whacka that he was not Ben's son, she could tell by his fingers, the colour of his hair, the shape of his mouth.

Ben read out parts of the letter. 'What happened in Wales? What's this walk in London Fields that Leo's referring to? What is it that Jan doesn't know?'

She told him. After half an hour he phoned Leo and demanded that he come over. Ben wanted to hear it from Leo's own mouth. He wanted another letter, also signed by Leo, to say that they had deceived him. Afterwards, Ben smashed his forehead against the table.

And now as she walked back down the Holloway Road from Archway she remembered the following morning, when she had gone into the garden to have a cigarette and found the burnt remains of a bundle of clothes, charred fragments of red cloth with gold embroidery: her wedding sari and Ben's silk Nehru coat.

Sixteen

'You know I've never seen Priya,' said Helen. 'I have a picture of her from things you've told me, but the last time she came to school I wasn't there.'

'She's much smaller than I had imagined her after that first encounter in Leone's room,' remarked Ben. 'Although I hadn't forgotten her deep reverberating laugh. She has quite a dark complexion, even by Indian standards, and jet-black hair.'

'Straight or curly?' Helen asked.

'Neither, really. It's thick and waxy, wavy in bits and straight in other bits, all mixed up, a bit like her temperament. She wears it quite short, bob length. How the hell did we end up here?' said Ben. 'The horrible Gibbs an hour ago, and now I'm in the middle of describing Priya to you. It must be because it's my son's birthday.' A childhood warning came to him: Don't get too excited, he heard his mother saying as he scampered round the tennis court for hours in a frenzy of delight. It will all end in tears.

'Soon after that night when I woke up to the funny side of things, I bumped into Leone. We had a coffee and I started asking her about her Indian friend. I wanted to see her again. I told myself I must be missing India. I found myself wondering where she came from and whether I would know anyone she knew. In India everyone of a certain class seemed to have some connection.

'I was working hard on my finals dissertation, looking at

early versions of the Arthurian legends, waking early, staying in the library from opening time to five-thirty.'

Helen gave him a look that told him that he was digressing.

'Then Leone invited me to the pub for her birthday drink. I went, and there was Priya. This time she was dressed differently. All in black – jeans and a stylish polo-neck sweater. We talked about the political situation in India. She made me laugh. She told me about her family. I told her about my time as a teacher at Mayo College. Talking to her at Leone's birthday was like being in India again. Priya knew people who had gone to Mayo, and yet it was different because Priya and I shared our Oxford world, where we both felt like outsiders. After closing time we went back with a group of women to Priya's room in Catz. It had a plate-glass window that looked out on to the greenest playing field you ever saw, or so it seemed to me when the light came up in the morning.'

'So you stayed the night,' said Helen, turning sideways to face Ben. 'I bet her friend, Leone, was overjoyed.'

'I didn't stay the night, not quite.' They were walking round the garden of St George's Square. On the pavement an elderly man in a mauve sweater and grey jacket was foraging at the bottom of the privet hedge, picking up bits of debris and shoving them into two overflowing Safeway bags. 'What's that man up to?' Ben asked.

'I don't know. Finish your story. What do you mean, "not quite"?'

'We sat up late drinking and smoking. One by one everyone left until there was just Priya, Leone and me. In fact, it was just Priya and me talking and Leone yawning.'

'She didn't want to leave the two of you together.'

'Right. She was very proprietorial about Priya. She felt she had to look after her. She kept hinting to me that I should go, but whenever I tried Priya insisted I stay and help her finish the bottle of whisky. So it went on until, it must have been at least three, when Leone left the room to go to the toilet. I wanted to stay up and I could see Priya was wide awake. I asked her if she would like to go for a walk and she said yes.'

'You went for a walk at three in the morning? Steven would never go for a walk with me even at three in the afternoon. He'd think it was a waste of time.'

Ben felt sorry for Helen, for her drab relationship. Almost immediately the sorrow was accompanied by envy: at least she didn't have the tearing pain that had dogged him this past year. They came back to the four-lane road by the river, where cars hurtled past towards the huge junction with Vauxhall Bridge Road. It was an unforgiving place to stand and talk. Ben thought of Helen's return journey across the river and through the featureless junctions of south London. Somewhere there, in a forest of alien, antagonistic streets, lived Helen. South of the river, Ben thought, was a foreign country of gas reservoirs, tower blocks, the Oval, the Elephant and Castle, the decrepitude of the Old Kent Road, Peckham, Deptford and New Cross. They turned back into a quiet avenue of trees and expensive cars on St George's Square. It was time to bring his Oxford story to a close. 'After that walk we didn't stop seeing each other for eleven days.'

'Eleven days!'

'Eleven nights and days. We couldn't stand to be apart.'

'That's love.'

'Yup,' said Ben wistfully. 'I don't know if it was obsession or love.'

'I want to hear more, but you'd better get going; otherwise you'll be late for the party.'

Once again, he felt guilty for having talked so much, thinking that he should make it up to her on their next encounter. 'Thank you for handling Gibbs so well and stopping me from losing my temper.'

'One more thing.' Helen smiled. She tilted her head back. 'I just wanted to say, you've got such a vivid memory. I really love your stories.'

Ben turned the key and pulled open his car door. Then, on a whim, he leaned over to his friend and gave her a hug.

'Have a good party,' she whispered.

Leaving her there on the edge of the pavement made him sad. Would she have run off with him if he had asked her to? He drove across Lupus Street and took a left past the church on to Belgrave Road. Helen was canny about people's emotions. It was as if she could read his soul and knew what he wanted. Priya and he had been together for the whole of the nineties. Their anniversaries were always a disaster. There was the night they had ended up sitting glumly in a Taco Bell off Piccadilly Circus. He went over the Eccleston Bridge hump and across Buckingham Palace Road. They had decided to stop these celebrations. There was something forced about these artificial effusions, Mother's Days, Father's Days, Hallowe'en, Valentine's Day. Perhaps they should mark that night they went on the Oxford walk, or the night when denim-skirted Priya came flying in through Leone's door. He cut into Belgrave Square, counting the squares he would go through or past on his way home. Belgrave, Grosvenor, Hanover, Cavendish.

On that spring night nine years ago in Oxford they had climbed over the gate of Catz and wandered aimlessly through the empty streets. Priya striding confidently in the glare of the street lamps. He had felt the rightness and the strangeness of things. She was telling him about her grandfather and his participation in Gandhi's civil disobedience movement, how, like many Indians, their family had collected all the foreign goods in the house and burnt them in the street. Her great-uncle had become the first finance minister of independent India. Stuck in a line of cars inching towards Hyde Park Corner, Ben remembered Priya telling him about the battered Budget bag her great-uncle had left to her. She had it in her room in Oxford. She sometimes felt it was symbolic of her family's high expectations of her. Her great-uncle would have been proud to know that she was completing her MPhil in Development Economics at Oxford.

They walked past New College porters' lodge. When he looked over at her he saw a face aglow. So much being expressed in these wordless moments. Never before had any-one made him feel so confident. It was as if, as they drifted through these cobbled lanes, their future were speaking to them in the voice of these blocks of stone, this old moon, this aged spire.

At last Ben nosed on to the Hyde Park Corner roundabout. He swung right and then left through the lights and the chicane that twisted past Queen Elizabeth Gate. This was his favourite part of the homeward route. He accelerated into the right lane. He could almost close his eyes and time the arrival of the turn from Park Lane into Upper Brook Street. A black cab slowed in front of him. He recalled how Priya had approached the Radcliffe Camera as the first light of dawn filtered through. For him, it was the English version of waking early to visit the banks of the River Ganges at Varanasi. 'Thou by the Indian Ganges' side / Should'st rubies find.' In India he had seen wor-shippers breaking the surface of the barely moving water, flicking droplets on to their glistening brown shoulders, whilst they, Ben and Priya, in the midst of love's long night, were paying homage to this knot of grand architecture, the dome, the stone carvings, the arches.

Priya said the words that were on his mind. 'During the day you never realize how fine these buildings are.'

'You never get to see them like this, so starved of people,' Ben had answered. Their half-whispered words tumbled, skating round the curves of the Radcliffe Camera.

The traffic took Ben through Grosvenor Square and past Claridge's and the glitzy boutiques on Brook Street. He cut left round Hanover Square, and crossed over Oxford Street. How many Oxfords were there in the world? Oxford, Mississippi, home town of William Faulkner. He swirled round Cavendish Square, with its cherry trees just coming into blossom, short-cutting through Chandos Street into Portland Place, emerging opposite Broadcasting House, where he used to stop and meet Priya for a cup of tea when she was doing a stint there. That brought back the pain. He pushed it aside and returned to his Oxford reverie. On the walk that night, they hadn't spoken much. From time to time they had caught each other's eye and smiled. He realized that when they were absorbing the architecture, the history, the grandeur of the place, they were also acknowledging their luck at having found each other. Ambling in the early hours of the morning, at the beginning, the very first day of love.

This was the person, the experience, he had been waiting for all his life. For once, he had felt free of his self-conscious agonizing, his stumbling over what to do next. Ben had buried this story so deep inside him. What happened in Oxford was love; sudden, sure and inexorable. There was no hurry to touch or hold or caress each other as they strolled and gazed, smiles wreathing their faces, 'the sweet breath of heaven' blowing on their bodies.

As he waited at the lights to cross the Euston Road, he remembered lines from *Hamlet*: 'meet it is I set it down, / that one may smile, and smile, and be a villain'. With that came a surmise about the two sides of Priya's character. Hidden behind her grin there was something rank, something rotten, something that had been eating away at his heart. She had caused him the worst hurt of his life, but she had also showed him something new, emptied the anger from him, he thought, as he drove on to the outer circle of Regent's Park, and these are experiences you can never lose. Once you have loved like that it can't be taken away. You may choose to ignore it, repress it, but you can't expunge it. Like the round pellets of sand dug up by a crab, still visible even after the nukes have fallen.

As he passed the wedding-cake façades of Cumberland Terrace he wanted simply to remember that time, those first eleven days in Oxford with Priya. Shafts of light shone on the budding trees. He passed by a jogger in shorts and vest. After the night of the walk they had parted in the full brightness of morning. Later she had told him how surprised she had been at her own restraint. It was as if they had been obeying a voice. Ben remembered not wanting to sleep or eat. No day after had ever offered more promise. Everything in Oxford, the trees, the buildings, the sky, even the privacy of his dreary room had been like a new joy. He had gone to bed beaming and woken at noon with the same smirk on his face. He had missed all his lectures. Taken his time getting dressed. All he could think of was Priya's face, her voice, her cheeks, her black eyes, her thick hair. He lay in the bath soaking in the anticipation of seeing her again. In the early evening his legs took him down the road and into the lane that led to St Catherine's College.

The memory of his younger self walking without a care past the porters' lodge made him wistful as he turned his car through Gloucester Gate. At the lights he checked the time. He passed Regent Books on Parkway at 3.41. Alan Bennett's face in the window. There was always a traffic jam here. He remembered his excited heart as he had approached Priya's college room. Suppose she rejected him? She hadn't been in. He had asked for directions to the dining hall. He remembered the hall so well, the tall austere Jacobsen chairs at high table. And there, after looking round the diners, he had spotted Leone and then, two seats away, his Indian queen: 'O, she doth teach the torches to burn bright!' It was only yesterday he had been trying to get his year 9s to understand the meaning of that line.

Priya had seen him coming through the rows of spoon-clinking undergraduates. She had stood up and pointed at him in mock surprise. Her face saying, Come on, I've been waiting for you. He had slipped in next to her, sheepish. She had heaped three spoons of sugar into her pot of yogurt. How exotic the food at her college had seemed. 'Can I come and eat here every day?' he had said, much to Leone's disapproval. It *was* a kind of folly. For eleven days, in the fog of their madness, they had inhabited a world in which they were the only citizens.

At Camden Town, Ben crossed through Britannia Junction while the lights were on amber. He looped into the left lane to get round a slow-mover, accelerating past the eighteen-aisled Sainsbury's. Leone had been grumpy and puzzled, and had looked at them as if to say, What the hell do you think you're doing? They laughed at her anger. He stayed in that hall talking to Priya until they were thrown out. Afterwards they had repaired to the bar until Priya asked him to show her his college, and they had both known as they staggered tipsily towards Keble that she was not returning to her room that night.

Down the Camden Road one-way system, past the red-brick women's prison, sneaking into the bus lane, Ben manoeuvred his car. He thought of Whacka's excitement as the rocking horse appeared through the door. It had started to rain again. He rolled up the window and waved away the squeegee merchants clustered at the Nag's Head lights. Little boys, ten or twelve years old, their faces smirched with grime and experience. Once, on a Sunday, walking past the window of Burger King, he had seen this group throwing chips at a Bangladeshi cleaner. He ran his fingers through his thinning hair at the memory of Priya doing the same to him as she had lain on her stomach, unclothed by his side on the single bed in his Keble room, with both bars of the wall heater burning red like radioactive centipedes. He remembered her tiny nipples with their large chocolate halos and the cries of satisfaction he was now so used to. They had had to strip the wet sheet off the mattress and push this on to the floor where they had slept until she had woken him in the middle of the night, wanting more.

Priya came to Keble breakfast the next morning. It was a very different college from hers. He had felt the eyes of several rugger louts on her. Nominally, it was still against college rules to have a partner of the opposite sex share your bed for the night. What would he say to his father if the college complained? Well, his father fucked up, didn't he? Anger came without a calling card. He recalled the lunch at his parents' Amersham home. 'I have nothing against Pakistans,' he said aloud, mocking his father's voice.

An articulated lorry with German number plates crawled

past him in the left lane on the Holloway Road, hydraulic brakes letting off steam. Talking to yourself keeps you sane, Helen had said once. She was right. Then his father's voice came back. 'You mustn't get the wrong end of the stick, Ben. I've always been good friends with old Faz. I have nothing against Asians. However,' he cleared his throat, 'however, it's a quite different matter when my only son, my only son,' he had this irritating way of repeating himself like a politician, 'wants to marry a non-Christian and my grandchildren are going to be half-Pakistan.' Ben had got up and left his half-eaten lunch. His mother had said nothing. A few minutes later, not knowing what to do with his rage, he had come back and sat down at the table. The subject had never been broached again.

Why had he never confronted his father? Why hadn't there been a quarrel? Why hadn't he shouted at him, You ignorant self-satisfied suburban middle-class twit, living in your fucking dormitory town and not even knowing that there is no such thing as a Pakistan and anyway Priya is Indian. Blood trapezed round his head. His father and mother would already be at the flat, waiting in their customary way. On seeing his father he would be gripped by that lifelong fear of authority, respect for your elders, decent behaviour. Or was there something else, he thought to himself, was there something to be universally cherished about such deference?

Imagine him, imagine Richard spying on what Ben had learnt to do to Priya during those eleven days in Oxford. In front of the long mirror, propped against Priya's desk, reflecting their mutual contortions, delighting in the sight of their tangled bodies; the minutiae of their entries and exits. On the last day of that eleven-day period, he had been sitting up in her bed, reading; she had gone to take a shower. While she had been away, he had been thinking of her, how much he adored her, how unhappy he was to have to return to the routine of his Oxford life. They had spent the days of leisure in frameless loiterings, sharing favourite spots and discovering new ones. Nosing in Indian grocers in Cowley, where Ben had shown her a seedy restaurant that served authentic Punjabi food. They had drunk in strange pubs. In one of them Priya had got talking to a giant Rasta from whom she had scored a lump of Afghan black. They'd stumbled upon an idyllic ale-house hidden away on the canal where they had spent hours getting sozzled with the eccentric owner. After a walk in the meadows behind Jericho, they had bought each other silly presents in Partytime, the toyshop on the corner of Kingston Road, and had filled their faces with homemade burgers smothered in garlic mayonnaise served up by the bearded Canadian on Wilton Street. They had escaped for a night to London, where Priya took Ben to meet Jocelyn for the first time. He had felt satiated, but worried that he had done no essays, no studying, and finals were not so far away. They had decided it was time to reenter the world, but all he had been able to think of were Priya's hips and breasts where he loved to sink his head.

Ben recalled how Priya had interrupted his thoughts, coming into the bedroom still wet from her shower. She was in a towelling dressing gown. It was early evening. He heard students' doors slam as they headed towards their dinners. They were living their lives and eating their mundane soup whilst here in front of him was a goddess standing in a blaze of evening sun, her brown cheeks, her black eyes and her teardrop ears aglow. In the centre of the room, Priya was combing back her dripping hair, her dressing gown ajar. He reached inside and kissed the scent of her warm belly. Flush with expertise, mouth burrowing in the delicious gloom, he awakened in her manifold threads of pleasure. Priya called out. Enjoying but not immediately responding to the urgencies that came from her, like a tennis player with perfect rhythm he bent to this enviable task. He liked it more than any tennis match and played it better. A sudden weakening of her knees, hands gripping his head, a tumescence flooding his burning, rocking face that was like a boulder washed by a surge of briny ocean.

Imagine that, Dad, thought Ben as he emerged from his orange car and headed to the door of his flat, heaving the rocking horse under one arm. That's who your son is. That's what your 'only son' can do. Imagine him on his knees, his face buried in the wet muff of a big Pakistan cunt.

Seventeen

Like mirror images husband and wife return home. At the door three-year-old Whacka trampolines himself into Priya's arms, shouting, 'Eddie the clown, Eddie the clown, not come.' Jocelyn Batstone, dressed as usual in her blue worker's trousers and lace-up shoes is busying herself in the kitchen trying to tidy up. A few minutes after four, Ben enters the flat.

'Where's the rocking horse?' Priya whispers.

'By the door,' says Ben. 'Let's give it to him now.'

'Whacka!' shouts Priya. 'Come and see what's here.' No response from the boy. 'I think he's just got engrossed in a game with Jocelyn.'

'Why don't we hide it in the basement and give it to him later.'

Ben stashes the horse under the basement stairs and then comes into the kitchen. 'Has the entertainer arrived?' he asks, popping a crinkled crisp into his mouth.

'I phoned him on his mobile. He's in Shepherd's Bush. He said he'll be here in fifteen minutes,' Priya replies.

'Shepherd's Bush is miles away,' says Jocelyn. 'It will take him forty-five minutes at least.' She and Whacka have finished their game and are helping Priya to wrap layers of newspaper round the pass-the-parcel prizes. Ben's parents appear in the doorway, mug of tea in hand. Mary smiles genially and gives Ben a kiss. His father, plaid tie hanging askew, is frowning at the camcorder hanging from his neck.

'Is that new?' asks Ben.

'Birthday present from Crispin. But I can't get the auto-focus to operate properly.' Father and son pore over the instruction manual.

'Oh God,' says Priya, 'somebody needs to get the kebabs and samosas I ordered from Turnpike Lane.'

At the mention of kebabs Ben waves his arm and mumbles, 'This is crazy.'

'But I've ordered them now,' Priya says plaintively, looking at Ben's mother for support.

'That means I'll have to worry about how they get here.'

Mary bustles round the kitchen table and starts to unwrap the sandwiches.

'Wait,' says Priya, unable not to interfere.

The doorbell rings and Ben rushes off to answer it.

'Mummmy, I wan my Batman costume,' says Whacka, tugging at Priya's hand like a rope-climber.

'You wear the Batman costume for half the party, but then for the cake-cutting promise me you'll wear the clothes Nani sent you from India.'

Ben introduces Raj, Amy's father, the earliest arrival, to his parents. Amy is again trying to hide between his legs.

'Do you remember, darling,' says Mary to her son, 'you got a Robin outfit for your fourth birthday.'

'I *do* remember that costume.'

'I'm sure I could find it if I hunted round,' says Mary.

The doorbell rings intermittently for the next fifteen minutes. Shepherding parents attempt to deliver up their offspring – a mixture of unruly and painfully shy toddlers who shed their coats and shoes by the door. Some hang round in their parents' shadows, some rush into the living room where their thudding feet shake the furniture. A frenzied running and screeching game begins, in which Whacka, now in the Batman outfit, is the leader.

Ben is being watched by his father while he dabs a spoon in the unctuous gravy for his biryani. Rings of purple onion are sizzling in a wok of hot oil. He adds a kettle of boiled water into a large pot bubbling on the stove. The rice is soaking in a bowl next to the sink.

'Chap came to see us the other day, nephew of the Williamses, you know the Williamses, Ben?' Ben nods. Why does my father have such an embarrassingly middle-class voice, he thinks. 'Well, he's just joined the police force and he's having an awful time. He says morale is very low and everybody at the station feels terribly hated.'

'Unlikely job for one of the Williamses' relatives, isn't it? I could understand one of them joining the army.'

'It's funny you should say that. They're always saying how surprising it is that our son has ended up as a teacher in an inner London comprehensive.'

'Who would want to be a policeman these days?' says Mary.

'Some of the kids I teach, for a start. The ones who can't get any GCSEs. It's a scandal really. You'd expect the police to require some passes at GCSE, but they're willing to take on recruits with minimal qualifications.'

'I have a friend,' says Raj, who still has his daughter Amy cuddled between his legs, 'who applied to join the police a year after graduating. We all thought him mad. One morning, a day or two before his interview, two officers came round to his flat at six-thirty. Got him out of bed and proceeded to conduct an interview.'

'Did he get the job?' asks Ben.

'No. He reckoned they spotted some grass by his bedside table.'

'I'm not surprised. The police are terribly suspicious of university graduates,' says Ben.

'No good with a truncheon,' Raj chuckles.

'There's this drama teacher at our school, half West Indian, half English. She used to be an occupational therapist with the police. You can imagine these young beat officers, some of them openly racist and sexist, having been in some harrowing situation, turn up for post-trauma support and find themselves sitting opposite a beautiful black woman.'

'How did they react?' Raj asks.

'By questioning her credentials,' says Ben. 'By questioning the whole counselling thing. But then once they started telling their stories and making themselves vulnerable, Sharon said, she found it difficult not to be moved by how innocent, brutal and thick they could be.'

Ben's parents look decidedly uneasy.

Priya opens the door to the garden. A fine spray, not really rain, floats down from the grey sky. She had hoped it would be dry so the kebabs and the chicken could be barbecued. Strewn all round the small patch of scrawny grass are various toys for the children, a blue plastic elephant see-saw, a mini trampoline, a red and yellow scooter and a plastic slide she has borrowed from a neighbour. The toys are wet. She spreads some newspaper on the carpet by the doorstep.

Ben is draining the soaked rice. He has laid out the crisped brown threads of onion on sheets of kitchen towel to one side of the cooker.

Priya puts her hand on his shoulder and whispers, 'Have you got your camera?'

'Let me just get this rice on.'

In the background he can hear Jocelyn holding forth to

Mary. 'In my day, we never had any entertainers. It was just cake and a few sweets. My father would be working in his study and he might emerge briefly for the singing of "Happy Birthday". My mother simply couldn't get her head round anything worldly.'

'What was she interested in?'

'History, especially African history,' Jocelyn explains. 'Lost in the world of academia – a scholar until the day she died. Spent all her time with her head buried in manuscripts at the British Library.'

'Wasn't it true', asks Priya from nearby, 'that to get away from the noise of the family and to be able to write she would buy a return ticket to Oxford and use the journey to work?'

'She used a variety of ploys. Every weekend she simply threw all the dirty clothes, sheets and towels into a bath of soapy water. An hour later she would let the water drain out. And as we grew older we had to go and pick what was ours out of the bath and hang them up to dry.'

The doorbell again. Mauro Sossi, Ben's friend and another tennis opponent, with his five-year-old daughter Michaela. Mauro's mother is Italian, his father is Scottish and he lived the first twenty years of his life in up-state New York. He has a worn artist's face and a Mediterranean complexion. A terrific tennis player, who gave up playing competitive tennis when he got a scholarship to Oxford to study English. It was on a tennis court at Oxford that he and Ben first met. In his middle twenties Mauro gave up his job as a graphic designer and turned to painting. He painted people: stallholders in Columbia Road market round the corner from where he lived in east London, schoolchildren coming out of the local primary, butchers slicing meat, Caribbean men outside a pub in Dalston.

He'd done a series of scenes inside and outside London pubs. There were tenderly observed portraits of his neighbours and his family.

Close behind Mauro and Michaela arrive Ben's younger sister Jane and her pompous husband Crispin, whom Priya insists on calling Charlie. They are all a little earlier than Priya had expected. People simply won't behave the way you want them to. Priya had specifically asked them to come after six o'clock. Here they are crowding out the kitchen, and the entertainer who should have been here an hour ago is nowhere to be seen.

Music comes on next door. Good, at least Ben is taking charge.

The fruity voice of Crispin greeting his parents-in-law fills the room. 'Good God,' he booms, 'what on earth is that?' He is looking over to where the onion rings have been laid out by Ben. 'Looks like the last cubicle in the men's bogs at work. Priya, you've really gone to town. How is it at the World Service these days? Did you see Pinochet tottering on the box the other day?' Crispin says the dictator's name as if it were some vintage French wine.

'Charlie, my dear,' says Priya, 'do me a favour, get some beers out of the fridge and offer them to the grown-ups.' Most parents have stayed at the party with their children.

Anya of the plunging neckline, who neglects her children but dresses them in expensive clothes, asks Priya, 'Would it be all right if I left Chile here?'

How could she call her daughter Chile? 'Sure,' says Priya, 'she can help with the games and the entertainer.' At least Anja has brought Ivana, her Slovakian au pair, with them. Priya sighs. At last, someone who can help her without having to be told what to do all the time.

Priya can hear Ben in the other room trying to get all the kids to sit in a circle. Thank God he is a schoolteacher – what would she have done with one of those other useless men standing round her? Doorbell again. She goes to open it, thinking, It's got to be the clown this time.

'Priyaaa, aaaaiiiiiii!'

'Patience, come in.'

'I told you I was gonna come. You see. How are you? How's the boy?'

Priya gives the tiny African woman a big hug. 'I'm so happy you could make it early. How are things at the hospital?'

'Yes, my dear, I am very well. I told you I was gonna come. Yes, I did. I wouldn't miss it.' Patience was the midwife at Whacka's birth. She has thin strong arms, short wiry hair and a wonderfully comforting voice. It is a voice that Priya could never forget. During her five hours of labour she owed so much to the expert handling of this woman: her strong back rubs, her constant chiding and cajoling, the balm in her voice, 'You're doing well, girl, breathe, away, breathe, away, breathe, away.'

Patience flutters into the kitchen, squeaking with laughter. Under one arm she holds a large present. 'Where is de birthday boy? Where can I find hiiiim? Where is the naughty lickle thing?' Her accent has been influenced by working with Caribbean midwives and nurses for twenty years at the Whittington hospital.

'Go in and see them. They're in the middle of a game.'

'I must see what mischeef he is getting up to.'

'Have a cup of tea first, Patience.'

'I will, later, dahling, later. You make yourself busy with the children's tea. What a lot of food you have been preparing!

Anyway, I'm glad, I'm starving.' She chuckles, rubbing her thin waist.

Ivana is offering cups of tea to all the adults, slipping round the guests like a silken skiff. Priya hears the music stop and pokes her head into the living room.

The toddlers are sitting in a circle. Ben is standing by the black stack of the Sony hi-fi, with his sister Jane and Patience next to each other, helping to make sure that every child is getting a present. Newspaper litters the room. Two children, Amy and Milo, stand outside the circle refusing to join in. Michaela, with the calm face, is overseeing the movement of the parcel from child to child. Whacka has fallen into one of his habitual open-mouthed stupors. Priya looks at him and feels a pang that takes her back to her childhood in her mother's Bombay flat, to birthday parties in which her hair was tied back in a ponytail with a red ribbon. When the children came through the door it was *she* who felt as if she were the outsider. Shyness and anxiety drained her of her usual exuberance. Her mother used to hire a man with a projector, to show the children cartoons – they thought of him as a magician. TV hadn't arrived in India, so it was an exceptional thrill to see Donald Duck and Tom and Jerry projected on to a makeshift screen in the living room. She remembers the giant shadows on the screen when someone stood up and got in the way of the projector beam. On this occasion Priya's mother has insisted on paying the entertainer's fee as a present to Whacka. There is my son, Priya thinks, and this is my home. How far away I have moved from my roots.

The diminishing parcel – it started out large and misshapen – arrives in Whacka's lap. Ben stops the music. People shout encouragement, 'Go on, Whacka, open the parcel.'

Patience kneels down beside him. 'Go on, Whacka, see what happen inside. What you find inside. Ya find something good?'

Whacka holds up a pair of plastic scissors. He catches his mother's eye and beams.

'What is it, Whacka?' asks Jane.

'Is for cutting things.'

'That's right, cutting and sticking,' Priya confirms. The music comes on again. 'The wheels on the bus go round and round.' Priya feels her spirits rise. It didn't matter what happened at the party as long as Whack had a good time. Kebabs, barbecue, drinks; the adults would take care of themselves. But where the hell was Eddie the clown? She looks over at Ben's parents, standing awkwardly in the corner. She beckons to them. Mary comes over as if she were being asked to perform some urgent task. 'Come and say hello to Mauro, you have met before, haven't you?'

'Of course we have. Now, you must tell me, how is your painting going?' Mary asks Mauro as Priya sidles away.

Jocelyn is talking to Crispin. Priya butts in, 'Are you any good at fires, Charlie?'

'Do I look like an arsonist?' He guffaws.

Priya gives him a fake smile. 'I mean lighting a fire for the barbecue.'

'I wouldn't say I'm an expert.'

'You just have to forget about the barbecue today. Look, it's still raining out there,' says Jocelyn.

Ivana has laid out the cocktail sausages, the Hula Hoops and crisps, the crudités and the sandwiches on the Spiderman party plates. Priya brings out the mangled jellies from the fridge. Squash is made up in plastic jugs. Food, voices and laughter. Priya would have liked her mother to be here to see all this. It was chaos, but what did it matter? It didn't even really matter that the entertainer was late. He would get here in the end. She could give the kids their tea and he could do his show after they'd eaten. It wasn't necessary for her to have an awful time.

Eighteen

Jocelyn moved in on the conversation Mauro was having with Ben's parents. 'Now, look,' she said, pointing her finger at him, 'what I really want to know is whether you're really any good at tennis.'

'Not as good', said Mauro stroking his portly belly, 'as I used to be.'

'You're not answering my question,' persisted Jocelyn. 'I've heard you're very good.'

' "Good" is such a relative word. Good compared to whom?' asked Priya, jumping in to save Mauro, of whom she was very fond.

'Do you beat Ben?' Jocelyn asked.

'I used to be good.'

'Do you beat Ben?' persisted Jocelyn.

'We don't play sets that much. We practise a lot.'

'But when you do, you always win,' Priya piped in.

'Is *Ben* any good?' asked Jocelyn.

'He has some lovely shots. But, you know, in tennis – I'm afraid you might find this boring,' he said to Richard and Mary, 'good tennis, it's all about movement and balance. If you get your feet in the right place then the shot comes automatically. The best players are always there to meet the ball wherever their opponent hits it to. If Ben were fitter, if I were thinner, we would both be much better.' Mauro's eyes brightened. 'I've had this painting on the go for about a month now. It's a spotted handkerchief, and although I was happy with the colours, there was something that disappointed me about it every time I went back to it. Just this afternoon, I realized that it was the frame. The painting needs a space to exist in. Getting your feet in the right place is the frame for the tennis shot, whereas the rhythm of the arm, the forehand or the backhand, are more like the colours in a painting: they come automatically. The frame makes the picture; without it you wouldn't know where to stop or start.'

Richard looked especially stolid, listening with great concentration, head bent to one side.

Mary had on a face of pretend curiosity. 'I can see what you mean about a painting having a frame,' she said. 'But in galleries these days you see all sorts of things, an old shoe or a half-eaten banana or a biscuit sitting in the middle of a huge white wall.'

'And what about all this installation art, then? Surely these things exist without a frame?' said Jocelyn.

'Every work of art has a space in which it should exist,' said Mauro. 'A kind of universe in which it has to float, like a balloon, until it finds its resting place. It takes time, but when it happens the piece of art stops floating. It comes to a standstill. It's suddenly able to say what it wants, using the most eloquent means.'

'Ah-ha, but what would you say about Hodgkin, who paints all over his frames?' Jocelyn retorted. 'I quite like the paintings but I really cannot see the point of splashing paint all over the woodwork.'

'I know what Mauro is saying,' said Ben, joining in the conversation. 'It's like a marriage, you need a frame for a relationship. That's why marriage is so popular, it's a social construct, but an extremely helpful one.'

'That's exactly right,' said Mauro, putting his arm round Ben. 'It's the potential space up to which a relationship can float.'

'What has all this floating got to do with tennis?' asked Ben.

'I'm surprised at you, pal, everything in life has got to do with tennis. I thought you knew that.'

Mary smiled at her son's friend. 'I used to have an uncle who always maintained that you could learn everything you needed to know about life from a game of tennis.'

'Interesting you should say that,' said Richard, pointing with the little finger of the hand that held a glass of beer. 'I wonder if sports, some sports at any rate, have a genuinely useful application in life. And another thing, Mauro. I wonder what you think – is it the loser or the winner who learns more at the end of the game, if you see what I mean?'

'No question about it,' said Ben waving his hand and sniggering at Mauro. 'It's always the loser who learns more.'

'But it's still the worse outcome,' said Ben's friend.

'I can't get to sleep at night sometimes thinking of the stupid shots I've missed against this colleague of mine I play at school,' admitted Ben.

'Ah, but equally,' said his father, 'you send yourself to sleep thinking of some brilliant backhand you hit past your opponent at the net.'

'Too true,' said Mauro.

'Dad,' said Michaela pulling at Mauro's arm, 'stop talking about tennis, just play, don't think about it, just do it.'

'These two are like heroin addicts. If Ben doesn't get his tennis every week he becomes a horrible, irritable person,' said Priya.

'It's healthier than heroin, surely,' said Jocelyn briskly.

'As long as you don't lose,' Priya came back. 'If Ben loses he becomes like one of those men who kicks the dog when they walk in through the door.'

'Rubbish,' said Ben. 'Let's give the kids their food now.'

'What about the cake?' asked Priya.

'Do the cake last,' said Jocelyn.

Ben could hear his father asking Mauro about his art. 'Do you find it's good to have a conversation with oneself when one is working?' He was surprised by his father's question. It was the perfect way to get Mauro talking.

'I find it's more like an argument than a conversation,' Mauro said.

Then Ben's attention switched to his mother's question to Priya. 'Do you find', Mary said, echoing her husband, while she and Jane were laying yet more food on the children's plates, 'that you miss India much?'

'I miss my mother,' said Priya. 'I wish she'd been able to come for Whacka's birthday, but I don't miss being in Delhi.'

'Yes, this *is* your home now, isn't it?' said Ben's mother.

'When I leave London, though, even when we come to you in Amersham, or when I go up north to Durham, or west to Exeter, I feel alien.'

'Really, why is that?' asked Mary.

'It's the monochromatic throng, the way I feel in a crowd of white people – looked at, odd, you walk into a pub and there's that momentary hush. It's not like the Holloway Road or even Oxford Street, where I feel at ease.'

'I'm surprised you feel like that after all these years,' said Mary.

Children streamed into the kitchen and jostled for places around the food-laden table. Some of the adults filtered out into the living room.

'Where are the others?' Priya asked Ben.

'I can't get them to come through,' he answered.

Priya went into the living room and found Whacka and five or six toddlers peering out of the bay window into the street. On the pavement a bizarrely outfitted man, in candy-striped stockings and a checked floppy hat, was pulling faces at the children as he finished getting dressed, dragging clothes and boxes out of the boot of his purple Mini, pulling yellow shorts over the stockings. Who's that weirdo? thought Priya. Whacka started shouting, 'Eddie the clown! Eddie the clown!' She had a job getting the group of children away from the window.

Ben stood with some of the parents while the kids ate their tea in eerie silence. This was most strange, he thought: party hats, Hula Hoops, jam tarts and total silence. At Whacka's second-birthday party there had been mayhem, with Whacka standing up and conducting an uproarious rendition of 'Happy Birthday'. Perhaps this is what growing up entails. Or was it, wondered Ben, that there had been real happiness in the air last year, but since the fracture between him and Priya the home atmosphere was a tense concoction.

Even the grown-ups had fallen silent as they watched the kids and had started to feel hunger scurrying round their stomachs like little mice. Ben took some pictures and Priya went next door to check on the clown. Very soon his red nose and painted cheeks appeared through the door. Amy started to cry. 'Frightened of clowns,' whispered Ben to Jocelyn. Eddie brought in his guitar and started to sing strange tuneless ditties to the children, whilst Ben completed the last stage of his biryani. He layered the rice, saffron, browned onions, nuts and then the lamb with its deliciously spiced curry, cardamoms, cloves, cinnamon wafted over the sickly sweet smell of cake and grape squash.

Edgy conversation restarted among the adults. Mary and

Richard were asking Patience about her son, who had just won a scholarship to Dulwich College. He was having to travel across London every day, from their house in Stamford Hill. 'All his friends are near home,' said Patience, 'but the boy likes it. He don't mind travelling, he's a good boy. I tell him he don't have to go to that school but he says he want to.'

Mauro was in conversation with Crispin about the stock market. Ben shouted across from where he was layering his biryani, 'But what about some trader going off on his own and causing huge problems, losing massive amounts of money like Nick Leeson?'

'There's always a risk of that,' said Crispin. 'A friend of mine in the City told me that last year a chap in Holland thought he might get away with a rogue trade while everybody was out of the office on Christmas Eve. He started selling at an alarming rate and when people here checked into their computers they couldn't understand what was happening. There was potentially a kind of panic-selling situation. Luckily someone noticed the irregularity and was able to trace the source to this trader in Amsterdam.'

'Sounds like a good idea if you've got the guts to make it work,' said Mauro.

'There's a thin line between guts and stupidity,' said Crispin.

Ben was half listening to the conversation between Patience and his parents. 'You see, we thought with our son that he would be happier and more suited to a boarding school. Richard was very keen on it, whereas I found it terribly hard to let go of him. I think you made the right decision,' Mary said, pointing to her husband.

'What's that?' said Ben, entering between them.

'We were just explaining to Patience how Jane was quite happy in the local school and she still has a lot – well, maybe not a lot – some friends who went there. Her best friend, Rachel, for instance.'

'The strange thing is I remember very little about my school,' said Ben, 'especially about the first three years. Priya often asks me about that time and there's not much I can tell her.'

'You told me about the way you felt at being left at the head teacher's house,' said Priya, joining in while chiding one of the boys. 'No need to grab at the jelly. There's lots left.'

'Eddie's throwing food, Mummy,' said Whacka, pointing to the clown who was indeed lobbing bits of bread at the children, some of whom were laughing, while others looked glum or confused.

'What was that about the head teacher's house?' asked Ben.

Priya felt embarrassed to be bringing this up now. 'I was just remembering what you told me about being dropped off at school for the first time. That it was the headmaster's policy that the parents should disappear without saying goodbye while their child was distracted. Do you remember that happening, Richard, or is Ben making that up?'

'I seem to recall it was the school's policy. Mind you, it may have made good sense,' said Richard.

'I can understan' that,' said Patience.

'But then the kid turns round and finds his parents have gone?' said Priya.

'Exactly,' said Richard. 'I don't see why you make such a fuss of saying goodbye when you leave Whacka with us, for instance.'

'Don't you think it might be a little disturbing for the child?'

Ben had sidled off back to Mauro and Crispin, where the conversation had switched back to Mauro's work. Hating to feel left out, Ben was constantly flitting about and talking to two people at once, while keeping an ear out for the phone and the door bell, supervising the food, taking photographs. The clown, who had a rasping chain-smoker's voice, was repeatedly starting the kids off on 'Happy Birthday', but every time they got to the end of the first line he would switch to a dissonant tune on his guitar and sing different words while surreptitiously aiming Hula Hoops at unsuspecting children. Even more mess for me to clear up, thought Ben.

The kids went into the living room with the entertainer. Ben now seemed to be occupied in there as well. It had stopped raining, but the sky was still grey and it felt decidedly chilly. Priya stood out on the garden steps. Enjoying a moment's solitude, she inhaled a deep breath of London evening and for a few seconds let her brain be empty. Then she came back in and heard raucous laughter come from the kids next door. She went in and saw Ben sitting cross-legged on the floor; the scarlet-coated entertainer was hitting him on the head with a long green balloon. Ben had a mock-grumpy look on his face.

Priya went to answer the doorbell. In came her writer friend Jehan and his beautiful psychotherapist wife Rebecca, who was wearing an elegant white shirt. A jade necklace adorned her slender throat, and calf-skin boots her feet. Jehan in his sharp brown jacket, hair combed back, purple shirt, was holding a bottle of chilled Chablis in each hand which he presented to Priya with an exaggerated flourish. He pulled out his cigarettes, Priya gave him a drink and he joined in Mauro and Crispin's conversation. Patience helped Ivana clear the kitchen table. Rebecca stood just inside the living-room door, watching the clown. Her lips looked troubled, her eyes flickered from sad to mildly amused. The clown was still using Ben as the butt of his jokes. He had stuck a pink and yellow fluffy wig on Ben's head and was now encouraging the toddlers to hit him with their balloons. Whacka sprayed strings of yellow gunk all over Ben's hair.

Priya approached Rebecca with a cup of tea. 'I don't think Ben is enjoying this much. Where did you find this fellow?' asked Rebecca.

'I saw him at one of the other kid's birthday parties. He's not that bad, is he?'

Rebecca gave her characteristic half-smile. She wasn't going to lie to make Priya feel better. 'It's nice for Ben to have his mother and father here. There's such a lovely feel to birthday parties when all three generations are present.'

From where he was sitting Ben had spied Rebecca watching the show. It was hard not to feel a little unsettled by her beauty. The brown eyes, the dark hair that fell in waves, the slenderness of her waist. He had been putting on an act for the kids – crying out in pain when they hit him, looking tearful while they sprayed him with coloured strings. Rebecca's gaze had made him self-conscious. He wanted to go and check on his biryani.

Nineteen

Jehan was short, thick-set, broad-shouldered. He had a big head of black hair, hooded eyes framed by expensive gold-rimmed spectacles. His words came out in a sonorous drawl with only the faintest trace of an Indian accent. He was in the process of finishing his fourth book. The second, an autobiographical work about a year spent teaching and travelling in China, had been a success in America, a success greatly augmented by being a choice in Oprah's book club. Jehan would often fly off to LA or Berlin or New York to give readings, sign books and be interviewed. Rebecca didn't go with him. She was strict about not missing sessions with her clients. Jehan's books were large, sprawling, ribald things – Ben recalled an inane review which described the first book as 'a huge multicoloured marquee'. Ben had found it difficult to read it through to the end. Terrific language, but few gripping characters. The opposite end of writing from the understated clarity of Priya's mother or Arun Sengupta.

Jehan was an admirer of Mohini Patnaik's work and had become a family friend. It had been the food connection that had brought Ben and Jehan together. Jehan's first book had a character with an eating disorder of comic proportions who was prone to orgiastic fast-food consumption in the middle of the night. At a party where Priya had introduced them Ben told Jehan how much he had enjoyed this food-obsessed creation. Later Ben had sent him a copy of his own book with an affectionate inscription inside. Jehan wrote back a letter in which he complimented Ben on his work and suggested that he might write a piece for an anthology of food writing his publisher was bringing out. Ben spent weeks composing the piece, but the publisher passed it over on the grounds that they were looking for pieces by authors who would not ordinarily write about food. Meanwhile, friendship between the two couples took root.

Jehan was four years older than Ben. When Ben was feeling particularly bitter he put Jehan's success down to the fashion for Indian writers in English. He couldn't help deluding himself that had he the right name and the required style, he too might sell a 100,000 copies. At other times, he had to admit that Jehan was a sharp writer, especially when he reviewed some new book or movie. His book on China was a triumph – part travel book, part political history, part autobiography, part philosophical tract.

Long thin spicy lamb kebabs and Martin Batstone emerged from the quiet corner of the kitchen. Priya placed a bowl of coriander, mint and garlic paste in the centre of a beautiful porcelain dish, while Ben spread quartered pieces of steaming nan round the bowl. 'Fantastic,' said Jehan as he took another bite. 'It's such a vivid green,' enthused Rebecca, scooping up some chutney with a piece of bread. 'Mmm, fresh coriander, that's one of the best tastes in the world.' The adults began to congregate round the dish of kebabs.

'The last time we met,' said Jehan to Mauro, 'I'm not sure if you remember it, you quoted something about memory. Something that stayed with me, but I couldn't remember the exact words. Something about the faster you move the more you forget.'

Mauro and Jehan liked to talk about the creative process. Unlike Ben, Mauro felt quite unthreatened by Jehan, perhaps because they were in different disciplines. Jehan's work had reached a wider audience, he'd had acclaim, and yet he showed a genuine interest in what Mauro had to say. He gave the impression that there were things he could learn from Mauro. They were both searchers, digging away in their little plot of land until they found some nugget to examine under a microscope. And they were both non-judgemental characters. Mauro took a cigarette from Jehan. Ben watched them with concern. He hated to feel excluded.

'I *wish* I had said it,' said Mauro, taking a long drag on his cigarette and speaking as he exhaled. 'It comes from Kundera's *Slowness*.'

'How does it go?' asked Jehan, cocking his ear.

'"There is a secret bond between slowness and memory, between speed and forgetting." To remember something you must slow it down, the faster you go the more you forget. On the other hand,' Mauro continued, 'I reckon if you slow something down too much a kind of torpor sets in. And then, an over-abundance of energy develops. I found myself doing everything very fast just to get rid of that excess adrenalin which can be counter-productive when you're trying to paint. You don't want to be jumpy in front of the canvas.'

'Dali was a bit like that?' asked Jehan. 'Rather mad. It does help if I'm excited about something I'm working on.'

'Don't you find it can interfere with your ability to spend long periods on it?' Mauro responded. 'I need to be relatively calm if I want to spend days and hours on a canvas. Excitement tires you out.'

Jehan laughed. 'I'm no good at working for long periods. I write in bursts and then go and do something repetitive and exhausting, like jogging or hitting a squash ball. I can't stand to idle in my study if I'm not making progress.'

'You idlers, you,' said Ben, sneaking up on their conversation. 'Some of us don't even have the time to pronounce the word. Let me recommend the kebabs that are now sitting on the table. I would hate for either of you to miss out on the earthly, or should I say the earthy, delights of Priya's delicious coriander chutney.'

'I've had some, but I'll gladly have some more.'

Everyone seemed to have their mouths full in the kitchen. White wine and beer were passed round to counter the heat of green chillis. The clown was giving out animal-shaped balloons to each child, producing new ones to blow up from inside his gigantic red boots, or from the legs of his commodious yellow shorts. He tried to satisfy the greedy children and pack his tricks away, in two battered suitcases, at the same time.

The Batman cake was waiting on the table with three unlit candles positioned in a triangle. Priya flung the leftover jelly into the bin. Ben was looking a little weary after his stint as the clown's assistant. He left Mauro and Jehan, grabbed a chair and took himself over to where Jane and Rebecca were sitting.

'We were invited to a party in Oxford last week,' said Rebecca, 'and this cantankerous college friend of Jehan's came up to him, and after not having seen him for years said, "Good God, dear chap, when did you last wash your hair? It's a complete mess. You'll have to give your life's savings to a barber to see to that."'

As Rebecca spoke, Ben thought, She has the most beautiful voice. And then there's her sculpted chin and the deep brown skin colour that dives down the opening of her white shirt. Don't look any further, he said to himself. Keep your eyes above the neck. It was as if her every word were a pebble that had been perfectly rounded by a running brook. Her lips delivered each one to you with passionate care. People were drawn in by the modulations of her voice.

Even Jocelyn, who had a mild distaste for anyone glamorous, joined the group. 'It has to be said, Jehan does have a pretty respectable shag pile growing from his head,' she snorted.

Rebecca carried on, giving Jocelyn her withering half-smile. She was not renowned for her sense of humour. 'The strange thing about Jehan is that he had the confidence to come home after that rebuke and carry on with his life as if nothing had happened. I would have been furious, but I would also have gone straight home, washed my hair and then had it cut as soon as possible.'

'Isn't that also the difference between men and women?' Ben asked.

'I agree,' said his sister Jane. 'Men are less bothered about their clothes. I rather envy them that.'

'In my experience men are just as vain as women,' put in Jocelyn. 'It's more to do with age. You young things care about your clothes and spend money at fancy designers. In my day one never bothered with what one was wearing as long as it was comfortable and affordable.'

'But isn't it the case that some people really don't care?' asked Jane.

'I don't disagree with that. Martin doesn't seem to notice, do you, Martin?' said Jocelyn, commanding attention from her husband. Without waiting for his reply she continued, 'For a long time, I thought everything I wore must be in some shade of blue.'

'Was he an academic?' Martin asked Rebecca. 'The man who felt it necessary to insult Jehan like that? He must have had an ego problem. It wasn't really about Jehan's hair. It was what you analysts call a projection, wasn't it?'

'That doesn't change the way one feels about it,' said Rebecca smiling.

'Doesn't being a therapist make your life any happier?' asked Jocelyn with sudden vehemence. 'I just can't understand why anyone would want to spend so much time thinking and talking about themselves if it didn't cheer them up.'

'It's not about being cheered up. That's a misunderstanding. It's about the ability to describe things in a different way. A continuous process of self-inquiry. An interest in the way people behave. What makes someone so contrary? Why so many of us seem slanted towards self-hate, self-sabotage. Therapists can't change the fact that life is always difficult, but they can sometimes make you more aware.'

Jocelyn looked thoroughly sceptical and seemed to be getting ready to unleash some wildly insensitive comment when Ben butted in awkwardly with the first thing that came to mind. 'I want to ask you something. I had the weirdest dream last night.'

'Tell me,' Rebecca said.

'Ben,' said Priya jumping in, 'we must get everyone in here for the cake.'

Babbling and screeching ensued as they tried to herd the children back into the kitchen. Each of them desperate to wield their own rabbit or dog balloon. Ben overheard Rebecca, beady-eyed as always, reprimanding the clown. 'Could you please give the next balloon to the birthday boy.' The clown's owlish painted face showed no perceptible change of expression. Rebecca waited next to him with folded arms. The parents who had disappeared for an hour came back in, looking exhausted and wet.

'My friend say the thing about children is they weigh you down with gold.'

'That's such a wonderful phrase, Patience. I wonder where it comes from?' said Jane.

'It come from my friend, a Spanish lady, very active in the church.'

With a collective sigh of relief everyone joins in singing the first line of 'Happy Birthday'. The thought flickers through Priya's mind that Leo and Jan haven't come, and when she looks over to Ben he is standing behind Whacka, smiling and singing, with one hand loosely draped round the boy's shoulder. Thank God they're not here, she thinks. In the third line of the song her eye catches a frown, a look of concentrated perturbation on Jocelyn's face. She too is standing near Whacka, looking grandmotherly, and squeezed up beside her Martin, holding her hand, also has a strange glow on his face. They only have granddaughters, thinks Priya.

The clapping and cheering urged Whacka to blow out the candles. Then Priya handed Jocelyn the first piece of cake to pass round. Doling out the rest of the slices, she made sure that Whacka got the piece of icing with Batman's head on it. Priya remembered the motherly way Jocelyn had looked at her and Ben when they were standing at the top of Primrose Hill three years ago on the day before Whacka's birth. Could she have known? Had Leo confided in his mother? Was Jocelyn able to detect her son's features in Whacka's face? She had been there at the hospital only hours after Whacka's birth. Priya had already told her she wanted her to be one of his godmothers. And Jocelyn had accepted the role with pleasure. As Priya passed her the slices of cake her panic subsided. She couldn't believe that Jocelyn would ever do anything to jeopardize her happiness. There are so many secret insecurities, Priya thought, that have to be carefully balanced within families that it's a wonder they don't all just spill out and ruin us. These thoughts were overtaken by noisy demands from the toddlers for sweets and party bags.

A fake-tan, low-slung, black-hammocked cleavage bent towards her. 'What a lovely party.' Anya's lipsticked face was by her side.

Priya noticed that the woman already had a drink in her hand.

'Was Chile all right?' Anya asked.

'Yes,' replied Priya. 'She and Michaela seem to have got on really well. Have you met Mauro?' She turned to introduce Anya.

'I haven't. And how do you know Priya and Ben?' She homed her lusting eyes on the polite painter.

Priya moved away, thinking how much she disliked that presumptuous question.

'I must tell you something funny,' said Mauro to Anya. 'I hope you won't mind, but I think it was your daughter I overheard. I was downstairs in the bedroom with two or three of the older children and they were playing with a toy. One of them started trying to pull the toy away from Chile and they started to fight. I said to Chile, who seemed the older of the two, 'Why don't you let Harry have the toy?' Or maybe it was a bit more like, 'For God's sake, let him have the toy.' At which Chile gave it to him, closed her eyes and said, 'I knew it. I knew that would happen. This is just the kind of bad luck that has been following me all my life. First my sister shouts at me, then my father takes over my computer, then

I'm punished in the playground, and now someone has to have the toy I want.'

Anya looked worried, as if Mauro might be accusing her of something.

As the parents bundled their children out through the narrow corridor the ever-smiling Ivana held out a tray of party bags for them to collect. The clown was sitting in a corner, knees drawn up, in his striped tights and his round-toed red boots, wolfing a mountain of children's food plus kebab and bread. Two sunflowers drooped from the lapels of his magenta coat.

Rebecca came over to Ben. 'You started telling me about some kind of dream you had.'

'I was on a tennis court,' said Ben. 'I think I was the umpire between two brothers who were playing a match. Then the most surreal thing happened – the tennis competition turned into a cooking contest. One of the brothers tried to cut himself open and stuff his stomach with food. I attempted to stop him, but I couldn't. It seemed like he was going to die unless I did something.'

Rebecca dropped her head to one side. Her eyes grew sad, and she spoke as if to soothe Ben. 'It's a dream about being eaten up inside by competition.'

'There were elaborate bits of cooking going on. Recipes from ancient times,' said Ben, thinking to himself, It wasn't just about my tennis competitiveness with Mauro and John – it's about my book I can't finish and about the job I lost.

'What happened to the man who mutilated himself?' Rebecca asked.

'His brother and I nursed him better. I helped stitch up his wound.'

'That's about the part of you that wants to look after

yourself. It's a fascinating dream because it represents – through the use of the brothers – the intensely destructive, competitive, driven, controlling side – the superego – and then the gentler, caring, communicative side, and you in the dream, caught in the middle, trying to mediate between the two brothers, but also nursing the brother who has tried to kill himself.'

'I think Freud got it all wrong about dreams,' said Crispin haughtily. 'I read somewhere that he thought dreams were an expression of repressed and unconscious desires.'

'That's a fair description,' said Rebecca sharply.

'But I don't think I have repressed anything,' said Crispin. 'Whenever I recall my dreams – and I don't have many – they tell me something about what I'm worried or anxious about. I already know what makes me anxious, I learn nothing new from my dreams.'

'All right,' said Jane joining in, a gleam in her eye, 'what about your dream of being in the car with your foot stuck on the accelerator. What's that about?'

'It's all about men and fast cars. It's a cliché, it's about how speed will kill you. I used to have a yearning for an open-top sports car.'

'Don't you think you're being a bit literal?' said Rebecca. 'How can you know that there aren't unconscious forces at play? By their very nature opaque to you?'

'I don't think that's right, you see,' said Crispin. 'I've given it a lot of thought and I can't find anything that I might have repressed or that might be unconscious. I *know* what I'm frightened of.'

'According to Freud,' said Rebecca, 'dreams about speed, speed and losing control, are often connected to a fear of impotence. Which reminds me of a joke I heard the other day. "Denial is not a river in Egypt."'

Crispin, Jane and Ben looked bemused.

'De *Nial* is not a river in Egypt,' Rebecca repeated loudly.

Twenty

Some time later the party had quietened down into the post-children dinner for the adults. A handful of kids had begun watching *Beauty and the Beast* in a corner of the living room while the grown-ups had settled into the kitchen round the granite table, when the doorbell rang. At that moment Ben had just lifted the lid on his biryani and was testing a grain of rice. Fragrant steam suffused with saffron and cloves invaded his pores, but the rice was still al dente and needed another ten minutes of cooking to fluff up. He sealed the pot quickly, remembering how the female servant at Priya's mother's house in India did it with a mixture of flour and water, wiped his hands on a towel and went to answer the door. Michaela came into the kitchen and asked whether Whacka was allowed to open any presents. Priya said, Yes, but he must choose three and she should make sure she knew who they were from.

The minute Ben saw the shadows behind the frosted glass he knew who it was. Leo's broad torso and Jan's long face. He pictured himself clunking Leo on the jaw, but Jan smiled, showing her perfect set of large teeth, and gave him sumptuous kisses on both cheeks. It was obvious she knew nothing, and Ben felt a pang of anger about his collusion in her happy ignorance.

'Are we very late?' she asked.

'No, you've timed it perfectly. Most of the feral children and their parents have gone.'

'Have we missed the cake and the singing of "Happy Birthday"?' she asked.

'Yes, but don't worry,' said Ben. 'Whacka is still awake.' Leo looked shifty, his head slightly bowed. It made Ben feel generous towards him. 'Come on in. There's lots of food and we're soon going to sit down and eat.'

Jan darted into the living room to greet the fading Whacka and give him his present. Leo stayed in the kitchen and Ben ushered him towards Jehan. Jocelyn came over and gave her son a kiss. Priya tried to control her pounding heart. She busied herself with washing the coriander for the onion and tomato *cachumber*. She felt almost certain now that Leo had confided in his mother. Jocelyn's bluster was so good. Priya peeled the skin off a purple onion. Suppose Ben were to explode? She wanted this party to be over. She wished they had all eaten their food and gone and she were lying on her bed downstairs. What were all these people doing in her home? She hated being the cause of all this potential drama. She quit the kitchen and went into the quieter room, where she found Jan kneeling next to Whacka, trying to interest him in the wooden puzzle she had brought him. It was a good present. Whacka liked puzzles, but he was too tired to do one now.

There was something reassuringly straightforward about Jan, like a cup of tea that always tasted the same. She shared none of Priya's interest in politics or feminism. Her concerns were closer to the inner world, the family, friendship, the home, Eastern religion. She could talk incessantly in those terms about the future, but went blank if the topic of conversation strayed beyond them. You'd think she had gone to a private school in Hampstead, but she turned out to have gone to a mixed comprehensive in Palmer's Green. She had started out training to be a dentist and ended up as a dental hygienist and was prone to giving the same advice to her friends that she gave her patients: scrub your tongue and floss twice a day, change your toothbrush regularly, and don't forget to brush for one minute on each side. Hygiene gave her enough time to follow her other passion, making jewellery. Despite the fact that Jocelyn and others sniggered behind her back about this hippy occupation, she was beginning to sell her ornaments to shops and was now making a tidy sum each month.

'I can't believe how much Whacka has grown. He doesn't even remember me.' Jan's long lashes flickered up and down like fairy wings.

'Whacka darling,' said his mother. 'You look so tired. Shall I take you down to your bed and read you a story?'

'Nnnno! Nnnno! I don *wanna* go! I *wanna* stay here.'

'Okay, okay, you stay here. I'll get you a blanket so you can fall asleep if you want to.'

'Nnno, no sleep,' Whacka said, rubbing his eyes.

'It's his birthday. I'm going to let him have his way,' she said, turning to Jan. 'So, how are you? What's been happening in your life?'

Jan moved to the window away from the cackling voices of the animated teapots and saucers in *Beauty and the Beast*. 'Actually, things have been difficult. I wanted to ask you a question, Priya. What do you do by way of spiritual life?' Jan craned her neck forward to anticipate Priya's reply.

Priya wanted to laugh. This was so like Jan. Straight in with the religion. 'Do you mean with Whack?'

'With Whack, but also for yourself,' she said, taking a sip of white wine with her long mouth.

'Whack has two godmothers, Jocelyn and Patience. You've

met Patience before, haven't you? She's had to go off to the hospital. She's on duty this evening.'

'The reason I'm asking is that Leo and I have been trying for a baby.'

'I didn't know that,' said Priya, amazed at her own ability to stay cool when she felt as if she might jump right out of her skin. 'I thought you'd decided you didn't want one,' she added, trying to figure out a way to respond.

'Well,' said Jan in her very proper voice. 'At first Leo didn't want to, but then he agreed, and it's now been almost eighteen months since we've been trying all sorts of things and nothing has worked. Recently I've become really depressed about it. That's why we haven't been seeing anyone, even good friends like you and Ben. Leo has been very down too. I think he thinks it's his fault, sometimes, and then at other times he goes back to thinking that we shouldn't have any children. I had an abortion in my early twenties, so Leo thinks the problem must be with him, even though our GP says it doesn't always work like that.'

'Have you tried . . .' stumbled Priya, because every kind of question that had flashed through her head she didn't want to hear the answer to. Jan was the type to describe at length the time of night, the temperature checks, and all the details of how they were supposed to have intercourse.

'I can't get Leo to come to the doctor with me. We might go the IVF route, we might adopt. I don't know, I need time to think about it. In the middle of all this my friends are all beginning to have children and though I don't believe in God in the traditional sense, I find myself asking, Why me? And then my best friend from school, Serena, with the big house in Kentish Town, has been dumped by her rich husband.' Crispin looked in at the door, realized they were having an earnest conversation, then turned and started watching the video with the children. He made a smart alec joke about one of the character's clothes which none of them paid any attention to. 'Serena had two kids, a third on the way,' Jan continued. 'One fine day her husband comes home and tells her he's having an affair with some nineteen-year-old floozie. How clichéd can you get? But that's not the end. A few weeks earlier they had found out that the baby she was pregnant with, that was about to be born, was severely brain-damaged. It will barely be able to see or speak. And still the bastard walked out of the door and has gone to some flat to live with his bimbo.'

'How is she coping?' said Priya. Laughter came from next door. 'Did she have a job? Is there any chance of a reconciliation?'

'They've tried all that. Marriage counselling. It's definitely over. He's gone. She's on Prozac and wouldn't have him back even if he tried. She's had to give up her job to look after the kids, especially the baby. He's got lots of money, so there are no financial worries, but she's had a horrendous time. You know what the first thing I thought about when I heard about Serena? I thought, Thank God it's not me. There was my friend, my best friend, so furious with her husband she wouldn't let him come near the children. I used to take her to the hospital for frequent check-ups during her pregnancy. Trying to find out if she could abort her baby. Feeling guilty about it because she was into the twenty-third week of her pregnancy. I couldn't even bear to tell Leo. I kept thinking, What if Leo did that to me? I don't think I could go on living. It's so pathetic. We don't even have any children. That's when I realized I needed help.'

In her head Priya was thinking, I must be in some kind of

movie or something. She was surprised to hear herself speaking normally. 'What you felt was like a kind of *Schadenfreude*. We all feel those things sometimes. It's not unnatural.'

'It was bad, Priya, really bad, it showed me that all I was ever thinking about was me. Even Serena could tell. One day I was sitting drinking tea with her and she sent me home, told me to fuck off out of her kitchen with my sick self-pity and my even-worse-off-than-thou-help-mate attitude. She didn't need it, she said. Somehow, maybe because I was so paranoid about it, she read my mind. I tried to see her again, but she wasn't interested. That's why I was asking you about spirituality.'

At this point Priya couldn't help overhearing the loud voices coming from next door. 'Poor Ted,' she could hear Rebecca say. Who are they talking about, she wondered. Priya made a mental effort to cut out the voices and concentrate on what Jan was telling her.

'First I thought of going to therapy,' Jan told her. 'I went to this man for about six weeks. He was worse than useless. His answer to everything I ever said was, "I know." "I'm feeling terrible about my friend." "I know," he would say. "I'm finding it difficult to get to sleep at night." "I know." He made me so angry I thought I might kill him. But then a friend at college – I'm doing a part-time degree in jewellery design now – this friend took me to a lecture at the Buddhist Centre on the Holloway Road by a Sri Lankan monk. That lecture changed me. For the past three months I've been part of a meditation group in Stoke Newington and I try to do twenty minutes of it every day at home.'

Priya's first thought was, What the hell can Jan understand about Buddhism? She didn't have much time for self-help types looking for salvation.

'It's not what people think,' continued Jan. 'Peace, calm,

relaxation. Those are stereotypical views of meditation. It's more about facing your fears; examining different states of mind; the aggression and competitiveness that bubble to the surface. I don't talk about it to most people. They just think it's universal-loving-kindness mumbo-jumbo.'

'Can you two break up your cosy chat and come through now?' called Ben. 'I'm serving up dinner.'

'I wanted to talk to you,' said Jan, 'because I know you studied religion at college.' They got up from the faded chaise longue and made to move towards the kitchen. 'If I talk to Leo about it he just switches off. He says it's my way of compensating for the disappointment of not having a baby. He hates the mention of religion. It's ingrained in him from Jocelyn. But it's not that I've given up my desire to have a baby or any of my other wants, quite the opposite. Buddhism works very hard at taking away the emphasis on self, which I find very useful. I can't get over the selfish way I thought about Serena, how it ruined our friendship.'

'The strange thing', said Priya, 'is that even though I studied religion and read quite a lot about it, I'm afraid I'm with Leo on this. I still am quite anti-religious, anti-any-god. I ended up being more interested in how religion has caused so much bloodshed, so much pain, war, indoctrination, nationalism; I became interested in the social side of religion, the politics of it. Even with Buddhism, which doesn't proselytize – and as religions go is nearer to a system of philosophy – in Mongolia and Sri Lanka, for example, monks who are meant to be non-violent have turned violent in the name of their faith. I became interested in the way religion oppresses rather than the way you see it as a liberating force. I suppose I'm very wary of Westerners or Westernized Indians ignoring the political problems in the world, and just sitting on a mountain top talking about lack of self,' she said. 'It just shows the different parts of the world we come from. Or maybe it shows I'm more cynical than you. I must go and help Ben or he'll be angry.'

The conversation had started Priya thinking. It had been so long since she had revisited her wish to do religious studies at school, when she had been absorbed not so much in the teachings of the Buddha as in his life. How he had slipped out of his palace one night when he was twenty-eight, leaving his sleeping wife and child, and gone off into the forest for the rest of his life. It reminded her of the way in which Plath had locked and sealed the door on her sleeping children, leaving them milk and bread. Both parents abandoned their families. Both then became famous. How could anyone bear to leave their children, and how could she have thought that Gautama was so noble for having done so? She wanted to think some more about it.

Hosts, friends and relatives sat round the large stone table. Everyone had their plateful of food. From next door came the muted voices of the video.

'This rice is fantastic,' said Rebecca. 'What have you got in here? Nuts, onions, and I can smell something rather unusual.'

'Saffron, or it could be the curry leaves I put in,' said Ben, loving Rebecca's caressing compliments.

'I can see the way the saffron is flecking some of the grains orange. It looks so beautiful,' she went on.

'Do you have this recipe in your book?' asked Jocelyn.

'Sadly, I don't. It's a bit too elaborate and I wanted to keep the recipes simple. I'm trying to include a version of it in the new book. In India they sometimes add rosewater to it, but I find the smell can be overpowering.'

'*Kewda*,' said Jehan. 'My mother used to spread this horribly garish beaten silver over the top.'

'At some weddings they put gold foil, just to show how rich they are,' said Priya.

'Never at a Patnaik wedding, I trust,' said Jehan.

'Especially at a Patnaik wedding,' Ben rejoined.

'In my grandfather's time you'd be lucky if you had a party at all. Everything was pared down to the basics.'

'So, Ben, how is school?' asked Jehan.

'I had a hair-raising experience today . . .' He began the story of Mr Gibbs and Marlon while noticing that Priya had started a conversation with Richard. He felt vexed by this. She knew nothing about how hard school could be, and today he had an awful incident to tell her about, and here she was treating him as if what he had to say was going to be boring. As he told his story he noticed with gathering irritation that Priya was still talking to his parents and that Jocelyn and Jan were also listening to that conversation.

Priya felt it was incumbent upon her to talk to Mary and Richard. They had been quiet for an hour or so, and her father-in-law looked decidedly stiff. 'So how are you occupying your time these days, Richard?' she asked.

'I have difficulty explaining it to myself. I haven't been able to get out into the garden much because it's been raining all the time. I'm learning about computers and there are the finances to keep control of. A few shares, that kind of thing.'

'Is that very complicated?'

'It shouldn't be, but I have to keep abreast of all the changes and every year there seem to be so many. You see,' he said to Leo, wagging his finger in the air like an admonishing priest, 'I was an accountant, and even after my retirement my extended family, of which there are many, expect me to do their accounts.'

On the other side of the table Ben was coming to the end of his story. 'It's only when things like this happen that one notices how difficult life in school can be. The other day a colleague and I' – he was careful not to mention Helen's name – 'were just leaving school when' – Ben noticed that more people round the table were tuning into his story – 'one of the teachers ran past us, saying that there was a gang of Bengali boys rampaging through the school with a long knife and some sticks. Apparently the gang were chasing two black boys. I looked at my colleague and said, "Let's get out of here before we get involved." As we were leaving we saw this six-foot boy legging it across the playground in front of us and then climbing a tree to try and get over the wall into the street.'

'But this is just the kind of vision of comprehensives that frightens parents from sending their children there,' said Rebecca with concern in her voice.

Ben laughed, and Priya said, 'Ben, you're giving everyone the impression that it's a jungle out there. Surely these are isolated incidents.'

'I'm only laughing because it was so funny to see this huge lanky black guy shouting at us from the top of a tree that his life was in danger with no one visibly chasing him. It took some time to get him down to talk to us. In a big school like Tachbrook there are fights, intruders, drugs, police getting called in – it feels inevitable. But then you go into your class and get on with teaching, and the students range all the way from girls going to Cambridge to girls heading for pregnancy at fifteen to boys who might be nicking stereos out of cars in their spare time. It's not a jungle, it's a reflection of what things are really like.'

'You really should try and write about this,' said Jehan. 'Forget about the East/West food thing for a while, especially if you're stuck. Everybody seems to be doing the East/West thing nowadays. The other day I saw cardamom-flavoured chocolate ice cream on the menu at some restaurant.'

Ben wanted to slide a long icicle up Jehan's arse. With one flippant remark he had torn into Ben's project, a project he had been struggling with for two years.

'But surely something can be done about all this gangsterishness? You can't just throw up you hands and let it happen,' preached Rebecca.

'Of course not. I hope I'm not sounding like an apologist. Teachers don't just throw up their hands. But you also have to recognize what the time limits are and where people are coming from. We've had CCTV put in at our school and at one time we even had security guards, though apparently having security guards made the whole situation much worse. The school got branded. It became famous for being a dangerous place, with fourteen-year-old National Front reps handing out leaflets in the corridors.'

Ben got up and went to the pot of biryani to serve people seconds. He found it alarmingly empty. Oh well, fuck them, he thought to himself, fuck the lot of them. Everyone's doing East/West cookbooks, are they? Well, mine's not the same, mine is different, it's going to set the world alight. Then a pain pierced the core of his stomach, the searing pain of self-knowledge, the pain of his languishing incomplete manuscript. What he'd done was not very good, and whatever it was, however good it was, it was never going to set the world aflame and he was never going to be as famous as Jehan, or have such a glamorous and adoring wife, who wasn't going to deceive him the way that Priya had done. 'There's some biryani still going. Who would like some more?' he forced the words out to stem the tide of morbid thoughts.

'You've excelled yourself, Ben. This is the best yet,' said Jehan, accepting his offer. Ben gave him a recklessly generous helping.

There was a momentary lull in the conversation. Mary broke the silence. 'Are you terribly disciplined?' she asked Jehan. 'Or do you have to make yourself sit down and write? I hear from Ben you've been working very hard.'

'To be perfectly honest, I've been sleeping a lot, staying in bed till eleven or twelve.'

There was laughter and Mary looked puzzled. Ben felt his mother's vulnerability.

'I have a minimum amount I try to achieve every day, which is two pages. If I write more, well and good, but if I nail my two pages then I'm happy.'

'Four hundred pages in 200 days. That's pretty good going,' said Ben in a despairing voice.

'Do you revise stuff?' Crispin asked. 'Or are you like the writer I heard on the radio the other night saying that she could never change anything because it would be like breathing the same breath twice?'

Ben noticed that Rebecca had drifted off like a tributary and was having a deep conversation with Leo and Mauro.

'I certainly don't subscribe to that view,' said Jehan, 'and I don't believe many writers do. Everything I write is endlessly revised. Three or four times. I have two readers I trust who always come up with good suggestions. Sometimes,' he said, turning to Mauro and trying to attract his attention, 'the first draft can be nothing more than the initial brush strokes in a painting. If you're very lucky the whole thing comes out as it should be. It's rarely like that. Sometimes you have to chuck it out and start again. Think of the mountains of insertions and corrections that Proust made, or the different versions of Wordsworth's *Prelude* . . .'

'You're not banging on about Proust *again*,' boomed Ben.

'The thing is,' said Crispin, 'I'm terribly interested in this business of revision. As a barrister, I have to prepare submissions and the way these are worded plays a big part in influencing the judge's mind. You have to condense a story into the space of a page, and tell it well, while making sure that all the points of law are included. The effect on the judge can make all the difference to the verdict.'

'I suppose it's like the synopsis of a story,' came from Ben.

'More than that,' said Crispin. 'You have to pare everything down to the bones, while also alluding to the relevant points of law. The French call it "zéro style".' He pronounced the words with panache.

'Terrific phrase,' said Jehan. 'Cortázar is a wonderful exponent.'

How the fuck does Jehan know about Cortázar when I've never heard of him? thought Ben. Why is he so clever?

'I'm no good at that. I just whip the horse and let it gallop and if it goes over the top I try to tame it with punctuation and the delete button. My stuff would be unreadable in the first draft.'

It's pretty unreadable as it is, almost slipped out of Ben's mouth.

'But I think that as a novelist,' said Mauro, 'or as any kind of artist, one *must* go over the top. If one didn't take risks how would one know where one's limit lies?'

Ben came round to their side of the table. 'I favour the Quiller-Couch dictum: "Murder your darlings."'

'What's that supposed to mean?' said Jane, who had been listening intently to these exchanges.

'Get rid of the bits that are precious to you,' said Jehan.

'But that seems like a foolish instruction,' said Mauro. 'Why would anyone want to do that?'

'What's your next novel about?' Jane asked Jehan. Well primed with drink and cigarettes, Jehan took a deep breath and seemed as if he were about to start on something when the Tennyson parents began gathering their things and wished everyone goodnight. Martin tried to get Jocelyn to go as well, but she wanted to hear what Jehan was going to say about his new book.

Twenty-One

After the Tennysons left more wine flowed. Mauro rolled a joint. He offered it to Jehan, saying it was quite mild. There was a general uncoiling and rearranging of tired limbs as coffee and tea, fruit and a box of chocolates were passed round. Ashtrays were emptied, plates cleared away. Michaela came in to hug her daddy and then slid back to the video in the living room. Chairs were pushed away from the table as the pace of the evening slowed and the mood grew more expansive.

'So.' Jocelyn prompted Jehan. 'We all want to know what your new book is about.'

Jehan smiled benignly, laid an elbow on the empty chair to his left and took a drag at the joint passed to him by Mauro.

'First person, third person, conventional timescale?' asked Jane, in her slightly drunk but still prim voice.

Jehan smiled. He didn't mind the attention, but he certainly wasn't going to hurry to give them any kind of answer. 'I'm fascinated by what you said, Crispin, about zero style. I want to try and see if I can go in that direction in my next book. What would it be like to write in a very spare, almost lawyeristic way? Could you fax me some examples of these submissions you write?'

'I'll tell you what the novel is about,' said Rebecca, breaking off from her huddled conversation with Leo. 'It's about masturbation.'

Consternation and laughter.

'A whole novel about masturbation! Woman or man?' asked Jane with a tipsy gleam.

'Both,' answered Rebecca.

'I suppose the woman is frustrated in some way?' Jocelyn put in.

'I protest,' said Jehan, 'she's not frustrated. You don't have to be frustrated to masturbate. Not at the end of the twentieth century.'

'It's a bit depressing, though,' said Martin quietly. Everybody looked at him because he hadn't spoken a single word in the last hour. He went a bit white as if he had been attacked by a bout of nausea.

'Quite the opposite,' perked up Jane. 'It's when you've got a good sex life that you masturbate.'

'I couldn't agree more,' said Jehan.

'Is Rebecca in it?' asked Jocelyn.

The smile blew off Jehan's face.

'I'd better not be,' warned Rebecca.

'*I* want to be in it,' said Jane. 'Can you give me a cameo role?'

Jehan tried to make a joke, but Ben could see that he was beginning to find this philistine behaviour embarrassing. 'I could try and give you a role. In fact, you might already have a role that –'

'You don't want to be in a novel, Jane,' interrupted Jocelyn. 'You'd hate it. I have a few friends who have written novels and I'm always turning the pages thinking, Is this me, is *this* me?'

'I've been writing a story,' Leo said suddenly. 'A kind of essay-cum-story about my time in Central America.'

Ben wanted to guffaw. Priya winced. 'Why is it that men always have the need to write something?' she asked.

'When I was in Belize,' Leo went on, undeterred, 'I recorded a lot of conversations and words from the local dialect, and I realized that they were using words completely differently. Not just words, but the concepts behind them were strange to me. For instance they call lies snacks.'

Everyone looked confused. Rebecca spoke. 'Exactly, that's what a snack is – a lie you tell to your stomach.'

Jehan looked bored.

'They have many other words like this, much funnier ones.'

'That's extraordinary,' Rebecca said, her eyes kindling.

Priya went into the living room to check on the kids. Rebecca and Leo continued their intense dialogue about the cultural specificity of words. 'Mind-fucking,' thought Priya.

'The other thing I realized while experimenting with trying to write this piece,' Leo pushed on, 'was that when two people are talking to each other in a story you can write about more than what they are saying. Like what's going on in their heads, represent their inner picture of the world.'

'Absolutely,' Rebecca said, her eyes dancing like honey bees in his direction.

'It made me think,' Leo continued, 'if in the story a Westerner is talking to a woman from Belize you can represent the way they understand each other, but also conceptually how they can never really understand each other because inside and outside they inhabit such separate worlds.'

Rebecca threw her hair back and reddened a bit. Others were beginning to become aware of the chemistry in the room. She and Leo had been talking to each other for most of the dinner.

'Do you find', Leo asked Jehan, 'that in your writing you can make characters think and speak at the same time?'

'Sure. It's what makes novels so pleasurable – the reader has access to the characters' darkest, most embarrassing thoughts. But I don't buy this idea that the characters in a novel take on a life of their own. I think the writer controls what the characters do and he must remain in charge of them. They should flinch every time he comes near them.'

Jane jumped in. 'Yes, but what novels can do is show us how there are some people you meet once or twice, at a party maybe, and then you have very little to say to them and they don't impinge on you in any way. They just interrupt the flow.' Ben's sister's speech was getting slurred and her elbow seemed to be sliding across the table towards Jehan.

'Why would you want them to appear, then? What would you say about them anyway?' asked Ben, reflecting the group's puzzlement.

'Novels cut out a lot of these inconsequential encounters, surely. That's why good novels are more interesting than life,' said Leo triumphantly.

'Quite the reverse,' said Jocelyn. 'No novel is ever as interesting as life, never as depressing and never as joyful. I think you're all quite mad and have had far too much to drink. The best novels are novels that give you some information, historical novels, for instance. *The Lions of Albion*, now that's what I call a bloody good read. Don't say you've never heard of it? Oh come now, Jehan. That's simply amazing. She is simply one of the best historical writers around. What I can't be doing with are novels about the trials and tribulations of middle-class north London couples. We've had enough of those to last us fifty years. Whingeing double-income liberal parents, please let us have no more of their banal utterances.'

'But I love novels that are set in the present,' said Jane. 'And I like novels that move me with their intelligence, the sheer force of their language, the power, the lucidity of language . . .'

'Jane, it's past nine, I do think we must be going,' said Crispin. 'Get the kids to bed.'

'I must ask Jehan one more quick question,' said Jane sliding her hand into her hair, leaning across towards him and sounding more and more like our mother, thought Ben. 'Do you think, Jehan, that all the characters novelists invent are like our dreams, versions of ourselves, as Freud would have it, or that they come from universal archetypes handed down through the ages?'

'I'm not sure Freud knew much about writing novels.'

'Or about art, for that matter,' said Mauro. 'Although he did say something interesting about artists in his essay on Leonardo. He said that he thought great artists were those who had some flaw in their vision.'

Half the group were gathering discarded shoes, socks, sweaters, coats. Jocelyn stood up. Martin was already by the door, saying to Jehan, 'Very nice to see you again.' Jocelyn joined them and wished Jehan goodbye, saying, 'I'm afraid to say I really don't think I will be reading your next book.'

Priya behaved as if she hadn't heard this comment and ushered Jocelyn, putting an arm round her waist, out of the door. She'd had enough for one evening. Thankfully, Jan and Leo left with his mother. Mauro collected Michaela, and as they left he and Ben discussed their next tennis engagement. Priya took Whacka downstairs to put him to bed. Jehan was finishing a joint in the kitchen. 'Come on,' said Rebecca. 'We must leave them.' But they stayed another five minutes, while Jehan gave Ben some advice about his writing. A cab arrived. Hugs and kisses. And finally, they have all gone.

The kitchen is glutted with debris: food, toys, dirty glasses, plates, cutlery, balloons, wrappers of all kinds, half-eaten sweets, ripped party bags, bits of clothing, hats, shoes, pots and pans, half a tray of grilled chicken, a mound of rice, curling sandwiches, cartons of juice, empty beer bottles, a couple of brimful ashtrays, slices of cake, half-chewed biscuits, jam tarts, cold clods of samosa, bottles of wine and whisky. Whack is asleep in his broken cot. A wild thing gradually renewing its energy for the new morning. The excitement of his birthday had ended in a fit of sobbing, a pathway from irritable tiredness to satisfying slumber. Priya remembers how he used to cry himself to sleep as a baby. The guilt she had felt at leaving him there with his long-drawn-out yelps. His third year is over, his day is over, only snapshots are left, a version of his life spooled up and laid to rest in little black canisters with grey lids. And what happens to adults, thinks Priya, as she comes up the stairs to the kitchen to sit with Ben, how are we meant to handle the end of a birthday party? The sense of relief she feels is almost the best feeling of the day. And yet a sense of anticlimax accompanies it.

Ben was sitting at the kitchen table greedily skinning up a fat joint from the little bag that Mauro had left him. Priya slopped some of the three-quarters-empty duty-free Black Label, brought by her brother on his last trip to London, into a tumbler that looked like hers. They both sat rather splayed in the kitchen. 'I'm so exhausted,' said Priya.

'So am I,' said Ben, reiterating the universal moan of the overworked, over-entertaining parent classes. 'It wasn't too bad, was it?'

'Your biryani disappeared.'

'I cooked too much rice. I had to leave a pile of it out of the mixture.'

'We can use it again, can't we?'

'Nah, it's overcooked and gloopy. That's a virtually terminal

state if you're a rice grain.' Ben chuckled. 'Terminal or unre-
solvable, which is the correct word?'

'The kebabs went fast.'

'Shame about the barbecue,' he lied. 'Half the chicken's
marinating in the fridge. We can use it tomorrow. If I can
cook anything ever again.'

'People always eat what's there,' said Priya taking a swig of
her whisky. 'Look at that empty fruit bowl.'

'That's Crispin. If there's fruit he'll finish it.'

'I normally hide some of it away when he comes round,'
said Priya getting up and taking a drag from the joint before
leaving the kitchen to go to the toilet.

Yes, but Crispin knows your hiding places by now. And so
do I, thought Ben, otherwise I never would have found Leo's
letter in your *Bhagavad Gita*. It was because I know she stows
letters and money in books . . . No, please don't go there
again, mind yourself, step back, stop. An end to quicksand
story lines and their dragnet questions. If you had never read
Leo's letter, would things have been different? Would it have
been better or worse not to have known? For the hundredth
time he asked himself. And then, like the smell of a poisoned,
decaying rat under the floorboards, something that you hoped
would go away, so you didn't have to rip out the nails and
scoop up the imploded entrails, came the thought of that
blood test, the one he had decided not to have. The reasoning
was simple. If he found out what he already knew in his heart,
that Whacka was Leo's blood, what difference would it make?
Would it make him relinquish his boy? Would it make him
love him less? Would he hate or love Priya less if by some
accident Whacka turned out to be his? Why does blood matter
so much? We're all the same bones, sinews, tissues, arteries,
the same shit, the same piss. Look at his students – he could

be the father of so many of them, the half that didn't have fathers. Whacka would always be his. He would never give him up. It was an animal thing. He was like the wolf in the story looking after Romulus and Remus.

His thoughts spun round on the carousel of his persecuting mind. Once again he felt like Milton's Satan wrapped in the adamantine chains of hell. 'Round he throws his baleful eyes.' He wanted to get free of himself. Focus on something else. What if he hadn't found the letter? And what if he could behave as if he hadn't? These were the questions Anouchka had asked him. While he had been going over his obsessional pseudo-philosophical rubbish about the importance of coincidence and contingency. Anouchka had said, 'I wonder, Ben, if you have ever considered what it might feel like to behave, to live, as if you hadn't found the letter. What if you could retrace your steps to the point where you opened the book and happened upon Leo's letter? What if you walked to the shelf where the book was and then remembered something you had to do?' 'Or something I had to eat,' Ben had joked. 'And then you forgot about looking in the book and life went on from there.' He had said, 'I would give anything for my life to go back there, to that very minute before I uncovered the letter.' At least an hour of each day since finding the letter has been spent thinking, If only that had never happened, if only he hadn't left them alone on that night in Wales, before the crater opened beneath his feet, before that moment of rupture, and still, he thought, he'd give anything to be back before the letter, never to have known the truth.

He heard Priya flushing the toilet. The millisecond before I opened that book and found the letter my life was the same as it is now, the same dissatisfactions, same worries, same obsessions, same guilt. Is that what Anouchka meant?

Priya yawned and stretched. She came up behind Ben and placed her arms round his neck. He stiffened slightly. 'Do you want a little more of this?' he asked, holding up the joint. Priya took it, smiled and sat down.

Twenty-Two

They resumed their post-mortem of the party. 'Whacka had a good time, didn't he?' said Ben.

'He had a brilliant time.'

'Did you see his face when he got the Superman suit?'

'We'll have to give him the rocking horse tomorrow. And the cricket bat. You must teach him to play cricket.'

'If it ever stops raining,' said Ben, looking at the tall spattered windows.

'The clown was weird. Did you see the way he was throwing bits of food at the children?'

'He didn't!'

'When the kids were eating their tea. God, I've become so English,' said Priya. 'I'd never have used a phrase like "eating their tea" in the first few years I was here.'

'When I came in,' said Ben, 'he was asking them, "Is it somebody's birthday?" and then all the kids shouted yes and he answered in a creepy voice, "It's not, no, it's not, no, it's not."'

'He didn't treat my boy special,' cried Priya in the upset tone of a little girl, 'like they're meant to.'

'I saw the clown giving him a big rabbit-shaped balloon. I think the clown was depressed. Did you see how he sat in the corner at the end of the party, knees up, scoffing a plateful of food. His painted eyes looked so sad.'

'They say lots of comedians are depressives. Rebecca was really worried about you. She kept telling me that the clown was treating you badly and that I should go and see if you were all right.'

'That's shrinks for you. What can I say? I was putting on that sulky face to make the kids laugh. It wasn't serious.'

'Your mother did well, jigging about with the clown's wig.'

'Watch it,' he said, passing her the joint.

'I thought it was very sporting of her.'

They both sat in silence for a while. Priya leant her head back and listened to raindrops spitting at the panes. The wind seemed to have come up and was whipping the windows, whistling through the gaps and cracks in the old sash boxes. She took a deep breath and let the air out of her lungs like a carpet being unrolled.

Ben found himself dragged back to his earlier thoughts. He remembered some lines from Leo's letter. Its contents were banal, reassuring even. Leo had wanted, in his letter, to confirm that he would never make any claim to Whacka or interfere in his upbringing. He'd wanted to reaffirm his friendship. He had apologized. He used the word 'sullied'. Something about regret for having 'sullied' what had been a beautiful friendship. He hoped that after months and years had passed their friendship might revive. Ben had used every word of Leo's like a stone in a sling, firing them at Priya's heart. As if she might have known the inner meaning, the alternative meanings, the implicit meaning, of each of Leo's utterances. Ben wanted facts. Not emotion, not subjectivity, not bullshit about friendship. As if, once he knew everything for certain his own course of action would suddenly become clear. He could feel tension seizing his neck.

The wind galloped at the side of the house. How like some kind of Judas in reverse, an emblem of self-deceit, he had kissed Jan when they had said goodbye at the end of the party.

She was the innocent angel who was being spared the ugliness of her partner's deed. How unjust, thought Ben. Why should that be allowed? Why hadn't he just taken her aside and told her? Instead of giving her leftover samosas in a bag, knowing that she loved Indian food. What had made him feel so generous towards them? Was it some kind of Christian self-punishment? Sometimes it felt as if he just couldn't be bothered. Hating someone involved effort, commitment even. Wouldn't it have been better to have had the balls to throw open the door and fling them out of the party. 'Just fuck off out of here, both of you, get out of my house! You're not welcome!' And then what? His son's birthday tainted with hate, with violence. Better to be like his father, who had never made a scene in his life.

'Jehan was nice today,' said Priya breaking into his thoughts. 'You two seemed to be having a heavy discussion.'

'Pompous bastard. Telling me how I should forget about writing my book and take a holiday. "East/West cooking is everywhere these days,"' Ben mimicked. 'As if that was going to cheer me up.'

'What did he mean?'

'I don't want to go into it,' said Ben, feeling a rising, vomitous aversion towards Jehan.

But Priya continued playfully, 'How can he say that to you when he produces a book a year?'

'There's more to life than producing a book a year.' Ben knew Priya so well. He could tell where this conversation might go. And still, like a child being invited into a dark chamber, he allowed himself to be led in. 'Anyway, it's not true that he produces a book a year.'

'Why don't you give up and stop torturing yourself about your writing?'

'I *have* stopped,' Ben lied. 'When did I last say anything about it?'

'I saw the look on your face when they were discussing Jehan's book.' Why am I messing with his mind like this? I should leave him alone, thought Priya. Let's just relax and enjoy this joint while the wind howls outside. 'Come on, Ben, tell the truth, you're a bit jealous, aren't you? You wish you could be like Jehan producing lots of books.'

'Me, jealous of Jehan? You're right, I *am* jealous of Jehan. I'm jealous of his wife. I'd like to give her one.'

Priya smirked. 'She's got no tits, what would you hold on to?'

'Now look who's jealous.'

'And no arse.'

'When she walks into a room everyone turns to look at her.'

'And everyone looks at Leo, when he walks into the room,' she mumbled.

'What was that?' he snapped.

'Nothing. I didn't say anything.'

'You bloody well did!' He was on the point of barking, 'I'm going to bed.' He was standing up. 'My son's birthday' – the irony of that phrase was never lost on Ben – 'on my son's birthday, you dare to mention the name of that disgusting, grovelling man with his flower-power wife?' He stopped by her chair. 'What did you say, anyway? Come on, say it. I missed the full import of your wisecrack.'

'Look, Ben, it was a stupid joke. I admit it. Let's not spoil the evening.'

'You coward,' he said, interrupting her contemptuously.

No man, no woman, no speaking thing ever got away with calling a Patnaik a coward. It was an issue of blood. Priya's family was being insulted. Her grandparents had gone to gaol for their truths, for their beliefs. Her mother had risked gaol – been divorced – outcast. 'To thine own self be true,' she'd always told Priya. Blood will have blood. It boiled in Priya's veins. She looked at her husband, harsh, defiant, reckless. It was almost as if they had been taken over by monstrous parts of themselves that had lain hidden all day, that had been successfully leashed. Now, just when both were exhausted, party over, guests gone, when it was time for rest, angry words like black bats flew out of their mouths. She weighted each syllable with venomous care. 'Everyone looks at Leo when he walks into the room. That's what I said.' Ben's face crumbled like a biscuit in a child's hand. Then she made to get up from her chair, but he grabbed her by the shoulders, and thrust her back. The push was not strong enough to throw Priya and the chair on to the floorboards, but Priya let out a histrionic screech and turned her descent into a topple and sprawl. There she lay prostrate.

Priya rose slowly, looking at him, a warrior, eyes flashing with indignation. Gongs of sound boomed at Ben from her bunched-up rabbit-like body. 'Are you going to hit me?' She leant forward, arms hanging by her sides, fists clenched. '*You* are the coward!' There was no thought now, just a sense of release, from the year of imprisonment. 'I'm going to say what I want to say. Why shouldn't I?' she shouted. An awful surge of power that made her body tremble as she spoke. 'The truth is,' she said, returning to her favourite phrase, 'you're the one who is shit-scared – you're shit-scared to own your son, to love him, to make love to me, to look Leo in the eye, to compare yourself with Jehan. You're like a weed when you're talking to Jehan. A pathetic weed. Afterwards it's all talk about how he's a bastard, but when he's there you would never dream of contradicting him.' She sucked air in through her teeth. 'If only you could allow yourself to be a little like your normal self with him.' Ben stood silent, stunned by Priya's swift hits. 'Too scared to write your book. You shit bricks at the thought of penning another recipe, for fuck's sake! Can't you see how pathetic it all is?'

He tried to compose a response, but all he could feel was his constricted chest, and a pain there that felt like humiliation. How could he put an end to this vicious attack?

'The truth is you think Jehan is like some kind of god. Your envy is so huge it stops you from writing your recipe book, you can't be content with enjoying your teaching or advancing in your career at school, and the worst of it is' – intoxicated now by her own eloquence, the eloquence that hits a reeling man – 'that you go on whingeing in therapy about how it's all my fault. My fault? Do you have eyes? All you're doing is making other people feel guilty. But then, that's what gives you most pleasure and that's why you won't stop.'

'I've had enough of this.'

'Let me finish.'

'No. I will not let you finish.'

But she had the louder voice. 'That's why you can't bear to leave because it might give Whack and me the opportunity to make something of our lives. And what has Whack done to you? You can't let us off the hook. You can't stop making us feel guilty, blaming me for everything.'

The words were rushing at him like a train. And though he felt disgusted by them he was surprised at himself for noticing the animation in her face and the way her black hair hung over the side of it. He had almost forgotten how beautiful she was. His indignation took over again. 'How dare you try and turn this thing round at me with your manipulative lies? I despise you for bringing Whacka into this. When have I ever treated him badly? I adore him, you know that. You're the one who got us into this mess, with your lustful cesspit of a sex-crazed body. You're a whore! You have no idea how much I hate you for what you've done to me, to my family. I can't think of any expletives bad enough.' (Or was it good enough, leapt into his pedant's mind.)

'I am not a whore.' She advanced at him and stamped her foot. 'There is nothing wrong with what I did. I just had to pretend to have regretted it to keep this hollow marriage together, just for Arjun's sake. Hear this now. I've kept it in too long. I am not sex-crazed, depraved or anything. I didn't grow up like you in a hell-hole of suburban Victorian hypocrisy and repression. My family were not ashamed of their feelings. They didn't spend their lives trying to cover up the reasons for their fourteen-year-old daughter's death.'

'Priya! Don't defile my sister's name.' His voice broke on the last word.

'She was not a saint, damn it!' Priya banging the table, tears in her eyes. She was treading on Ben's hallowed ground. 'And I'll say this as well. I had sex with Leo. Not just once but twice. I had sex with a sexy man. A man who is my friend. It was a mistake. That's all there is to it. I don't love him. I'm not going to run away with him.'

'Stop it now!' Ben yelled. 'Or I'll leave the flat, I'll leave the room. Go and tell somebody else! I don't want to hear another word.'

'Threaten me as much as you like,' said Priya menacingly.

'Priya, I'll leave. This will be the end of us for ever. If you say another word that will be the end of us. It will be over. I beg of you, I can't stand it.' His voice started to break again. She must be stopped. He would be destroyed. Everything would be destroyed.

Ben moved towards the door. Priya sprang there first and cut him off. She barred his exit by placing her back up against the little rectangular coloured panes of glass set into the door. She grasped the handle behind her back. Her voice was husky, clenched, but as soon as she made to speak he plugged his ears with his fingers and started to hum loudly, as he used to do as a kid when his sister was teasing him. Priya had been here many times before, and normally she'd stop speaking and walk out. But now she started the most blood-curdling speech. She went into her orgasmic, prehistoric yell. This was a voice that had pedigree. Its forefathers had given speeches to thousands of freedom-fighters, to village meetings, had calmed the unrest of angry masses. Ben could not test his hum without removing his fingers from his ears, and that would let in Priya's simple message. Every cell in Priya's body pitched into her voice. 'It was good. I don't regret it. It was good. Do you hear?' That was her mother's old-fashioned phrase, and it came to help her at her moment of truth. 'It *was* good. The sex was good.' Eleven months she had waited to let this out. Whatever happened now it was out there in the world and she wasn't ashamed of it. So intoxicated was Priya that she almost missed the shape of his fingers making for her throat. For a second she thought she might have driven him to kill her.

But he was still trying to plead with her. Out of sync now with the portentous words that had left her mouth. 'Priya, the neighbours are banging on the ceiling.'

'I sucked his cock.' Like soup being spilled from a bowl, her madness splashed on the floor. Maybe I want to destroy everything, she thought. Like a child who dared herself to do something stupid and has done it. A picture is always the worst. Storyboarded by her, the image would never leave his head.

Ben thought he would strangle the words back into her throat. They had spilt out and he was going to squeeze the poison back into its bag. He would push time backwards, down her gullet, spoon the gall back into her mouth and make her swallow. All his effort spent trying to hold himself together, and here, with one swipe, the gash had been opened again. Unless he could somehow force the words back.

He really had gone mad. How could he ever have thought that something good was going to happen today – wrong, wrong, wrong as usual. How could he have thought that this woman could make him happy? It was this thought that made his hand smash at the glass pane behind her. The first time he aimed at a red pane and broke it. He could feel his right knuckle was cut, but the injury to the door was minor. Barely visible. Now he went at it structurally. He aimed his tennis hand, his hardest serve, straight into the thin wooden frame that held the glass, remembering to keep his hand on the other side, so he wouldn't tear his wrist pulling it back. He used his hand like an axe. One side of the framework shattered into bird-bones of glass and metal. It was frightening for Priya to have to look into his frozen face. She remembered her dream, where Whacka had come crashing through a glass door in the aftermath of an explosion. 'Stop it, you bastard!' she howled.

He finished the job by tearing out the last bits of dark blue pane using his fingers. I must get my hand through that door, open it from the other side and get out of here, he told himself. As he made to do this he was disturbed by a crash behind him. Priya had somehow managed to heave their granite-top table and throw it over on to the wooden floor. 'I'm not going to be treated like this. I'd rather be a rat, a dog, anything, but not this. You are not going to shut me out.'

Ben glanced at the broken plates and wine glasses, the

floorboard into which a corner of granite had sunk. Their most expensive possession misaligned. They had saved for it and had cherished it. 'I don't care,' he snorted. 'Do what you want. I'm leaving.' He turned on her with a look full of hate, and spoke in a way he had never spoken before. 'You whore!' Then he disappeared down the narrow stairs that hid Whacka's rocking horse to the basement where the three-year-old boy was sleeping through his parents' trauma.

A mad impulse-vision entered Ben's mind. In it he was smashing all the windows in the house. He would wake all the neighbours. He would wake Whacka. He would rouse the street with ambulances and police cars. Should he try and bundle him up and take him with him now? Where was he going? He thought of driving to his parents' house. He had school tomorrow morning. He would not take the day off. No, he would go to Mauro's. Or should he wake Jane? He couldn't stand the thought of Crispin's face. He would leave Whacka for now, the boy was exhausted. He would be bewildered to be woken. There would be some kind of terrible struggle with Priya. No, it wouldn't work, he must go on his own, he would sort Whack out later. Thoughts came to him of negotiating times when he would be dropping off Whack at Priya's door. Why should she have the flat? Let her roam the streets and sleep on friends' floors. The divorced father, picking up and dropping off the children. A fate he'd always wanted to avoid.

He had stopped outside Whack's bedroom, wondering whether to peep at his sleeping face, when the voice he least wanted to hear rushed at him like a tornado. 'Don't even dream of it. If you want to take your cowardly self off, then fuck off, I don't want you here. But don't you even dream of touching my baby.' Out of kindness to him it was always our son, your son, not *my son*, *my baby*. Now she said it with serrated emphasis.

'I don't need you to tell me how to treat him. I'll come back for Whacka when he's awake. And, oh, while I'm away, you can suck as many cocks as you like, but I will take my child as far away from you as can be.'

She thudded down the stairs after him. Ben was ready. This time he was going. Priya convinced herself that she was having her child wrenched away from her. She saw Whacka's fiery eyes when Patience swooped him out from between her legs and put him on her chest, still bloody and squashed-looking, Whacka gazing up at her. His black dots of love branded in her heart. For that look she would endure any pain, any anguish, any struggle. Amidst this ocean of trouble it was him she would cling to until her last drowning breath.

Twenty-Three

Ben found a bag, an old black sausage-sports-thing. What a pigsty this bedroom was. He started thinking of what he would need for the next few days. What does it matter what I wear? I must go into school. He picked up socks, pants, a shirt. Priya was at the door watching. He wasn't going to be able to find anything he wanted. There were kid's costumes and toys mixed in with torn pieces of wrapping paper and discarded presents from the morning. He picked up a damp towel and shoved it in his bag. He gave up trying to get it right. A couple of T-shirts, odd socks, a pair of boxers that might not be clean, an unsuitable tie. He gave the room a last swivelling glance. Goodbye, mess. 'Never again,' he said out loud, 'will I have to live in this shit hole.' Priya was silent.

Get out of here, he told himself. But, still, he couldn't help wondering if this time it would be for good. He couldn't keep up the charade: sacrificing everything for his broken ideal of a family. He would get custody of Whacka. He would fight till his teeth were broken. What would happen to their sessions with Anouchka? He didn't want to go to them.

Ben made to leave the bedroom, but Priya was standing in the doorway and he could tell from her posture that she was not going to move. She looked at him with hatred. He tried to shield himself from it.

'Why don't you take your book?'

'What book? What are you talking about? Could I please be

allowed to leave?' he said in the horrid cold-soup voice of his father.

'What will you do? Will you push me again? Will you smash up another door?'

'I am not a violent person,' he said.

'So I'm the evil one?'

'You said it.'

'Yes, because that's how you have always painted me. The "bad sister" you once wrote on a card you sent me in Oxford. I don't want to be the "bad sister" for your convenience. It's always me. I'm the one in devil's clothing driving you out of the door.'

No way, thought Ben. This is her sorcery. Trying to suck me into a discussion. 'Okay, I'll admit it,' he said in as calm a voice as possible. 'You have ruined this family. You have destroyed our marriage, and yes, in this instance, it *is* all your fault. And, I hope you never forget it. I hope when Whacka grows up you don't feed him lies about what happened between us.'

'So, if a woman or a man makes a mistake they must pay for it for their entire lives? Is that your philosophy?'

'I'm not falling for that rhetorical crap.'

'You're too scared to listen to me, as Anouchka keeps telling you, because you know it will hurt. You just want me to button up – right? You want to run away. You want to put your fingers in your ears like a child and scamper out of the room. If I *am* the bad one, how come it's so difficult for you to hear what I have to say? Why do you always have to shun the truth?'

'You couldn't have put it better. What I'd like you to do is button up, leave me alone and let me out of this house. You're nothing to me any more, not even a bit of dirty chewing-gum on the floor. You're a piece of nothing.'

Once again he tried to get out but she stood firm, glaring into his eyes. She knew from the look on his face that he was loath to touch her. 'Fine, go. But before you go, just tell me one thing. Do you really think that when one person in a marriage is unfaithful, do you really imagine all the blame lies with that person? Do you really think – just do me the favour of answering this question honestly – do you really think that it is all one person's fault? Do you not think that the other person in the couple had a part to play? Did you have nothing to do with what happened between us?'

'Please move and let me out of this door,' said Ben in a voice that he recognized as being schoolteacherish.

'So, the fact that you were depressed, that you could think about nothing but your stupid book, that you often stayed up late at night watching television or reading rather than coming to bed with me, that when you did, you finished in two seconds flat and left me to my own devices – none of these things, according to you, made any difference?'

'Don't talk to me about "your own devices",' he mocked. 'And don't try to drag me into some pointless debate. You're a cesspit of lust.'

'I am a cesspit of lust that awakened you to sexual enjoyment. Do you remember how I found you and Leone lying on the floor in Oxford, frigid with anxiety? Do you remember? Who taught you about sex, for fuck's sake? Your mother? Your father?' It was her turn to mock. 'Your repressed homosexual schoolmasters?'

'Don't you dare talk like that about my mother and father. My mother is a decent honest person. What about honesty, Priya? What about *trust*? What about the fact that I can never trust you again? That every time you go out in the evening I still have a horrible panic in my stomach that you might be getting in between the sweaty sheets of some . . . Out of my way!' he shouted. 'I WANT TO GET OUT!'

'OF COURSE YOU DO! YOU WANT TO GET OUT OF YOUR SKIN. YOU BASTARD, YOU WANT TO GET OUT OF YOUR RESPONSIBILITIES. I don't want to be left here with a wrecked house. To wake up to glass all over the floor and a boy to whom I have to explain the whereabouts of his missing father.'

'Let me out,' said Ben, simmering down. 'You know you can't stay up all night like this. I *will* leave in the end and this is only making it worse.'

'I'll let you out when you answer my question.' Her words came fast and furious. 'When you stop persecuting me, when you stop calling me a slut and a whore.' She lunged at him with her right arm. 'You bastard, you fucking bastard.' Pushing him on to the bed, she tried to bite his arm. Ben grabbed her wrists and forced them back. That's where Whacka gets his ferocious strength, he thought. But his tennis-playing hands were too strong for her; he prised her arms apart as if they were a lizard's feet. Forced her hissing face off him and rolled her sideways on to the bed, all the time being very careful to avoid getting her body in a wrestling grapple.

She sprang back to the cupboard. This show of revulsion, this lofty aversion made her hysterical. 'Have you fucked Helen?'

Ben didn't answer.

'Have you fucked Helen, you bastard? Have you got your hands up her skirt yet?' She said 'bastard' in her old Indian accent.

'Of course I haven't, you know that. You have no right . . .'

'I have no right, only you have the right. Why haven't you fucked her? Is it so that you can hold all the moral high ground?' She grabbed hold of his jumper, a maroon V-neck he had had for many years, and as he tried to break free she ripped it down the front. 'You think I haven't read the filth in your notebooks, your pathetic fantasies. Just because I made a mistake, just once, went ahead and did something. What is the difference between my infidelity and your days and nights of head-fucking?' She caught hold of his ripped sweater and as he tried to push her away she tore it from his neck.

'I don't believe it, you've been snooping in my notebooks!' He was trying to recover from her violence, scared to leave her like this. 'How can you sink so low? Once! Once, was it? What about Marcus? How stupid I was to forgive you then? This is my punishment.' Then he did a terrible thing. He couldn't stop. He didn't mean to do it. He laughed. It just came out. Nervous laughter like frothing milk. It was more callous than anything that had gone before. He felt as if he had been wandering in a snow-covered field for a long time trying to find a way out. He had seen the exit now, it was freezing, he mustn't fall asleep, he must make for it without getting deflected.

'I didn't snoop. I just read a bit of the filthy meanderings on an open page,' she said scornfully.

'I'll tell you what the difference is between what you did and my notebook fantasies, you brainless baboon. You did something and I didn't. You tore up the trust, you made a hole, you destroyed things, and I, I haven't done anything. Have you never heard in your high-falootin' BBC world that thinking about something doesn't make it a crime? Thinking is not the same as doing.'

'Yes it is! You are too much of a coward to follow your gut. Your biggest fucking explosion is on the tennis court versus John Welsh or Mauro. The difference is that you want to do it to Helen, but you don't have the courage to follow your instincts. You're a dithering gentleman from Amersham who can't make up his mind which phrase to use and you will always be that. Hypocritical, afraid and self-righteous. Your parents don't even bother to go to church any more but they act like saintly fucking Christians and you, you are the product of that same double-standard lot. I loathe you, I loathe the place you come from, and the only mistake I made was to think that whatever happened I loved you. I want to make sure you understand something once and for all. I don't love Leo, or even fancy him any more. I loved you and you couldn't even see that. For a year I've been trying to get you to stop, stop persecuting me' – her voice broke – 'stop persecuting yourself, stop persecuting our son and our family, but no, you won't let go, because you can't let go of your petty self-righteousness, 'your "what will *my friends* think, what will *my family* think" attitude. Will my father gloat because he told me not to marry a Paki? *We* are your family damn it, Whacka and me, I loved you, Whacka loves you. Why wasn't that enough?'

'That's exactly what I want to know. Why wasn't it enough for you? Why did you have to . . . ?' He trailed off because he was aware of being dragged back into the argument. This was the same old road; he was losing sight of the gate in the snow-covered field. 'Okay, have you said what you want to say? Can I go now?'

'You can go now,' she said, beginning to cry, moving away from the door and sitting down on the edge of the bed.

As Ben went up the stairs he spoke to himself, loud enough for her to hear, 'What a waste of time.' His brain began to churn with the difficult prospect of what he might do when he went out of that door. He glanced at his watch and saw that it was ten minutes past eleven. He saw himself sitting in Mauro's dingy living room watching daytime television. *Supermarket Sweep. Ready Steady Cook.* No, he would go into school in the morning even if he was up half the night. Should he phone Mauro now?

Get out first. Just fleetingly he thought of the warmth of the bed downstairs. His bed, their bed. As he reached the door of the flat he stopped, wondering if he had forgotten anything essential. In his head was a voice saying, Don't stop, just go, get out. There were two doors to pass through. At this point he heard the beginnings of a cry, like a jackal in the desert. *Lost in the Desert*, about the boy in the Kalahari with his dog – he'd seen it three times at the local cinema in Amersham. Howls punctuated by sobs. Priya's footsteps plodded up the stairs, bringing her crying with her. He made for the door to the street.

Bag in hand, he went down the dingy-carpeted communal corridor. Behind him he saw Priya crouched down on her knees, her head sunk in the palms that lay in front of her, like someone praying to Mecca. She let out the most piercing howl, like Calypso being left on her island by Odysseus. They had not married for convenience, they had married because of their difference, they'd been a swivel of black and white chocolate, a multiracial lolly – the way Ben had imagined them in the early hours of this day. They were nations joined together, not just people. They were the hopes of humanity reaching across thousands of miles of separating ocean. Their love was post-colonial, post-modern, post-everything. This was their nationalism, their pride, their today, their tomorrow. Not like the sister who had abandoned him without expla-nation, not like the mother who had left her for four months without explanation. The feminist radical, the anti-racist marcher, the reader of Gramsci and Marx, Foucault and Fanon, was laid up on the floor, head in her hands, wailing without restraint like a wolf torn from her cubs. Fingers crawled up the inside of her neck and she wanted to push them out, like giving birth, but worse, because here was no hope, no sense of imminent relief.

Ben stood in the open doorway, robbed of the ability to feel or think. His wife was crying as he had never seen her before. His black sports bag propped open the front door through which a wet London wind was blowing. He leant his back against the wall and tried to muscle decisions out of his brain. He heard a door slam upstairs and a set of feet came thudding down. Mick's drunken red face appeared, his hair a mess. 'This is too much! I canna get to sleep. Carol is tired. Have you not heard me banging on the floor? You'll have to stop all this right now unless you want me to call the police.'

'Ben,' said Priya, 'will you please shut the door and tell him to go upstairs.'

'Tell *me* to go upstairs? You canna be serious. You don't own the place, you know. You owe me an apology. You're not in India now, love. We have our rights too.'

'Mick,' said Ben with controlled anger in his voice. 'I'm sorry about the noise.'

'I'm going upstairs and if I hear any more of yous I'm gonna havta phone the polis. Get a divorce, for Christ's sake. All this shouting and screeeming and cryin',' he muttered as he went up the stairs.

'Yeah, why don't you drink a little less,' Ben muttered back.

'What did you say?' threatened Mick coming back down the stairs. 'I've got your number . . . You're a marked man, Johnny.'

'It's not Johnny, it's Ben. And while you're at it, why don't you stop making Carol cry every night?'

'I'm phoning the polis, I'm phoning the focking polis,' shouted Mick.

'Leave it, Ben, for God's sake, don't be stupid,' said Priya.

'Okay, mate, I'm sorry, all right. I'm just a bit upset, that's all. I'm sorry we've kept you up. I'll keep the noise down.' Thus placated, Mick went back up to his flat and left Ben standing in the doorway. The front door was still propped open with his bag. What should he do? He didn't want to leave Priya like this. Again the voice in his head said, Go, Ben, go. Take yourself out of that door. His feet moved him to the front steps, but when he got there a sharp wind blew him back. He'd been so sure a minute ago. How can things change so suddenly?

He can't possibly go back. What is this scribbling inside him, a child's scribbling, round and round? He knows Priya has heard him drop the bag. All the words he is able to think of seem absurd, corny. She is still kneeling, head on her hands, hands on the carpet. The same carpet that so many children and their parents have trodden on today. It's as if everything is rushing out of him, as if he were a punctured tyre. 'Priya,' he says, 'are you . . .'

'Go, or don't go, but don't say any more. No more. I can't stand it.' She was using his words.

He wants to say something, he can't believe it, but he wants to comfort her, to touch her. Involuntarily almost, he moves towards her, crouches down, he knows she can hear him and is reassured by the fact that she doesn't flinch. She shudders at his touch, but not much. What was happening to him? How had he got from the open doors, the smashing, the screaming, to this? He can't square his head with what's happening, but if he lets go . . . if he lets go. Let it die. Let go.

He places his hand on her back. She barely moves. It's so

easy now. Now he knows what to do. He's home with the body he knows best in the world. Like a healer he moves his hand down her back, rubbing slowly. Moans leap out of her like frogs. He physics them down, tries to bleed away the pain with his palm. Relief, like rain, like tears, comes over him. Something is being washed. Tears that allay fears. He joins his magical tennis hands on her shoulder blades and rubs in small eddies all the way, very slowly. She allows a big exhalation. As if to join her he lays his head in the small of her curved back, brings his hands down round the backs of her thighs and stays there breathing lightly. From the street a fresh breeze blows in through the open door.

Twenty-Four

Two glasses of whisky, ten minutes to twelve, clasped hands, a sofa, refrigerator hum, thermostat click, train rumbling the foundations, cars sluicing through ocean night.

'I'm so lucky to have you.'

He tried to answer. 'I feel . . .' then thinks better of it. Too much said. Let the thought rest. Too much misconstruction. 'Some of what you said downstairs was right,' Ben said. 'I *am* frightened. It's easier for me to pretend it's your fault or someone else's fault.'

'Sometimes,' she said, 'we behave as if there are two columns: "Right" and "Wrong", "Fault" and "Faultless". When I was at school I had to put everything in one or the other. One gets used to it.' What's in the middle? Priya wondered to herself. Maybe that's what she should be exploring, even fighting for. The space between right and wrong. She turned to look at him. 'I can't remember what I said, but I'm sorry.' For a minute or so they both sat and absorbed the night sounds: a plane droning overhead, the creak of the floorboards above, a door slamming shut, a young woman's voice as she passed their window, talking on her mobile.

'I don't want to think any more,' he said, looking at the mirror over the mantelpiece. 'I just want to sit here.' He wanted to say it was what he had always wanted. There was a silence, then he added, 'Next to you.'

'I've never seen you so angry,' she said.

'I've never seen you so sad.'

He's right, Priya thought. Why do we always have to do something, fix something? Why not just sit? The way we are now.

'I'm sorry about the door.'

'Never mind,' she said, squeezing his hand.

Lying next to Priya listening to the rain. He felt his doubts dissolve like sugar. He had reentered this cluttered room, thrown his clothes on to a chair, adding to the mess with a wry recollection of his earlier thoughts. He imagined himself in the back seat of a cold taxi smelling of deodorizer, stopping at Dalston Junction, on his way to Mauro's flat, where he didn't want to be. Was it the comfort and security, this warm bed, the familiar smell, that had made him stay? Flight from the inconvenience and embarrassment of separation? Part of him didn't care to answer that question. Fuck it. He didn't need to. He felt like a man who had, for almost a year, ever since the day he had found out about Priya and Leo, stumbled through a wasteland and reached a crossroads. Ever since then he had been pacing around, clinging to the intersection, tormented by indecision. But now, in the last hour of his son's birthday, he felt as if the clouds had cleared and revealed the whole spread of the city that he had been searching for. It was still miles and miles away, but it was there. He was sure of it.

With a smile he takes Priya's hand under the duvet and feels himself striding down his chosen path. He feels light, happy, curious. Why has it taken this long? Why did I wait at the crossroads for so long? And why did I, in my imagination, wander down the wrong path through broken, desolate fields? Why did it take so long for the horizon to clear? Was it my fault? Am I that slow? Will my book also clear up like this one day? Does everything have to take this long and be this difficult?

Priya went with her gut. It was easier in the gut. She still had doubts, but they mattered little to her. She was a believer – she believed in causes, in people, in principles. In her gut she arrived at the place where she had fallen in love with Ben on that balmy night amidst the ancient Oxford colleges. Not, of course, ancient compared to Indian temples of learning, she thought, in parenthesis. She needed him, his gentleness, his pedantry, his whistling and humming of silly tunes, his irritations, his difference. Her infidelities, in the end, only seemed to reinforce the sense that Ben was the one she must return to and stay with. She was still angry at her self-destructive urge and resolved in the future to quash the need to immerse herself in it, to inspect the brickwork of her fatal urges. It was a good fight and she would win, she told herself.

And her mind had been pricked by a new thought. The middle way. All her life she had shunned the idea. It reeked of mediocrity. Of boredom. Of suburban self-satisfaction. But tonight it felt like her own discovery, a minor epiphany, a departure, this idea that you could paddle your boat in the middle of the river where the currents were weakest and where you could see more of the landscape round you. Turbulence was not necessarily life-enhancing. Like the losing of her scarf after her excited imaginings on the tube. Unlike the pleasure she had got this morning from just sitting in the kitchen looking out at the cherry tree.

Ben pressed his palm into hers. She turned on her side and laid her head on his shoulder. His arm flowed round her back. What if tomorrow she woke up and he were gone? She tightened her embrace, pressing her cheek against his hairless breast, listening to the rise and fall of his breathing. There was some cliché that we should live each day as if we were going to die tomorrow. The thought of tomorrow rushed up her body like a jet. She felt her beating heart rising from its quiet place. She wanted her world to stay like this, cradled under Ben's right arm, the soft of his shoulder for a pillow. Tomorrow she would wake to the chirping of birds, the spring buds dripping, the rubbish bags in a heap on the street, Rosa's accordion awaiting her nubbly fingers, the hiss of the pistons in the rubbish truck, the shout of the gloved men as they signalled to the driver to move on, the swish of cars. Lone footsteps on the wet pavement clacking towards work, clink of bottles, electric whine of the milk van as it pulls away, newspaper being pushed through the letter flap by a Nigerian boy in an oversized anorak, insistent hammer banging, pootle of a scooter, roar of the arterial road. Click of the radiators, dripping tap, damp seeping through the bricks, scratching of mice under the floorboards, ginger cat with one leg missing scrabbling for food, creaking wood, alarm ticking its way to the inevitable digital bleeps, a sharp eddy of wind in which a bit of newspaper with some of last-night's-sauce-smothered chips stuck to it flaps down the pavement towards a red crisp packet and the amber glare of the street lamps quite suddenly fades out.

' 'Night,' said Priya.

Ben heard it and he tried to reply. A strange blurry sound crossed over from his liquid world of sleep to the breathing world of light and emptiness and air.

Nothing more blissful than bed when you are exhausted, when you are weary, when you have said all there is to say, at least for that day. The couple uncurl from each other and repattern their bodies when their heat is up. It is still raining

Acknowledgements

A special thank you to Jenny Richardson who became my friend five years ago, at the time when this novel was in its difficult gestation period. Our walks and talks were and continue to be a great source of sustenance and encouragement. Thanks are due to Chris Cramer, my long-time friend and supersonic tennis partner, and to Marcus Verhagen for his intelligent and sensitive readings of draft versions of the novel. Thanks also to Jane Miller, Sam Miller, Shireen Vakil, Elisabeth Merriman and Charlotte Gardiner for reading incisively and making useful suggestions.

I am indebted to Susanna Abse and Lesley Bell for asking important questions and showing me new ways to listen; to Simon Prosser, my editor, for being patient and for believing in me, and to Rose Gaete for shepherding me past cul-de-sacs in the final stages of writing. Many thanks to Jessica Morris, Ed Pilkington and Anita and Amir Samaan for loaning me spaces to work in, and to Jean Lebrecht, Headteacher at Hornsey School for Girls, for being supportive. I am grateful to the students at all the schools where I have taught for their stories and their laughter.

From the start of my writing career Karl Miller has provided a superb editorial filter and in doing so has taught me more about the fine points of the English language than any teacher before. To him I give thanks and pay homage. The last thank you goes to my gorgeous daughters, Tara and Natasha, whose presence beams a constant brightness into my life. A big kiss to them both.